PRAISE FOR KAREN KONDAZIAN'S

THE WHIP

"You won't know what *The Whip* means until you read this fascinating book. It's a piece of the Old West, a part of America's past, told with amazing authenticity."

—Thomas Fleming, *New York Times*
best-selling author of *Conquerors of the Sky*

"Take it from someone who's had firsthand experience with great art exploring the human spirit in a Western setting: Karen Kondazian's *The Whip* is just that. This is a story that cries out through its adventurous surroundings—a call from deep in the human heart, a call for understanding, for love, for identity—and it does so through the skill of a magnificent writer. (It also cries out to be a movie. It's that rich, visual, and dramatic.)"

—Jim Beaver, star of HBO's *Deadwood* and
author of *Life's That Way*

"Karen Kondazian's *The Whip* is a cracking good story with more twists and turns than a wagon trail through the mountains. Kondazian takes what could be a hackneyed adventure tale of Charley Parkhurst's gender-shifting revenge and imbues it with surprising tenderness and yearning."

—Edward Achorn, Pulitzer Prize finalist
and author of *Fifty-nine in '84: Old Hoss
Radbourn, Barehanded Baseball, and the
Greatest Season a Pitcher Ever Had*

"*The Whip* is one of the best books I've read in long time...a real page turner. I didn't want it to end and it stayed with me long after I put it down. I've noted quotations from the book that I continue to revisit because they struck such deep chords in me. I laughed and cried. The experience reminded me of reading *Lonesome Dove*—you go on a true journey with the characters, especially our hero/heroine, Charley Parkhurst, and you don't have to be a fan of Westerns to love it. The novel is inspired by the extraordinary true story of one of the first stagecoach drivers of the Wild West, so you get a bit of a history lesson, and the writing is poetic and poignant, making you feel as if you are right there with the characters—feeling what they're feeling, smelling the smells, seeing the sights, tasting the grit, and experiencing their love, joy, pain and the all the nuances in between. The story is unusual, complicated, fast-paced, and beautifully written. It's quite simply, epic. I can't wait for the movie version!"

—Elise Ballard, author of *Epiphany*

inspired by a true story

THE
WHIP

A NOVEL

Karen Kondazian

HPG

HANSEN PUBLISHING GROUP

The Whip by Karen Kondazian
Copyright © 2012 by Karen Kondazian. All rights reserved.

19 18 17 16 15 14 13   5 6 7 8 9 10

ISBN: 978-1-60182-302-1

This is a work of historical fiction and includes background material about the historic stagecoach, freight and banking company called Wells Fargo & Co., which was active in the American West in the mid-19th century. No sponsorship or endorsement by, and no affiliation with, the contemporary company known as Wells Fargo is claimed or implied.

The epigraph for Book One: Louis L'Amour, *Lonely on the Mountain*, Bantam, 1984. Reproduced by permission.

Book design and typography by Jon Hansen
Cover design by Jeffry A. DeCola
Back cover photograph by Ed Krieger

Hansen Publishing Group, LLC
302 Ryders Lane
East Brunswick, NJ 08816
http://hansenpublishing.com

For my mother Lillian Marie and my father Varnum Paul...

for giving me the resources to find my way in this world,
for helping me to understand, as Charley Parkhurst did,
what one must sacrifice
to embrace a life of freedom.

In Blackwater Woods

Look, the trees
are turning
their own bodies
into pillars

of light,
are giving off the rich
fragrance of cinnamon
and fulfillment,

the long tapers
of cattails
are bursting and floating away over
the blue shoulders

of the ponds,
and every pond,
no matter what its
name is, is

nameless now.
Every year
everything
I have ever learned

in my lifetime
leads back to this: the fires
and the black river of loss
whose other side

is salvation,
whose meaning
none of us will ever know.
To live in this world

you must be able
to do three things:
to love what is mortal;
to hold it

against your bones knowing
your own life depends on it;
and, when the time comes to let it go,
to let it go.

In researching this book, I found many contradictory statements regarding the facts and dates surrounding the life and legend of Charley Parkhurst and of the history of the Old West. I chose to come as close to the facts as possible while still staying true to the story of Charley's life that I imagined. Some historical details are invented.

—KAREN KONDAZIAN
November 2011

Of course great curiosity is excited as to the cause that led this woman to exist so many years in such strange guise. There may be a strange history that to the novelist would be a source of inspiration...

—WATSONVILLE PAJARONIAN
from Charley Parkhurst's Obituary
January 1, 1880

Letter to the Reader

Boston, Massachusetts
January 27, 1901

As a young man, in the year of 1879, I made the trek out West to California to write my first article for the *Boston Globe*. The point of my journey was to interview the last of a dying breed, the stagecoach drivers or whips as they were called. I was instructed by my editor to listen to their stories, to hear their true voices, in particular around the subject of the demise of the stage-coaches—which were being devoured by the railroads, bite by bite.

Whilst on my job there, I met a fellow, an old timer and well known whip from the Wells Fargo line, one Charley Parkhurst. He gave me his voice on these matters, but more vital than that, he gave me the unique understanding of how adventure, freedom and loneliness seem to go hand in hand.

Less than eight months later, on the morning of December 31, 1879, I read an obituary on Charley. He had passed away at the ripe old age of 67. His mysterious and out of the ordinary life reminded me of a quote by Sir Arthur Conan Doyle—"life is infinitely stranger than anything the mind could invent." It got me to thinking that someday I wanted to write a novel about Charley and of that fabled time in our history.

And so, after years of procrastination, of struggling to put pen to paper, I now deliver my book to you. My genuine hope is, that in this tale you find not only some entertainment and pleasure but more important, that Charley's story might illuminate as Shakespeare wrote, "What a piece of work is a man…"

—Timothy Byrne

BOOK ONE

*There will come a time when you
believe everything is finished.
That will be the beginning.*

—LOUIS L'AMOUR
LONELY ON THE MOUNTAIN

One

California
May 8, 1879

He looked like a craggy yellow toothed god. One-Eyed Charley sat high up on the driver's box balancing the reins of the six-horse team. He pinched out a chaw of tobacco and placed it in his cheek. The stagecoach was swaying, cracking, bouncing—wooden wheels sloshing on sun parched earth turned to mud. The horses executed his commands with precision. His twelve foot snake whip snapped over their heads as his shouts and curses drove them forward.

Riding in the honored seat beside Charley, on his run from San Juan Bautista to Santa Cruz, was a young journalist, Timothy Byrne.

Byrne snuck a look at the driver.

Charley sat holding the reins in his gloved hands, chewing his tobacco, staring raptly ahead, a black patch over his left eye. He had a polished granite face, a natural man whose features were etched by careless exposure to sun, wind, and rain. He was covered from head to toe with dirt and mire, a notable contrast Byrne thought, to the precision and elegance of his hand movements. The way he fingered the reins brought to mind a concert pianist. Byrne had heard that old Charley Parkhurst was one of Wells Fargo's most adept drivers…that he could get his coach along twisting roads in the dead of night as a dog can follow a trail by his nose. He had heard Parkhurst could swear the dust off the streets. And he had heard of his sterling reputation for safety, punctuality, and for dealing with whatever came along—floods, rockslides, bandits…even neophyte newspapermen from Boston.

Byrne tried to shout out his questions to Parkhurst. Much to his chagrin, the earsplitting sounds of the coach made it impossible for him to make clear a full sentence, let alone to hear an answer. He would just have to find a way to get his interview at the end of the journey…maybe buy the whip a whiskey or two at the local saloon in Santa Cruz.

Since there was no possibility for a conversation at this juncture, Byrne sat looking out over the passing terrain…engulfed by all the sensations of this vast, unencumbered land. Some senses were familiar, like the pungent smell of horse and the musky scent of old leather. Some foreign…flowers and plants of various sorts, wet sweet grasses, sagebrush maybe? And then there was that sky. He had never seen in all his life a sky hanging so near. It was as though all that heavy azure might wrench itself free from the Good Lord's hand and plummet to the earth. The blue was dotted with Mourning Cloak butterflies. It took his breath away. He wished his Elizabeth were here to see it.

Out of nowhere it seemed, a pair of eagles appeared in the sky. They were clasping talons, yelping, squawking, and spiraling towards the ground.

"What the hell are they doing?" he shouted over the sounds of the wheels and hooves.

"Fucking," Charley yelled back.

"In the air?"

Charley ignored him. Then he saw why.

They were fast approaching something of a disturbing nature, a creaky and most dubious looking construction of boards spanning a roiling gap. According to his calculations, this must be the California Pajaro River. He shot Charley a tentative look. Of course Parkhurst wasn't really going to try to cross. God Almighty, he himself wouldn't have walked across that bridge.

He saw Charley raise the long whip, cracking it over the heads of the horses. And with a terrifying jerk that raised the hair on his balls, the stagecoach picked up speed. The team plunged ahead with a wild leap onto the rotting, weather-eyeleted bridge. The brown waters, swollen from yesterday's rain, were edging toward the bottom of the rickety boards. The horses were pulling like all creation.

Charley shouted at the top of his lungs, "Hang on everybody. We'll save what's left of you."

From inside the coach came a great feminine scream, broken off no doubt, by the very sort of dead faint that Byrne himself felt half-inclined to fall into. The sound of the coach wheels clattering over the bridge and the pounding of the hooves vibrated to his bones. He could not help but think of the weight—there was almost a full load of passengers plus luggage. And Oh Mary, Mother of God, wasn't the bridge sagging below them? Wasn't that a snapping noise? And wasn't that the groaning of wood?

Frantic, he turned to look at Charley and saw an amazing thing, a face transcendent with pleasure, a face living a perfect moment in time. He turned to look back over his shoulder. The bridge was already disappearing, its supports tumbling into the water, the water splashing up and gulping it whole. But now, thank Heavenly God, below him, the comforting sound of hooves on rock-solid earth.

His heart was pounding so violently in his head that he was aware of nothing at all except that he was alive. Oh God, yes. Yes. He would marry Elizabeth, give up journalism and write his novel. If he could just stop panting.

Charley reined the horses down to a slow walk.

At last Byrne could pry his frozen fingers from off the guard rail.

"Close call," he said. His mouth was so dry that his teeth caught on his lip.

Charley gave him a wide cheerful grin. "Not to worry. Never had an accident on a run. Mean to keep that score." He pinched out a fresh chaw of tobacco. "And I'm also damn careful who I take a bath with."

Byrne tried to laugh but instead, a peculiar sound like the breaking of wind came out of his throat. He reached into his coat pocket and pulled out a small silver flask and held it out to Charley.

"Not on the job, son. Apologies if you had some anxiety. That goddamn bridge was hale and hearty when we crossed over her last week. Never know what the damn weather will do to them."

Charley then with great care, almost delicately, spit his tobacco juice at a passing bush. "But hell, been doing this so long, just trust in my craw to get me through. Never let me down yet."

Just then the stagecoach hit a chuck hole in the road. Byrne couldn't help it…his stomach rose to his throat. He grabbed onto the guard rail and began to retch over the side.

Charley laughed and laughed, the sound, a deep croaky hoot.

In a few minutes Byrne sat up straight again. "Sorry about that. I don't know how the hell you can do all this every day."

"Shit. You been doing this as long as I have, your guts would love it too." Charley gave him a smile. "And you know what, son? I done my share of thinking about life, the way a man does when his clock starts to winding down; and whilst I never been one to be shook hard over heaven, I do believe we are guided at times by an invisible hand."

"Well, here's to the invisible hand." Timothy raised his flask and took another swig of whiskey.

Charley gave a loud whoop, cracked the whip and the coach lurched on towards Santa Cruz.

Two

The banker was twiddling his gold pocket watch which he had just removed from his well-stuffed vest with figured silk stripes. His fingers were like little juicy pork sausages dangling from the big well-dressed sausage of his body. Call him Mr. Sausage Man—all the children did.

He stood before the Wells Fargo Office in Santa Cruz, a red brick building with green shutters. He was waiting for a shipment from San Juan Bautista to arrive. Light from a gas lamp illuminated his round face and the round face of his watch.

It looked like the coach was going to be late, he noted. Mr. Perfect Parkhurst, always on time, was going to be late for once. That one-eyed high-and-mighty everybody idolized. That yardbird his wife always asked after. He smiled with smug satisfaction.

But wait, damn it. He heard the whip's bugle announcing the stagecoach arrival. The pounding of the team—he could hear it now—and way down the long street the smell of the rising dust. The stagecoach was coming. The whole world was dust and pounding, pounding and dust. And now, like filthy little fairies, the bloody children were coming. When Parkhurst arrived they always came. Their faces were gleaming like little planets through the dust—the nasty urchins.

The stagecoach approached at a dramatic gallop and stopped right in front of the banker. The horses grunted. There was dust everywhere. And in the midst of it, Charley Parkhurst. The whip raised his battered hat with a gallant flourish.

"Evening, Sir," he said, with a grand broken-toothed stretching of his mouth. His face was open, a study of frank planes—but then there was that black eye patch and the dark mystery beneath.

The banker raised his hand limply in greeting, but the runny-nosed creatures had surrounded him and were jostling him on every side. He winced and retreated with some difficulty to the back edge of the crowd.

"Charley. Hey, Charley," a scruffy towheaded boy shouted. "Got any candy today?"

As Charley reached into his coat pocket, something like pain crossed his weary face, followed hard by his usual two-chaptered smile: the quick smile, then the slow smile...taking his time at it.

Charley threw down a large handful of wrapped sweets.

"Candy," shouted the boys.

The candies scattered every which way. One landed in the brim of the banker's hat.

"Got it," shouted one of the older boys as he jumped for it, knocking the hat off the banker's head. "Sorry, Mr. Sausage Man."

The banker seized his disrespected hat from the ground. "My name, Lester, is Mr. Middleton." He glared all around him.

Boys were scuffling in the dust, grabbing candies from the dirt and from each other. They were tumbling over and wrestling each other.

"That's it, boys. No more candy," said Charley above the din. "Time to run along. It's getting late. Must be past your dinner time."

The boys began to wander off, the volume of their voices lowering little by little with the distance. Below and behind Charley, the passengers were departing the coach. A winsome female in her voluminous packaging was being extricated with the help of some of the male passengers. As she was lowered through the doorway and her feet touched the ground, she wilted, frail and exhausted from the grueling trip. Two of the men moved in closer to her sides and held her upper arms to buoy her.

She was whimpering. "Oh goodness, I was jigged, tossed, bounced to the ceiling, tumbled to the floor, wedged against a window, and scattered in all directions."

The two young men ushered her down the street...doing the duty of obliging young men, holding between them a gratefully murmuring bouquet.

Charley watched them go for a moment.

Off to one side, two girls had arrived and stood in the outermost corolla of the glow cast by the gas lamp, their dresses drained of color in the darkness. They whispered and giggled and touched their hair. Charley glanced over at them. One of them was holding a covered plate. She met his eyes head on, and then, blushing, dropped her eyes down. Charley considered her, considered them both, a tolerant and amused expression on his face.

Byrne, still sitting on the spare end of the driver's seat, was feeling his old self again.

"Now I know why you like being a whip, Charley. I see you have a couple of admirers waiting for your attentions. I have an idea. Why don't you join me at the saloon for a drink...and bring the girls along with you."

"You been drinking too many nips out of your little silver flask, Byrne. Hell, you don't bring nice girls into a saloon. And look at me...I'm old and ugly enough to be their grandfather. Every run there's always girls waiting with plates of cookies or some other damn thing. It happens to all the whips. Just part of the job."

A loud throat-clearing from the banker and Charley and Byrne began to clamber down from the coach.

As they disembarked, Charley continued, "But I'll take you up on that drink. Always end my runs with a shot or two anyways. Tiny's Saloon is just down the street on your left. Can't miss it. I'll be there soon as I'm done here."

"Right. See you there after I check into the hotel."

Byrne heaved his luggage off the back of the coach and headed down the street.

Two burly bank guards came out single-file through the door of the bank, reconfigured themselves to walk side by side to the stagecoach, and then stepped forward to remove the armored box from under the driver's seat.

Charley walked a few steps to the lamp. He moved with a noticeable limp. Now off the coach and on solid ground, he seemed older, more fragile.

The guards, carrying the strongbox, vanished into the bank, followed by the banker. The door clicked shut. Now just the two young women were left. They were having a hurried whisper and then one of them, the bold-eyed one, stepped forward into the gaslight right beside Charley, holding out the cloth-covered plate. Her dress was deep blue that set off her eyes, with ribbons shiny and dark green.

Charley noticed her lips quivering.

"Hey, Charley," she said. "I baked you some more biscuits."

"Thank you for your kindness, Miss Abigail," he said taking the plate.

Way back in the beginning, when he first clomped off a stagecoach, he would blush at the rosy pink attentions of women. There was no natural way to be. He was either rude or gruff with them, or on the other hand, erred by affecting a crude lasciviousness. Women thought him odd then. Now they found him to be a gentleman. They approached and he backed up, and they took his politeness and distance as respect for their sex.

The girl spun around, her face clouded with complicated emotions, and looked to her friend. They exchanged an anxious glance and rushed away in a fresh gale of giggles and whispers and swirling of cloth.

The wind sighed and Charley shivered, chilled to the bone. Now they were gone, too. Everyone was gone. The street was empty; it was as if all sound had leaked from the world.

One of the lead horses whinnied a quiet reminder and Charley moved to his side and stroked the damp flesh.

"Yeah, ole Jasper, I know. We both feel like shit. My bones are hurting too."

Charley's discourse with the horse was interrupted. Strident female voices were cutting through the night...singing...

> *"We were so happy till Father drank rum,*
> *Then all our sorrow and trouble begun;*
> *Mother grew paler, and wept ev'ry day,*
> *Bessie and I were hungry to play.*
> *Slowly they faded, and one Summer's night*
> *Found their dear faces all silent and white;*
> *Then with big tears slowly dropping, I said:*
> *Father's a Drunkard, and Mother is dead!*
> *Oh, is it too late? 'men of Temp'rance,' please try,*
> *Or poor little Bessie may soon starve and die..."*

Bang.

A door must have swung open down the street, for there was a brief cut-off roar of sound—glass clinking, people bellowing, loud, tinny piano music. A male voice screaming, "You damn singin' sage-hens. You're blocking the entrance. Get the fuck out of here."

The door closed. Silence.

Charley looked up. The silhouette of the young stock tender was advancing down the street towards him. The boy approached, his features still cast in shadow. He nodded to Charley, and without a word climbed up onto the driver's box and took hold of the reins. The tired horses clopped away. The stagecoach rolled lifelessly behind.

Charley sat for a minute on the steps of the bank, sweating in the chill air. He was sapped, depleted. His body felt like a stranger, his breath shallow and hard, his chest tight. He waited for his body to return to him. Shit. He'd been having these damn spells the last couple of months. It was time he went back to Doc Plumm. He had been putting it off. He would walk down to the doctor's office and see if he was there before meeting Byrne at the saloon.

THREE

Doc Plumm always seemed on the verge of narcolepsy in mid-sentence. But today he was mindful and alert.

"The sore on your tongue is very serious Charley. Last time you were here I made a point to tell you to come back in two weeks if it didn't go away. You didn't follow my advice. It's been well over five months since I've seen you."

"Hell, it didn't hurt, so I figured it wasn't anything to worry about. It's just these damn spells I've been having."

"Well, they're both something to worry about. You've got advanced tongue cancer. And your heart isn't doing so well either."

"What the hell does that mean?"

"I'm so sorry Charley. It means that if you don't have an operation, your throat and tongue will swell up and you'll suffocate. Or if you're lucky, your heart will take you first."

Charley stared down at his worn boots for a minute, as if taking in each crack that creased the old leather.

"What's this operation of yours?"

"Well my procedure can cure the cancer but the operation will swell the throat up so you can't breathe. We'll have to order a silver tube from San Francisco, have it inserted in the windpipe below the cancer, so you can breathe during the operation."

"Fucking tube stuck in my throat? You know what Doc? I sure as hell ain't doing that. It's liable to kill me anyways, so what the hell. Pray for me that my heart stops before this fucking cancer suffocates me to death."

"You're wrong Charley. I advise that you have this operation. Your neck is swollen pretty bad on both sides now and your heartbeat is erratic."

"How long do I have if I don't do it?"

"If you're lucky, about four or five months. If you insist on not having the procedure, I'd say that you better put your affairs in order. I'll give you some opium tablets for the pain. You'll need to find a doctor closer to you in Watsonville, who can give you more as you need them and take care of you. And when the time comes and it gets bad, you'll want some morphine. Come and see me whenever you need to."

There was a long silence as Charley stared out the doctor's window.

"Are you okay Charley? What can I do for you? You want a whiskey?"

"Shit, no. I'm not okay…But hell, I've had much worse things happen to me. Maybe I'll survive this too. Never gave up in my life. I'm just gonna continue down the road I've been living. And if and when it's time to go, it's goddamned time to go. Nothing I can do about it. Nothing any of us can do about it. Just do what you have to do to survive. Give me the goddamn fucking opium tablets and let me pay my bill. You're a good guy Doc. I appreciate your offer of the operation and the silver tube and all. But I want to go all in one piece…no holes, no parts missing."

Charley tried to laugh but then the tears came.

***

It's true that we're all children disguised as adults…When age and illness embrace our body…when disease and pain overcome, our eternal youth within begins raging, stamping, praying. Please dear God who lays me down to sleep…an awful mistake has been made…I was just now learning to feel safe beneath this fragile skin, trust within this prison cell. Just now my eyes are open to the world…Just now I feel the earth beneath my feet.

FOUR

In God we trust. All others pay cash. Two young boys had positioned themselves under the sign beside the doorway to Tiny's Grand Central Saloon. They darted round and craned their heads inside with longing and inquisitiveness each time anyone came in or out of the swinging door. Bright lights and glassware, shouting and spitting and music. Little tables and rich spilling aromatics. And, most curious, were the women. Women of a new sort, women with pillows of soft dimpling flesh quivering out of the tops of their tight, low-cut bodices. The children saw a man with his face buried in the cushiony breast of a woman, and the woman's face looking straight towards the door when they peeked in. She was smirking and grinning and most unlike any mother either of them had ever seen. It was thrilling. It was bewildering. It was wonderful.

Then out of the darkness, Charley appeared. "Lester...hey, Weldon. You boys still around? I told you to go home to dinner. Nothing in here for you...not yet anyways. Now get going."

Charley put out his right hand to enter—with his left hand he carried the covered plate of biscuits. But at that very moment the door swung outward with a shock wave of brilliance and loudness exploding towards him, and a flood of liquid pouring over his boots. He jumped back. "What the hell—"

The barkeeper was advancing with vigor, wielding a large jug before him, sloshing beer over the floorboards at the saloon entrance. He looked up.

"Oh shit, sorry about that, Charley. Have one on me. It's just them goddamned Daughters of Temperance females. Won't none of them be kneeling in prayer or song out here again tonight.

Worth the damn beer not to have them disrupting business and the good times."

Inside, the long mahogany bar was lined with lonely drinking men, huddled together like cattle along a stream. Off to the side, Tiny Crutwell, the proprietor, all three foot ten inches of him, was pounding with gusto on an old upright piano. Charley passed behind him, greeting him with a pat on the shoulder. He continued on to the bar and set down the biscuit plate. In an instant, the biscuits disappeared, snatched up by rough weathered hands. He plunked himself down on an empty stool.

Behind him at a nearby table was a preacher in black tails and a stovepipe hat. Lit to the gills, the preacher raised his glass. "Proverbs 31, verses 6 and 7," he intoned. "Give strong drink unto him that is ready to perish, and wine unto those that be of heavy heart. Let him drink and forget his poverty, and remember his misery no more!"

A roar of cheering and clinking of glasses swelled up.

Someone down the bar reached behind the shoulders of his stool-mates to offer Charley a cigar. "It's a Partagas…your favorite," the man said.

Charley nodded his appreciation—he didn't recognize the man—but accepted the cigar anyway, leaning forward to tuck it into his pocket for later.

A short heavy glass of whiskey, delivered by the barkeep, appeared before him.

"Thanks J.D." Charley raised it in a silent toast and downed it in a single gulp. He thumped the glass back down onto the bar.

But who was that? *Who was that?* With a sudden moment of shock he'd caught sight of his own worn and unfamiliar face in the large gilt-edged mirror in front of him. Oh. Yes. That's himself. Charley. Charley. The edges of the crowd pushed into his vision and the swirling of all his senses ensued. He downed another shot.

Then he heard a cheery voice. Byrne, with two shots of whiskey in hand, appeared next to him at the bar.

"Here I am Charley. What the hell took you so long?"

"Hey Byrne…you roostered yet?"

"Sorry?"

"Drunk. You drunk yet?"

"Not yet…but well on my way. Roostered. I like that. Going to use that in my article."

He handed Charley one of the shots and raised his glass high.

"Here's to being single…drinking doubles…and seeing triple!"

They tossed back their drinks.

"Hell then, come on," said Charley. "Let's get your damn questions over with. If you keep buying the booze, I'll keep answering the questions."

"Deal," Byrne said, and ordered another round. As he pulled pencil and paper out of his jacket, he observed Charley staring into the mirror. What was he looking at? He looked like he was in a bad mood.

"Alright Charley, so how much longer are you planning on coaching?"

"Shit…apparently not much longer," muttered Charley.

"What? What do you mean?"

"Don't mean nothing…I'm an old-timer, Byrne. Don't travel like a colt no more. Besides…not much coaching left with the railroads 'n' all. You can get from New York to San Francisco in eight days now. Imagine that. Took me four months to get here in '49. Had to sail down to Panama and back up the west coast. I was so goddamn drunk the whole time, I don't even remember most of it."

"Four months on a ship. Hell. My stomach wouldn't have made the trip. Why'd you put yourself through that? What made you come out west?"

Charley hesitated, fiddling with his shot glass.

"All I knew and loved were horses. So I took a job as a whip. I wanted the freedom. I wanted the adventure. You know?" He downed his shot.

Byrne noticed Charley's unease…he seemed to be having a conversation with the glass in front of him instead of with Byrne. Something odd and melancholy about this man. Couldn't put his finger on it. He decided to change the subject.

"So what are you going to do with yourself when you give up stage coaching?"

"Give up? Fuck, I bet I'll die still holding the reins on some damn coach somewhere." He motioned for another drink. He was starting to feel warm and relaxed.

"Hell, there were a few times I damn well thought I would die holding the reins. There was this fucking cholera epidemic in '50. Killed over a thousand people in three weeks they say. Me and the boys must have driven half the population of Sacramento fleeing that goddamned plague. And then there was that fucking fire that scorched the city."

He threw back another drink. "Yeah, a couple of friends went that way."

Charley looked like he was going to pass out for a minute, but rallied. "Where was I? What did you ask?"

"I just wanted to know what you were going to do when you can't coach anymore."

"Oh that's right. Point of fact, I'm not coaching much these days anyways. I tend to my horses and my apple orchard, and when the sciatica isn't laying me low, I do a little lumberjacking for the extra dollar. And I'm a member of the Independent Order of Odd Fellows."

"You're an Odd Fellow? What the hell are Odd Fellows?"

"Hey don't laugh Byrne; we do all kinds of charitable shit. It's a great group of men who love to be of service. It's an honor. Have to be invited to join. We just raised enough money to help a young widow and her kids from losing their place."

"You're not as tough as you appear to be, are you Charley?"

The barkeep appeared once again and refilled both of their glasses.

"Here's to you changing the world. One widow at a time." Byrne winked at him and laughed at his own joke as they downed the shot.

"Changing the world," Charley slurred. "Oh, shit yes...if I was young and strong again, I'd run for bloody President."

"What would you do if you were President Charley Parkhurst?"

"There's lots of bad things out there I'd fix. Stomp out what's left of the fucking Ku Klux Klan for one."

They were then interrupted by a thin, crusty-faced man. "Hate to tell you gents but I just overheard what you said, and you're fucking misinformed."

The stranger was already in his cups, sitting slouched on the bar stool behind Charley.

"The great Klan is gone," the man said. "Fucking Republicans took them down...threw 'em all in jail. When I get back home to Louisiana, I'm going to join the White League and help the good ole white Democrats get these fucking Republicans out of office. No matter what it takes. Long live the White League. Goddamnit, we sure as hell won't lose *this* war."

"Is that right?" Charley growled."I say, long live the Republicans. About time we took the fucking Klan down." He turned his back on the man and continued his train of thought to Byrne.

"Goddamned stranger...You know, first time I ever voted was Republican. For the great General Grant back in '68. Took a bath, slicked back my hair, put on my best suit and headed into Soquel."

He stared into space.

Byrne waited.

Out of the clear blue Charley started laughing. "Yeah, got to the Tom Mann Hotel and there was this gaggle of suffragettes screaming in my ear."

Byrne wished he knew what was so funny.

Charley continued on, "You know what? Put my first mark on a ballot at the ripe old age of 56. Would've voted for Lincoln back in '60 too, but always seemed to be on the road voting time."

The stranger leaned toward Charley and interrupted again.

"Lincoln? Grant? Those cocksuckers. Horatio Seymour should have won against Grant. He had a great slogan…*This is a white man's country, let white men rule.*"

Charley turned back, his voice quiet and cold. "Guess you're not too happy about the 14th Amendment then are you? I hasten to remind you, Negroes are full American citizens now."

"If you're not careful you piece of shit, with your nancy-boy politics, I'm gonna have to shut you up…gonna shove my fist down your fucking throat."

The man stood up knocking the bar stool over, and stepped forward towards Charley. But as he raised his fist, he lost focus, stumbled backwards, and collapsed into a drunken unconscious heap on the floor.

A few men began to gather around Charley and Byrne.

"Hey J.D.," Charley shouted to the barkeep. "Get out your broom. Somebody here needs to sweep up the white man who rules."

Byrne started to hoot.

Tiny, who had stopped playing piano in all the commotion, hopped up on the bar, and walked along the top of it pouring a round of celebratory drinks for everyone.

"Free shots for all Republicans," he yelled to the crowd. "And a double for my buddy Parkie."

After the double, Charley tipped himself down from the stool. His eyes caught the empty biscuit plate sitting there. He grabbed it. With Byrne in tow he staggered through the crowd of men towards the door. He caught sight of a nice-looking young man, a regular he knew from the saloon, and he thrust the plate at him.

"Hey William, do me a favor and see to it that Abigail Simmons gets her plate back."

The man looked up surprised, his hands accepting the plate. "Abigail Simmons? Are you sure Charley?"

"Oh yeah, I'm all set that way myself," Charley said.

The young man gave an insinuating smile and thanked him. Charley stumbled onwards through the door, Byrne right behind him.

"I'm going this way to my hotel Charley. Where you headed?"

"Gonna bunk down in the stable tonight. Ride home in the morning."

"Well…thanks for the terrifying coach ride and almost getting me beat up in the bar. I'll never forget it or you. Oh, and I'll get a copy of the article to you when it's published."

"Hell, don't worry about that. Just be sure you make me look good."

Charley turned and tottered off in the direction of the stables and his horse, away from the noisy brightness and loneliness of the saloon.

***

And Byrne began his article this way: Imagine, he wrote. Imagine if you will, the last of the great stagecoaches thundering by in the dark of night: the whip and horses as one; the words "Wells Fargo" gleaming above the door, stenciled in gold. Two lamps swing from hooks on the front. No one sees the stagecoach but a lone wild dog pacing through the scrub.

FIVE

Watsonville, California
December 28, 1879

The table was covered with a red cloth and set for two. The interior of the small cabin glowed in the candlelight. Homemade curtains rippled from the dark recesses of the windows inward towards the illumination. Deliciousness hung in the air; something savory was cooking. Anna bent over the wood stove for a moment, adding fuel, the glow of the fire playing over her face.

Close to sixty, one could still see in the secret places of that face, covered over by shadows and hard lines, what a beauty she must have been…a pressed rose now lost in the dusty pages of some nameless book.

Anna heard the familiar sound of slow hoof beats approaching the cabin. She reached up to smooth her hair, her dark eyes tightening, apprehensive.

A few minutes later the door of the cabin opened and Charley entered. Anna put her hands, protected by two checkered cloths, around the rim of a steaming tureen of soup, and carried it from the wood stove to the table.

Charley reached with difficulty to hang his coat and hat on their customary hooks beside the door. He paused to rinse his hands and face in the basin of water, then turned and limped toward the table and sat down. Anna watched him with concern. Not a word had been spoken.

Charley brought the spoon to his mouth, blew on it to cool it, and then tried to sip the broth. He could not swallow…the liquid spewed from his mouth. The exertion brought on a racking cough. Pain clouded his eyes.

"Please let me help you. Let me go get the doctor."

The music of Anna's Sicilian roots still, after all these years, colored her husky voice.

Charley's face was ashen, sweat beading down. When the cough subsided, he grunted, "No."

He heaved himself out of his chair. Anna watched him as he moved in a slow painful shuffle toward their bedroom; Anna's lips pressed inward, her mouth a shadowy slash against pale skin. He vanished into the room, closing the door behind him.

Charley sat on the bed patting his pockets until he found matches and a cigar. He bit off the end, lit the cigar and took a deep draw. His exhalation became another wrenching cough.

Anna stood up and made her way to the closed door.

"Charley? Why won't you let me help you?" She tried the knob. The door was bolted. "Damn it, you answer me."

"We all got to go sometime." His voice was raspy and winded.

"This is not a joke. Why do you lock the door?"

There was no reply.

"Alright. I don't care. Even if you don't like it, I'm going across to the Harmon's, so George can go and get Dr. Irelan. Just lie down on the bed and rest. I will be back soon, I promise."

Still there was no response. Frustrated and helpless, holding back tears, Anna slapped the door with her hand. She grabbed her coat and walked out of the cabin.

A moment later, when Charley opened the door, he saw that she was gone. He turned back, shutting the bedroom door again. He started to take another pull on the cigar but his lips had no strength. His arm felt heavy holding it. The cigar fell from his fingers to the floor. He stared down at it. He put it out with his boot. A stabbing pain ran down his arm.

He sat back down on the bed…his breathing still labored, his throat tight. He took from his pocket a small tin. Sliding open the top, he removed several opium tablets from inside. Somehow he managed to swallow them. He bent and pulled off his boots. He felt winded…like he had been kicked in the gut. With great expense to his body, he dropped down to the floor on his knees in front of the bed.

Reaching well under it, he pulled towards him the little trunk hidden there. He brushed a thick layer of dust off the top and stared at it for a moment as though it were a stranger. He took a little key from his pocket, turned it in its lock and then raised the lid. Reaching in, he pulled out something small and fragile and red. He held it up in his hands. It was a tiny embroidered homespun dress…the dress of a small child.

Charley lifted the dress to his face, breathing from it as though it might give him life. He put it down on the floor alongside him and reached back into the trunk: a tiny pair of crocheted shoes. With care, he placed them below the little red dress. His shoulders rose and fell. Next, a tattered copy of Emerson's *Essays*. And then lastly, a coiled dusty old whip.

It meant something, Charley thought, that he'd held onto these souvenirs from a life that had long since ceased to be his.

He pulled himself up from the floor.

He was feeling ensnared beneath his garments. He felt he might smother within their bindings. He had to remove them and free himself from their grasp. He stripped off his shirt. His back and chest were wrapped round with wide bands of cotton stripping. He began to unwind the coarse cloths that bound him, and they fell in loops onto the floor.

In a moment he was finished. Fighting against the waves of nausea and vertigo, he bent down to remove his pants and under-garments. His breath was short and strained and made a hollow yellow sound in his chest.

He was naked now. He felt liberated, weightless, euphoric.

In the dark glow of the candlelight, he stood in front of a small silver framed mirror perched on his bureau. There he watched himself remove the last bit of cover on his body...the black patch from his left eye, revealing an opaque, sightless orb.

Next he took the mirror, his hands trembling, and moved it all around his body, every inch that he could see. He put the mirror back in its place.

He took his hands and moved them to his waist and onto the hair of his groin. His hands touched the softness of his chest and then the roughness of his face.

Unexpected tears came to his eyes.

He lay down naked and spent on top of the blanket and looked up into the shadows of the air above.

In the distance, he could hear his breath rattling.

How strange it was. All that seemed to be left of this world now was breath.

Then a sound came to him. A whistle. And fluttering...tiny flapping—orange against the blue.

The candle next to the bed sputtered, struggling to stay lit.

Warm blood escaped from his mouth. He sensed now, that he was a stranger to that flesh beneath, to that final intake of breath. Without fear, without surprise...the realization that in that moment he was about to die.

Six

Boston, Massachusetts
March 1812

It was March of 1812, the month when wagon-ruts were filled with cold, dark puddles—the month of mud and suicide in New England. Inauspicious thunder rumbled that morning from dark, low-hanging clouds. The rain was freezing. It came down slanted. A wagon clattered up the road toward a dreary-looking institution surrounded by barren winter fields. It was the Boston Society for Destitute Children.

From a distance the building looked bleak—somebody's old mansion converted by committee work to a good cause. From closer up the building looked not merely bleak but stricken. Shutters hung off. Paint peeling. A child's rag doll was disintegrating in one of the puddles that pitted the front courtyard. The granite vases flanking the stairway were broken into great pieces.

The wagon stopped in front. A young blond woman in a dark shawl, hugging a straw basket to her chest against the rain, stepped down and hurried toward the front door. She raised her fist and pounded hard against the peeling paint. Without waiting for a response, she knelt and placed the basket down on the topmost step. She had tucked a rag poppet inside the basket with her baby. She'd left a little note with no information of any earthly use. Neither of them, baby nor mother, was crying.

The young woman returned to the wagon and touched the back of the hand of the older man beside her. He grimaced and slapped the reins across the back of the nags.

The door of the orphanage opened and a man, the headmaster, appeared. Seeing no one in front of him, he looked down for a baby. Indeed, there it was. Another one. He bent down to pick it up. He held it so that it might also see the wagon moving away down the road.

"Wave good-bye to mommy," said the headmaster. "Wave bye-bye. You'll not see her again."

SEVEN

That night it was still raining; it had been raining for days. A flash of light, followed by a deafening crash of thunder, illuminated the room revealing long rows of crude beds, each with one or more sleeping children.

The noise awakened the baby, hemmed in by pillows on a bed. She rooted for a breast. She thrashed her little hands out and grasped nothing. The baby whimpered, then started to wail. In a moment she was screaming, hot and red-faced.

All up and down the rows, the screaming ignited the other children, who burst with some relief into tears. How they needed to cry, those children. Some of them had not even awakened. They were crying out loud from their sleep, crying their hearts out, knotted up in their coarse white nightclothes. It seemed there was not a dry eye or a closed mouth in the place.

A fleshy, greasy-haired woman in a soiled nightdress appeared in the arched doorway, carrying a candle. She cast a grumpy eye over the room. Her mere appearance was enough to silence the children. They buried their faces in their pillows to stifle their sobs. The general racket died down, leaving a single burred, ear-splitting wail that moved up and down the audible registers: the baby, still screaming among her pillows.

The woman lumbered over to the bed. For an instant the baby was diverted by the flickering candle in the woman's hand. Curious, she paused her screaming. Then she caught sight of the woman's big face coming closer and closer to her own, and howled even louder than before…with terror this time.

The woman hoisted the baby up like a small plank onto one rolling hip. "We'll have none of this now, missy," she said. "Don't I need my beauty sleep like anyone else?"

Carrying the squirming, screaming bundle under one arm she strode past the rows of beds. As she passed by, the children in each row feigned sleep, holding themselves still, not relaxing nor peeking out from their pillows till they knew she'd gone.

Lee Colton however, a skinny somber-looking boy of four, slipped out of the bed he shared with another boy, and followed at a canny distance. Curious where the mean fat lady was taking the crying baby, he continued to follow them. He tiptoed through another room of beds, and then down a long hallway, past a heavy mahogany wardrobe, and then further down the hallway at the end of which there was a door.

The woman held the child against her hip with her big elbow and pulled the door open. Inside was a cramped, dark space filled with shelves of stained linen. She set the baby into a laundry basket on the floor. "When you stop your bloody caterwaulin', then you can come out."

She stepped back, yawned, and closed the door. A moment of silence, and then the muffled sound of redoubled screaming from within. In the laundry closet, utter darkness had descended.

The woman turned, grunted with exasperation, and lumbered back down the hallway.

Lee had drawn himself into a corner where the mahogany wardrobe met the wall, and now he inhaled and held his breath. The woman moved with much slapping and sliding of her flesh against itself. She wheezed and she thumped, too. The light from the candle illuminated the high parts of the walls and then the lower parts. Lee closed his eyes. In a moment she had heaved herself by him. He could hear her belabored passage into the dormitory, and then into the one after it. He could hear the final closing of the door. The children in their rows of beds were now breathing, unclenching their fists. Lee opened his eyes. He knew the children were whimpering themselves to sleep now.

There was a little moonlight filtering in through a window, and he could make his way by it. He moved to the closet door and stood outside it for a moment. He listened to the frantic cries of the baby. Standing there in indecision, he hoisted up his baggy long underwear. He put his hand on the closet door handle. He had to stop the crying, he had to save the pretty baby. Turning to look once more behind him, he slipped inside.

Early the next morning the fleshy woman reappeared, in an acre or so of apron, sighing, put-upon, dragging with her through the rooms and hallways a mop and a pail of dirty water. She paused at the laundry closet, put her hand on the knob, and yanked open the door. She stopped in mid-movement. Inside the closet, Lee was sound asleep, the baby, safe in his arms, staring up at him.

EIGHT

A cloud of dandelion fluff floated through the air.
"I'm making a wish. I'm making a wish," sang little
Charlotte.

Lee was keeping his eyes protectively on her as she played in
the spring grass freckled with milkweed and wildflowers. At eight
years old, he was still skinny and small for his age. He was pale
and intense.

Charlotte was four now. She was happy looking, with a sweet
face and bright periwinkle eyes framed by an angelic cloud of
flaxen hair that seemed to harbor the new sunlight. She looked
up and saw a butterfly. She fell to the ground and began to wiggle
her little body. "Look. I'm wiggling. I'm a pillar."

"No, I told you. It's called a caterpillar."

Charlotte held her breath till her face was red. Then she jumped
up and started to run towards the butterfly. "See. Now, I'm a
butterfly. Look at me, I'm flying," she squealed. At the last moment she swerved, swooping at Lee with playful mischievousness,
knocking him sideways.

He let himself be knocked over and then, as she attempted
to climb over his legs, he sat up, pinned her down, and plunked
himself upon her, triumphant. "I win. I'm the winner," he shouted.
He lifted one fist towards the sky.

Charlotte, face-up under him, giggled. "Look. Look." She
pointed at one of the butterflies.

In the moment that Lee was distracted she managed to wriggle
free. "Can't catch me," she taunted, and teetered away.

But Lee had lost interest in their game. He was still staring
at the butterfly, fascinated. It was hovering just over him. It had

orange translucent wings, veined with black. The wings were glossy, like paper soaked in oil, but also—he had just sensed—there was featheriness there. He wanted to see the wings even more close up. He wanted to touch it.

Charlotte looked back over her shoulder at him and came to a halt. She trundled back, disappointed. "Lee," she said. "What is it?"

"Look up," he whispered.

She saw the butterfly hovering just over his head and jumped towards it, reaching out with her pudgy little hand.

"No," hissed Lee between clenched teeth. "You must not touch it. If you touch them, they die."

She looked back at him, surprised by the thought that her touch could make something die. But regardless of the danger, she defiantly stuck out her finger.

"Silly baby Charlotte," said Lee. The butterfly was leaving anyway.

But no, it wasn't. It was moving over to the spot just above Charlotte's head.

"Don't move," he whispered.

The butterfly hovered for an instant before spiraling down to her hand in a single smooth arc and, to the absolute surprise and delight of both of them, alighted on her finger.

Charlotte and Lee stared at the little creature, amazed.

Then, just as quick, the butterfly floated off her finger towards the sky.

"See. See it didn't die," she said back to Lee.

NINE

O ne morning, just after dawn, Miss Isabelle Haden appeared at the orphanage. She was a gaunt, carrot-topped woman with high moral zeal. One might picture her marching out of some misty Dickensian orphanage of collective nightmare. As she clipped her way down the corridor, her footsteps became more and more determined, her face drying up and her lips tightening. She was attended by the scurrying headmaster. He was carrying a sheaf of paper...scribbling notes while she barked out instructions. She turned to frown at him for a moment. "Please man, keep up."

They continued down the corridor until they descended upon the dormitory. She paused in the doorway and surveyed the still sleeping children with pity.

The fleshy woman appeared behind them laden with her cleaning equipment.

The headmaster turned to Miss Haden. "Allow me to introduce one of my staff. This is Parthenia. She does the general caring for and cleaning up and looking after of our unfortunate wards."

Parthenia gave a timid smile.

"Parthenia, this is Miss Haden, who has been sent by our beneficent new owner, Mr. Dyer, to assist us in our efforts here."

"Pleased to make your acquaintance, mum," said Parthenia, with a bob that thickened her girth.

Miss Haden ignored her. Looking at the headmaster she said, "Do the boys or the girls sleep in here?"

"Why the..." he stammered. "The younger ones...they all do."

"Shocking," uttered Miss Haden. She turned on her heel and clicked on up the corridor. The headmaster scurried after.

"I can see I've arrived not a moment too soon," she continued. "I shall have to inform my superiors of conditions here. And of all the frightful disorganization I have observed."

"But, Miss Haden, we—"

"The first and most important thing to accomplish is that separate quarters are to be constructed for the boys. All children will learn to read, and they will all attend church services every Sunday. And the girls are to be instructed in the domestic arts, that they may someday prove of value to their husbands."

"Forgive my asking, but why the sudden interest in—"

"The state of Massachusetts wishes it. President Madison wishes it. Mr. Dyer wishes it. It is important that we educate our youth...even the lowly. Of course, you shan't be here to see it. You're being replaced."

She swept out of the room, leaving the headmaster standing there in the dust motes.

TEN

Wisps of Charlotte's hair floated like spun gold through a shaft of sunlight and settled in feathery piles upon the planks in the dusty attic storeroom. Lee was cutting little Charlotte's hair. He cut it in a rough boyish style, close to her head. Charlotte clutched her tattered doll. She was squirming all over, infuriating Lee, whose fierce concentration was something to behold. He sucked on his bottom lip as he snipped.

Charlotte was dressed in boy's short pants. She tugged at the crotch. "I don't like these clothes," she pouted.

"Be still," he said.

From outside the open attic window came muffled sounds of hammering. Lee glanced toward the noise. He stepped back to regard Charlotte's haircut, the heavy iron scissors hanging from his fingers.

"Tell me again," he said to her. "What's your name?"

She rolled her eyes, ignoring him, dancing her doll on her knees.

He grabbed the doll away. She cried out, reaching for it.

"What's your name?" he demanded.

"Char…lee," she said, her eyes riveted on her doll.

"Good. Lee, like me, remember? Char"—he pointed at her— "Lee"—he pointed at himself. "Charley."

"No, I'm not. I'm Charlotte. I don't want to be Char-lee."

An angry look came into his eyes. He strode over to the attic window and tossed out her doll.

Charlotte screamed, hurling herself towards the window. "That was my mommy's doll."

"Your mommy left you in a basket on the doorstep."

"Well your mommy just left you on the ground."

Lee caught her by the shoulders, shaking her, his eyes burning into hers.

"It's not a game Charlotte. They are separating the girls and the boys. They want to take you away from me. You'll sleep alone, forever, with no one to take care of you and protect you. You will be all alone. Is that what you want? You are mine. Don't you understand that? You want them to take you away from me?"

Charlotte's eyes filled with tears, her lower lip trembling. She shook her head no.

Outside, the doll had fallen unobserved amongst the workmen who were still putting finishing touches on the separate quarters. Not one saw a poppet whizzing through the air, nor noticed the collision of soft doll and hard ground.

Miss Haden and the new headmaster, Franklin Meade, were otherwise occupied; they flanked the new entrance, welcoming a line of boys carrying small bundles of their possessions. The boys were moving forward one by one.

Lee and Charlotte appeared from a side door of the girl's dormitory and surreptitiously joined the line at the end. Charlotte wore her new short hair and boy's clothes. She was feeling hostile. Each time Lee pushed her forward a bit, ahead of him, she planted her heels in the ground. He shoved forward. She resisted. Still, in a short time they'd arrived at the entrance.

"Name?" said headmaster Meade, looking down at Charlotte with a warm smile.

She just stood there.

"What is your name young man," he said. "We need to put your name on our list. Wouldn't you like that?"

"Char—," She looked up, a faint glimmer of fear crossing her face. Then she glanced back at Lee, who met her eyes with a warning stare. "Char-lee Durkee," she finished.

The headmaster wrote her name down and looked past her to Lee. "And yourself, young man?"

"Lee, sir. Lee Colton."

"Fine manners you have," said Mr. Meade. He looked back down at the two children. "Go on, then. Next."

Lee took Charlotte's hand and they moved past the headmaster, wending their way through and around the line of boys. They smiled at each other and exchanged a conspiratorial glance.

In a moment they stood in the boys' dormitory, amongst rows of beds with crisp new white sheets and wool blankets.

"Here," said Lee, putting his bundle on one bed, and gesturing to the next one over.

Charlotte was about to swing her little bundle over on top of the taut grey coverlet when they were startled by a sharp voice behind them.

"Not so fast, boys…"

It was Miss Haden. She grabbed each of them by their ears and tugged, maneuvering them toward another room.

"Ow," shouted Charlotte in a tone of girlish injury. Lee glared at her.

In the center of the next room were positioned several large cold-water wash tubs, each enclosing its own shivering, naked victim. Snaking from each tub was a line of boys waiting to be washed and deloused. Miss Haden, with a final twist of her fingertips on the lobe of each ear, deposited Lee and Charlotte at the end of one of these lines before sweeping herself back into the other room with a missionary zeal for more stragglers. Lee and Charlotte looked at each other. They knew they were in for trouble.

And indeed, it was just about ten minutes later that Miss Haden, her mouth set in a hard line, hurried Charlotte's small towel-wrapped body out of the boys' wing and marched her over to the main house in front of the shocked new headmaster.

Some of the girls who were outside playing saw it all. They pointed at her short hair, laughing. One of them dangled Charlotte's doll, taunting her with it. "Come here little boy... come and get your dolly."

The doll had marks across its face and its dress was half-torn off. Heartbroken, Charlotte started to reach for it but then forced her hand to her side. She made herself look away. She was trying not to care—but at the last moment, just as Miss Haden was about to drag her in through the doorway, Charlotte slipped from her grasp, bit the offending girl's hand, ripping the doll from her astonished grip. Part of the poppet's dirty dress was clutched in the thief's fingers, but Charlotte did not care. She had succeeded. She had taken back what was hers. Miss Haden swooped on her prey and grabbed her by the arms, giving her ear a resounding snap. It hurt but Charlotte did not cry out. Lee would be proud of her. She was feeling strong and brave for the first time in her four years of life.

 ELEVEN

That night, in the girls' dormitory, he came to her. The cavernous room had been tidied and painted, and the girls now slept one to a bed. Charlotte was curled on her side, her body damp from the summer's heat. She couldn't sleep. It was strange and lonely not to have Lee next to her in the bed. Then she heard the sound of a low, melodious whistle and her eyes opened wide. Lee. She sat up.

He was in his nightclothes, climbing through the open window. He slung one leg over the sill and dropped to the floor without a sound. He'd already seen Charlotte's silhouette and, raising a finger to his lips in caution, he tiptoed over to her. No one else stirred.

She lifted the sheet open and wrapped her arms around him. With glee and relief she kissed him on his cheeks as he climbed in with her.

He kissed her face and all over her soft body. He hugged her close and they fell asleep in each other's arms.

It was, of course, Miss Haden who discovered them at dawn. At first she couldn't quite believe what she was seeing. She stood as if paralyzed for an uncomprehending moment, a candle guttering in her left hand, a scandalized expression on her pinched face.

In her right hand she held her new silver wake-up bell. Coming back into herself, she began to ring it, tentative at first and then more and more, working herself into a frenzy. Tinkle. Tinkle. Tinkle.

It was a devilish, loud, persistent sound. The girls began to wake up, lifting their heads, rubbing the sleep from their eyes—

confused by the strange loud music. Tinkle. Tinkle. Tinkle. Some
of them, out of habit, swung their feet out of bed and began to
put their shoes on for some drill or other. Then they could see
Miss Haden, standing in the middle of the room, staring with
wide shocked eyes down at Lee and Charlotte together in bed.
Some of the girls began to laugh, relieved that it was someone
else that was in trouble.

Parthenia arrived in her dirty shift and a moment later was
followed by Mr. Meade, pulling the edges of a chenille robe over
his nightshirt.

Lee and Charlotte looked at each other in despair. All the
girls were giggling, and some were whispering "tinkle, tinkle,
tinkle." But the faces of Miss Haden, Parthenia, and Mr. Meade
were white and grim with the direst of prediction.

Miss Haden escorted Lee later that morning to the headmaster's office. She waited in the corridor outside, a small smile of
satisfaction on her face.

Headmaster Meade looked up at Lee as he came into the office.
"Please shut the door behind you Mr. Colton."

He pushed his two hands against the top of the large mahogany
desk and rose from his chair. Lee watched as he walked the few
steps to where a leather strap hung by a hook on the wall. He
removed it and turned, flicking the strap against his palm. He
seemed distant and detached.

Lee shrugged and then turned around, holding onto the back
of a chair.

The headmaster looked at Lee's slender, straight back. He
raised the strap. Lee's hands tightened around the back of the
chair. The headmaster snapped the strap hard. At the very last
moment however, he deflected the blow onto the desk. It was a
resounding strike. Lee turned around, astonished.

The headmaster spoke in an even voice.

"Boy, why did you go into the girl's dormitory? You know it's not allowed."

Lee, his face flushed with feeling, looked up at him.

"Charlotte needs me. She doesn't know how to sleep alone. She's scared of the dark."

The headmaster nodded. He didn't say anything for a long minute. He examined Lee's face.

Lee, his heart still pounding, waited.

"I see," the headmaster said. He looked down at the strap and then back at Lee. "Don't do it, Mr. Colton. Even once more. If it happens again, I'm going to look a fool and then you know who will be doling out the punishment. Do you understand boy?"

Lee nodded. "Yes, sir."

The headmaster gave him a little half smile, then moved to the door and pushed it open, standing aside. Lee dashed out of the room.

Through the open door the headmaster's eyes met the dogged gaze of Miss Haden. "I shan't think we'll have any more problems with him," he said.

Believing the boy had received his strong discipline, Miss Haden's eyes shone at the headmaster with the highest of regard.

TWELVE

Miss Haden...it was she who discovered them together again that very next night when Lee crept back into the girls' dormitory, back into Charlotte's bed.

Charlotte had welcomed him, nervous but grateful. She'd tucked her head into the spot under his arm. He'd put his arm around her. He had meant to leave in a moment and she understood that, but it was too warm, too familiar, too safe. They fell asleep like that.

Charlotte awoke with a start. A moving pool of flickering light was illuminating the walls of the corridor. She shook Lee.

When Miss Haden arrived, pausing in the doorway, lantern in hand, all at first seemed to be in order. She turned to go. But then something caught her eye. The window was open. Miss Haden's lips pursed. She swept towards Charlotte, who appeared to be sleeping, her face buried in her pillow.

Miss Haden stopped at her bedside. In the silence, she could hear a soft fast breathing from beneath the bed. She knelt down with her lantern and peered under. A pair of bare feet and a huddled form could be seen in the space between bed and floor. Lee's defiant face looked out at her. Her hand reached toward him and then all of a sudden she withdrew. She hurried out of the room, her shoes clicking expeditiously across the floor.

It was the rope, Charlotte later thought when she could understand such things, that took whatever good there was in Lee Colton and killed it that very night. Where had Miss Haden gotten the rope, the great thin coil of it? She must have had it ready somewhere nearby—a rope to catch a child with.

She returned to the dormitory, carrying the rope over one arm and intercepted Lee in the act of trying to leave the room through the window. One leg was already out. In this awkward position he was indefensible. Miss Haden got a good fix on him. She looped the rope around his two wrists and pulled it tight, tying it with expert speed into a packing knot. The knot held. She began to pull on the rope.

"You think you're going to get away from me, Mr. Colton? Then you have another thought coming."

All the girls in the dormitory were awake at this point. They were sitting up in their beds; they were staring with dropped jaws at the great drama unfolding before them.

"Help me, girls," demanded Miss Haden with clenched teeth. "Help me pull."

A couple of girls swiveled to their feet, and tripping over themselves in dutifulness, rushed to take hold of the end of the rope.

"Pull, girls. Pull."

Together they dragged Lee in through the window, over the sill, and onto the floor.

He was swearing all the curse words he'd learned in his nine years—mild stuff, but nonetheless goading to Miss Haden. She realized then that the new headmaster had failed. That he was both weak and ineffectual in the face of sin and here, corroborating her with every foul word, was the very incarnation of sin. It was she who would have to save him.

Charlotte was screaming and crying. She pulled on Miss Haden's dress to no avail. She was swatted away like a naughty puppy.

Miss Haden pointed toward two of the older girls. "You two bring the lantern and follow me. And the rest of you go back to your beds."

She dragged Lee out of the dormitory, through the front door and down the porch steps. Then she pushed him toward the old basswood tree that stood in the middle of the bare yard between the main building of the orphanage and the new boys' wing.

He wasn't fighting back anymore. He was refusing to move unless pushed or dragged. He was sullen, and his sullenness as it turned out, was the greatest insolence of all. She missed the glorious sensation she'd had a few minutes earlier of battling with her archetypal enemy. He was deliberately denying her that; she understood, and in retaliation she pushed him a little harder than was necessary so that he fell to his knees at the base of the tree.

She wrapped the long end of the rope around and around the tree and finished it off with a series of duplicate knots strong enough to seal a fate.

"I will not tolerate this shocking and deliberate misbehavior," she said. She was panting.

Lee just stared at the ground.

"This cannot go on," she continued.

The tiny purple vein that followed the length of her neck was throbbing. "You don't like your own bed, Mr. Colton? Fine. You may spend the night out here, and as many nights as it takes to teach you the difference between what is right and proper and what is wrong and evil."

Some of the girls were coming out of the front door, and they were collecting, barefoot and silent, on the entrance stairway.

Then there was movement in the crowd: Charlotte pushing her way through. In a moment she emerged in the front and stood alone there, sobbing before she made her way to Lee and Miss Haden.

"Lee," she said whimpering. "I love you."

He wouldn't look at her.

"Charlotte," said Miss Haden. "Be quiet. Go back in. Get into bed. Girls, all of you, go in. There is nothing to see out here. Nobody to see."

"No," cried Charlotte. "I'm going to stay out here. I want to help my brother."

Miss Haden snatched her arm and brought her own face down right in front of Charlotte's.

"He is not your brother," she said. "I cannot and will not allow this unnatural relationship to continue. You are not to speak to him. You are not to play with him."

Charlotte spat at her.

Miss Haden slapped her hard in the face. Shocked by the blow, Charlotte just stood there, blinking.

"It's for your own good. Lee is a bad boy. You can't understand this, but someday you will thank me. Now, get back into the dormitory. This instant."

At the sight of Charlotte being struck, Lee thrashed about, trying to get loose, screaming curses at Miss Haden.

She ignored him. She grabbed Charlotte by her upper arm and began to frog march her back towards the entrance. The girls were at the window, looking out at this thing that was happening, this thing they could not understand.

"Girls. Get into your beds."

They scattered back, where they lay with open eyes, anxious, staring into the darkness.

Miss Haden, still holding firm to Charlotte's arm, escorted her back to her bed.

A voice came through the window. "Charlotte. Charlotte. Don't believe anything she says."

Miss Haden went to the window and slammed it shut. She stared out at Lee, his arms tied behind him, pulling like a wild animal against the rope tied to the tree.

With satisfaction, she saw that he was crying. She returned to Charlotte's bed and sat at the bottom end, clearly intending to remain until the girl fell asleep.

Charlotte lay there weeping, covering her face with her arms.

From his window in the boys' wing, Mr. Meade was watching Lee. He stood there looking out at him struggling in the yard. He stood there for a long while.

The following evening, when Lee, his hands and wrists raw and bleeding, was untied, the headmaster stroked his head in sympathy.

Lee drew back from his touch. There was something new in his eyes…something dark and closed and vicious.

THIRTEEN

Charlotte wasn't much good at sewing seams. She lacked the patience for it; she lacked the inner drive to stitch the neatest, straightest row. When it was time for the girls to be communing with their needles, she tended to drift. She was drifting now, her eyes flickering around the room—girl after girl bent over their work. From where she sat she could see the backs of their bent necks—bent necks in neat rows. The girls were for the most part kept in rows and seemed not to mind it. Try putting the boys in rows. They'd not stand for it long. Imagine Lee and the other boys sewing or knitting or darning, all in a row. What a funny sight that would be. Of course, she'd seen Lee with sewing shears once. That corner of the attic over there, with the big mending workbasket, that was where Lee, so long ago, had shorn her hair. What a terrible trouble that had been.

She touched her hair, lifting her hand from the length of muslin sheet she was mending. Her hair was long now, in two blonde plaits. Little blonde wild wisps always materialized over her forehead. She was pretty, the other girls said, always adding, "what a waste." Well, they could go to hell. If getting a husband meant spending her days sewing, cooking and cleaning, then she would be quite happy just to be with Lee for the rest of her life.

It was so hot up here. All the heat in the world rose to that attic and was trapped there, shimmering. It baked her. It baked the unsealed eaves. The pine knots were beading with resin; the wood didn't know it was long dead. Sweat was beading on her temples and behind her ears. Sweat slid down her neck. They had been in the attic for an hour already and were to stay for an hour more. In the meantime, the boys were outside, free, shouting and clomping; she could hear them in the yard below.

And then she heard the low, melodious whistle—Lee's whistle for her. At this she rose from her seat and wandered to the open window. One of the other girls gave her a warning look. Charlotte ignored her.

Down there in the yard Lee whistled again, waving a stick, enticing her. He wanted Charlotte for a game of stickball.

Now fifteen, Lee was insolently handsome and despite all expectations, tall enough for a girl to feel she might lean against his shoulder. He had long blond lashes. His nose was broken at the bridge.

The girls kept their eyes on him. The boys kept their eyes on him; they couldn't help it. There was something magnetic there, something tense and compelling. It was anger of course, showing off its sexual side.

He had a disconcerting way of looking at people with a squint, as though he was looking into the sun. But now he was grinning up at Charlotte in a fetching, lopsided way—his impish smile, the smile he reserved just for her. The others, boys and girls, got smirks and suggestive looks.

Charlotte made her way back to her chair and her hated sewing basket, picking up the long sheet of muslin she had been working on. It was linen for the orphanage. They had to make all their bed sheets, aprons, dish towels and napkins. She sat there for another minute holding her breath tight with fervent anticipation and then leapt up, knocking her pins to the ground and plunging towards the attic door.

One of the girls shouted, "Charlotte. Don't."

They were appalled by her sometimes. She was always keeping company with Lee. She was always skipping out on church and chores. And there were rumors that she was a bad girl…that she and Lee did bad things together. She was irresponsible and impulsive, and was always getting in trouble for it. She made that much more work for the rest of them, too—like now. Pins were spread out all over the floor, in the cracks between the rough planks.

Charlotte streaked down the two flights of stairs and out the front door and into the midst of the group of rough-housing boys with whom Lee was playing stickball. Her eyes were shining and her face was full of mischievous pleasure. She dashed in and grabbed a stick from a boy twice her size. She didn't register the boy's perturbed face. She just saw how Lee grinned at her.

"What took you so long?" he said as he tossed her the ball.

Charlotte swung and smacked it grandly. It flew through the air to the farthest part of the yard. But no one ran to it. The ball arced down, thudded into the caked earth, and rolled, slowing to a stop.

What? Charlotte looked around, dismayed. The other boys had stopped playing the moment she'd taken the stick. They were looking at her with disgust. They were glaring at her. She met their glares with a glare of her own.

The boys began to mill about, resentful, grumbling amongst themselves, coalescing into small grumbling groups.

Charlotte looked at Lee. They met eyes across the yard. That look…everyone always said it was as though they had a secret language between them, that look.

Lee approached a group. Charlotte followed him.

"What the hell's the matter?" Lee asked one of the boys.

"We don't play with girls," the boy declared. He gave Lee a challenging look.

"She's not a girl. She's, you know…Char."

"She's still a girl."

"No, she's not."

"Yes, she is. Why do you always have to play with her? Why don't you go up to the attic and sew with the girls if you like her so much?"

There was a sudden swift blur as Lee swung his stick and in a fierce, cruel move—an unexpected move—savagely hit the boy in the forehead, inflicting a bloody gash.

For a split second nobody moved.

Maybe it was Charlotte's imagination. But no—there was the boy, bleeding from his forehead, not sure what had just happened. There was Lee with the stick, breathing hard, a wide grin on his face. The boys around them were stunned; it had happened so fast.

"I say she's not," said Lee.

Words broke the spell. The boys were coming back to life. The boy who had been hit was lifting his hand to his face. It was wet. He looked at his hand. His hand was red.

Charlotte stared at Lee, shocked.

"You bastard—" roared the boy. He stepped forward, clenched his fist, and took a swing at Lee. The rest of the boys formed a ragged circle around the two, egging them on.

Lee, still wielding the stick, plunged forward.

"Lee, no," screamed Charlotte.

She dove in and clutched at the end of the stick. He released it and, howling like a wildcat, leapt upon the boy. They were both on the ground now, the boy squirming under Lee's punching fist. Charlotte jumped at Lee's back, trying to grab his shirt.

The boy under Lee, kicked Charlotte in the stomach.

Incensed, she kicked him back. She tumbled away from them, her dress ripping. Another boy jumped on her to even out the fight.

At the front of the main house the door was opening. The toe of a shoe. A dark hem. Miss Haden. What's this? Fighting. Boys. Shouting. Pounding. A boy with blood covering his eye. Blood. And that Lee Colton. That Lee.

Miss Haden lifted her skirt with one hand, beetled down the front stairs, and began to run toward them. At these times she came alive.

"Headmaster," she shouted as she ran. "Headmaster." A formality, as it would be she and not the headmaster who would stop the fight. How brilliant she was at handling moments like these. "Headmaster."

In his office Mr. Meade heard her cries. He let out a sigh and rose from his seat. He shuffled to his door and made his way down the hallway. Children were dashing beside him towards the front door. They were not allowed in the yard at this time of the day— the girls, the younger children, the boys with chores—but they bulged outward from the doorway anyway.

"Children, children," he said, already defeated. Of course they ignored him or moved left or right so as to make no difference. He turned then to make his way, bent-shouldered, overwhelmed. Miss Haden would take care of it. She had an instinct for high drama; she'd wait for the height of the battle before stepping in. He should arrive just at the end to pronounce the godly benediction. But he could take his time. He should take his time.

Faces were appearing at the upstairs windows and then turning round to inform the others: a fight—a real good one. Lee Colton. Blood.

Miss Haden was panting at the outskirts of the melee, dust was rising, and she scanned the scuffling crowd. Boy. Boy. Boy. Lee. She started to position herself. Boy. Boy. Girl. Girl? It was Charlotte. It was time.

She stepped forward, grabbed a collar, and stepped back in triumph with her prize—Charlotte indeed. At that, the tussle stopped. She hadn't even needed to speak. The dust was already settling and boys were shrinking backwards, chagrined.

Miss Haden looked down at Charlotte, but Charlotte was staring at Lee. Lee, whose lips were tightening into a straight white line...his face holding the same willfulness as Miss Haden.

The headmaster came round the corner of the building. Now it was his time. He straightened up to full height and quickened his pace, trotting across the yard to the scene of bedlam and disarray. "Well, what's this?" he demanded in full voice. "What's this?"

FOURTEEN

"So Charlotte, you like to play with boys, do you?" said Miss Haden. A smile flickered across her face. Her eyes, her body energized, aroused. They were in the headmistress' office.

With an insolent smirk, Charlotte stood with her hands on the back of a chair, waiting to be whipped.

"So you like to play with boys," Miss Haden repeated, tearing off each word. Charlotte said nothing. She looked straight ahead.

Behind her, Miss Haden was lifting the leather strap from the hook where it hung on the wall. She ran her fingers over its worn edge. Then in a single, almost balletic move she turned and swung her arm forward. She was a decisive woman, one who took pride in persevering, in getting results.

The strap connected with Charlotte's back. Miss Haden paused, observing her, awaiting some reaction, getting none. No scream, no cry, no begging. She raised the strap again.

"What sort of playing do you do with the boys, Charlotte? What about Lee Colton? What do you do, Charlotte?" Now she was whispering. "What do you do together? What do you do to him?"

She swung her arm again. And again.

Charlotte flinched, clenching her teeth, but she would not cry out.

Mr. Meade had paused in the hallway outside the closed office door and was listening to the sound of the repeated blows. His face was twisted with anguish. He couldn't stand it anymore. He opened the door.

Miss Haden, her arm raised, looked up, surprised. Mr. Meade gave his rare headmaster look. She dropped her arm, defused. Charlotte turned her head around then, saw the headmaster, and removed her hands from the back of the chair.

There was a silence.

"May I go?" she said to Mr. Meade.

The headmaster kept his eyes on Miss Haden.

Miss Haden paused, twisting the strap back and forth in her hand. "Fine. Go."

Charlotte walked out, closing the door behind her.

"Why do you let those two get away with such bad behavior?" snapped Miss Haden. "We should have thrown the Colton boy out years ago…and she is no better than he is. She and that boy are cut from the same cloth; miscreants…mark my words."

Mr. Meade answered with his rare headmaster voice. "Don't get bellicose, Isabelle. It is my decision. They are both staying until they are sixteen or until they are adopted, married or have an outside job. You know the rules. Just as it is for all of our wards here."

"Don't you reprimand me, Franklin. I know the rules here."

Miss Haden's eyes glittered with an idea; she was an imaginative woman; no one could suppress that imagination of hers. "She shall have to be broken then, like a colt."

FIFTEEN

Fresh from her beating, Charlotte was led across the yard by the iron clasp of her headmistress at a great pace. The stable yard at night might have been nightmarish—all those long shadows, the soughing in the branches, the sudden mad motion of the underbrush shagging the margins; but strange though it might be, Charlotte felt at peace. Being led at all by someone felt good.

In the distant past, Lee would wrap his larger hand around her smaller one and guide her through the skinny legs and knocking knees that jammed the orphanage hallways. He would lead her across the yard of the orphanage through a barrage of snowballs. Now it was Miss Haden leading her through the thrashing wind that whipped the trees about. Why was she taking her out here?

At the stable, Miss Haden pushed Charlotte in front of her and through the doorway, soft lantern light seeping out as they entered.

The horses munching, looked up.

Jonas, the groom, looked up from the harness he was cleaning, quiet surprise in his dark eyes. A girl? Here at the stable, at night? Then Miss Haden loomed in…her right hand closing, talon-like, on the shoulder of the girl. She pushed her forward. The girl stumbled.

Charlotte, entranced, had stopped to look all around.

The horses were nickering and shifting their flanks…their hooves stamping on the resonant, straw-strewn floor. The groom, his coal black skin burnishing in the glow of the candle lamp, smiled at her. Multiple parentheses of wrinkles appeared around his eyes. He had salt-and-pepper hair cropped close.

"Jonas," said Miss Haden, "allow me to introduce you to your new stable boy."

Jonas regarded Charlotte with curious sympathy.

Miss Haden glanced at the horses in their stalls. "Which of these creatures is most difficult to control?" she asked.

"Why, ma'am," responded Jonas without pause, his voice a soft even keel, "I'd have to say that'd be Beelzebub."

"Beelzebub," she said, delighted at the name. "Where is he?"

Jonas, who was used to swiftly sizing up horseflesh—their stance, their spirit, their nature; who had long ago assessed the headmistress, and was now already almost finished sizing up the girl, turned and indicated a fine looking black stallion. The horse appeared calm enough at the moment, but his eyes were feral and untrustworthy.

"Yes. Perfect. Beelzebub, chief of the devils," said Miss Haden. She turned to Charlotte. "Everything that goes into that horse, and everything that comes out is to be your responsibility. If he is difficult, if he disobeys…you, not he, are to be punished."

Charlotte could not take her eyes off the great black horse.

"Now, I am nothing if not reasonable," continued Miss Haden. "Be informed that you may return to us at any time, under condition that you deliver to me a profound and heartfelt apology for your unruly and disruptive behavior, and that you vow to dedicate yourself to the acquisition of the womanly arts."

"Yes ma'am," Charlotte murmured, her eyes still transfixed on Beelzebub's lustrous dark coat.

Leaving Charlotte with the horses, Miss Haden walked out, inclining her head empress-like for Jonas to follow her. They stood outside.

"Now Jonas, I expect you to do as I have instructed. Do not go easy on her. She is too stubborn, too rebellious, and too independent, for her own good. We must help her find her way."

"Yes'm," said Jonas nodding.

He was noticing something, a sound that wasn't the wind, a tree branch, or the motion of an animal. He turned his eyes towards the sound without moving his head: he could just make out a shadow that didn't belong. It might have been that of a boy or young man. It was stepping back into the woods. It was gone now. Miss Haden was still speaking.

"Don't be concerned," she said, granting him a painful little crease of a smile. "She shan't be with you more than a night or two. One taste of shoveling manure and she'll be begging for a needle and thread."

"Yes'm," said Jonas, inclining his head in outward agreement. Had Miss Haden been a reader of eyes, she'd have seen that he wasn't so sure. In any case, Jonas was now looking over to where the shadow had been. He couldn't see it now. He'd warn her anyway.

"Ma'am, I..."

"No complaints, Jonas. I trust that everything is clear and that there is no need for us to prolong this unpleasant conversation any longer. She is your responsibility. I am leaving her in your care, and I am leaving now."

"Yes'm, Miss Haden."

She swept off, pleased with her handling of it all.

Inside the stable, Charlotte was walking around peering into the different stalls. It was so cozy in here she thought...the warm musky smell of horse and hay.

Charlotte entered Beelzebub's stall. Cautious, she approached him. She stood in front of the stallion, looking him in the eye. She raised her hand up toward his nose.

"There now," she said. "You're not so mean, are you? Can I pet you?"

The horse lunged his head down and nipped Charlotte's hand hard.

She cried out, falling backward into the hay.

Jonas entered the stable, ran into the stall and kneeled down next to her. "Are you alright? What happened?"

"He bit me," said Charlotte, confused. She started to sob. And once she started she was unable to stop, her thin shoulders shuddering.

He laid a gentle hand on her back and she winced in pain. He then noticed the tear in the back of her blouse and beneath it; he saw her back covered with angry purple welts. Jonas, who was past being shocked by anything other people did to the creatures in their care, knew what to do. He stroked her head comforting her, letting her weep.

Unseen by either of them, Lee was standing in the shadows of the doorway, watching. Charlotte was laying her head on the groom's chest. He was stroking her hair, murmuring something to her. She was sobbing in his arms. He was holding her close and she was letting him.

In a furor of conflicting emotions Lee turned and ran away into the darkness.

Jonas heard a sound and looked up, but seeing no one, he turned his attention back to Charlotte.

"You will like it here, missy," he said to her. The headmistress hadn't even told him her name.

SIXTEEN

It was dawn of the following day. Charlotte was dressed in some of Jonas' old clothes, a wrapping of bandage around her hand. She stood there for a moment watching Jonas, who was humming a soft tune as he brushed Beelzebub. With great care, she cut a wide berth around them, moving from stall to stall feeding the horses just as Jonas had instructed her. She finished with the last horse, placing the feed bucket down and touched her wounded hand, flinching. Seeing all of this out of the corner of his eye, Jonas stopped his work and went to her.

"Alright now Charlotte, if you are going to be around horses you got to understand something. When a horse don't know you yet, never stare 'em in the eye. And make sure when you offer your hand to a horse, it's curled into a soft fist with your palm facing down. He led her over to Ginger, a good natured mare and demonstrated.

"Why do you have to do that? she asked.

"Otherwise, the horse might think your hand is a claw...that you are being aggressive towards her. That's what old Beelzebub must have thought. That's why he bit you. Horses are just looking for safety. If they feel safe, then you're safe. When you approach them, you must be calm, always respectful and have the horse's well-being in mind. They're just like people."

Charlotte wanted to feel the mare's soft coat. She closed her eyes to calm herself and thought of what Jonas had just said. She took a deep breath and began to pat Ginger's neck.

Jonas stopped her. "No, not that way Charlotte. Horses hate to be patted. What you need to do is rub on them firmly; stroke them following their hair. They like that."

Charlotte's small hand copied Jonas' strong stroking movement. The horse began licking and chewing.

"There you go. Old Ginger's relaxing. That's how horses show they're comfortable; they lick their mouths and chew."

Charlotte began to giggle, "It's like she's smiling, isn't it?"

How easy it was to make a horse smile Charlotte thought…to make them happy. Easier than people. She grabbed a handful of oats and held it up to Ginger. The horse nuzzled Charlotte when finished…pushing her lips against her with great eagerness, almost knocking her over.

"Now what's she trying to tell you, that mare?" asked Jonas.

The horse's mouth was still inspecting Charlotte's hand. "Oh, she wants more," she said.

She gave her another handful of feed and stood there breathing along with Ginger. The mare raised her head and smelled Charlotte breathe, her huge nostrils working like soft bellows.

"See there. You're doing right," said Jonas. "You know, everything in God's creation has a language, and its own ways. Animals, crops, people—even the stars in the sky—all of them, shouting out their secrets every minute to anyone got eyes to see and ears to hear with. Trick is you got to pay attention. It's like, how can you tell if that dried up old prune of a headmistress is mad at you?"

"Well…her lips go together in a straight line, and her eyes go kind of pink all around like a rabbit, and her nose, her nose goes out like this. And she starts her sniffing." Charlotte imitated her as best she could.

Jonas laughed. "You got it right, much as I know. I seen her look like that as well. Now, would you go up and give her a pat on the cheek if she looked at you like that?"

"No."

Jonas nodded. "Well, that's what you did with old Beelzebub last night. He was telling you plain as day he's not no easy friend. You just couldn't read the signs, because they was in horse."

"Can you teach me horse?"

"Well, I don't know. Some things can't be taught. Some you have to be born with. And some of it Charlotte, is up to the horse."

So Charlotte stayed under Jonas' tutelage—for a day, then a month, and another, and another, until a year had passed.

She approached Beelzebub with trepidation at first—learning to read him, letting him read her, allowing her body to tell him she was his friend…that she was safe. Given both their histories, that took time.

 Seventeen

Another Sunday morning and another church service Charlotte had been able to elude. Jonas came back from his church to find Charlotte brushing Beelzebub in his stall.

"Hey missy. You didn't go to church again this morning did you?"

"Nope I didn't. Much prefer the company of horses than Miss Haden and the stupid tattletale girls. Don't believe in that stuff anyways."

"You don't believe in God?"

"I don't think so. I can't figure out who God is anyway. The minister says that he's up there in the sky…looking down on us, taking care of us. I don't believe him. Otherwise, Lee and I would have parents. And awful things wouldn't happen…like Lee being tied to the tree. How come you believe in God?"

"Well, I just do I guess. Always have…makes me feel safe. It's called faith."

"Why did my mama leave me then? Was I bad? Was that God punishing me because I did something wrong?"

"I don't know why those things happen Charlotte…why your mama did what she did. That was a terrible thing. But I bet it didn't have anything to do with you. She must not have felt like she had a choice. Everybody is just trying to do the best they can with what they got. I think God sometimes gives us trials and tribulations to see what we do with 'em. But I don't believe for a second that God punishes you."

"Well maybe he doesn't, but that's what it feels like. I wish I could feel safe like you."

"You know Charlotte, God isn't just up in the sky. He's down here too. I see him in my horses. I see him in you. That's what makes me feel safe."

Charlotte scrunched up her nose. "That's funny. You see God in me? In Beelzebub? What about in old Miss Haden? Do you see God in her?

Jonas chuckled. "Well, maybe not Miss Haden. But even when we don't like someone, we gotta treat them with respect. With compassion. Humans and otherwise."

"I'll never respect Miss Haden. Not ever."

"All comes down to treating people the way that you want to be treated. It's the old do unto others…like the Bible says? Miss Haden doesn't understand that. Maybe you will though some-day…Come on now missy, guess you just got your church for today. Let's wash up for lunch."

 EIGHTEEN

Two years later Charlotte was still at the stable, waking in the cold mists of the morning, washing herself in the frigid water of the barrel, mucking out the stalls, exercising the horses, currying them, feeding them. She'd learned to ride. She could ride Beelzebub now; she could ride him with effortless grace—stallion and girl, one coursing creature.

The horse had tested her and found in her a likely student of himself, and then with a delicacy and mystery, he'd instructed her. In the end there was a deep and wordless communion between them, borne out of a hard-won trust. Jonas saw it come to life out of nothing. He watched it. It deepened and widened and then swirled around the two of them so palpably that you had to stand back if you were not to be pulled into the powerful vortex of it.

And Miss Haden? Any inkling of a thought about the boyish girl approaching and she willed her mind to go blank. Let her stay in the stable and sling the horse manure. If that's what she wanted her life to be, then so be it. She was Jonas's problem. The same could not be said of Lee…that wretched boy was still hanging around the main house. Headmaster Meade had inexplicably given him a job as handyman. She was sure that damn man gave him the job just to spite her.

And Lee? Lee never stopped thinking of Charlotte. At seventeen his thoughts had been murky and sultry. At eighteen they grew precise. They grew urgent.

One afternoon, Lee was leaning against the stable door, watching Charlotte ride up on Beelzebub.

"Let me get on," he said as she approached.

"I don't think so. You'll get hurt." She swung down in a dismount.

Lee grabbed the reins from her.

Beelzebub whinnied in protest, tossing his head.

"No," shouted Charlotte, grabbing the reins back. "Don't pull on him like that. You'll wreck his mouth."

"What do you know?"

"A horse's mouth is very sensitive, just like yours or mine."

They were standing very near each other. Lee leaned into Charlotte, his gaze traveling down the curve rising in the front of her shirt, then up to Charlotte's lips. "Oh?"

"Yes," she answered. "You should always ride with more legs than hands. If you yank too hard on the bit it hurts him. He won't feel the feel anymore. His mouth can get numb and pretty soon he's no good because he won't respond to the reins. 'Cold mouth,' is what Jonas calls it."

"Your mouth ain't cold…is it?"

"Stop it, Lee. I'm busy."

She stepped back. She could feel the rough stable wall behind her.

"You weren't too busy last week for it. Let me see if your mouth can follow the feel."

Lee stepped forward to kiss her. He was staring at her mouth as if hypnotized by it. Charlotte turned her head away and licked her lips. She saw its effect on him: a wild agitation that seemed to flicker all through his body. Curious to test her powers, she licked her lips again, slower this time. He seized hold of her wrists with a pincer grasp.

"Charlotte," he groaned.

She tore her arms away from him. "Stop. You're hurting me."

Jonas heard Charlotte cry out. He appeared from inside the barn, taking it all in.

"You come to help today, Lee?" he asked.

"Nah." Lee turned and shuffled away, pausing to give Charlotte one last quick glance over his shoulder. She met eyes with him and for a moment they stared at each other. Then he turned his head down, spat on the ground and left.

NINETEEN

That night, Charlotte slept as she always did, with Beelzebub. She slept under a blanket on a small pile of hay in one corner of the stall. The stallion snorted from time to time. Under his lids his eyes were moving back and forth, back and forth. Charlotte's sleep was also restless that night; something in her dreams of Lee kept not happening.

Just short of midnight she woke to the sound of a low melodious whistle nearby. She opened her eyes and saw light. Looking down at her over the front of the stall, grinning his lopsided grin, was Lee, lantern in hand. She realized at that moment that she was not surprised. Hadn't she been waiting all night for him? Hadn't she known he was coming?

Awake now, Beelzebub's nervous hooves started to dance towards Charlotte's head.

"Beelzebub," she hissed. She rolled out of reach just in time to avoid being stepped on by the stallion. She let herself out of the stall.

"What are you doing here?"

Lee placed the lantern on the ground. She saw he had a small bundle with him, tied together with rope. He gave her a wan champion's smile.

"They finally kicked me out. No more work here. Let's go," he said.

"Go? Where?"

"Anywhere."

Charlotte slumped against the stall, her blanket wrapped around her.

"I'll take care of you," he said. "Didn't I always take care of you?"

"I can't," she said in a tiny voice. It had all just washed over her, the dreams she'd had, what she'd thought of doing with him.

"Why not?"

"I can't leave Jonas and Beelzebub and the horses," she added.

"Who the hell cares about them?"

"I do. I'm not going to run away."

Lee turned around and punched the stall door hard with his hand. The stallion pinned his ears and whinnied. For a moment it looked as if Lee might hit Charlotte too. But instead the intensity drained from his face and was replaced by an icy casualness. He leaned in very close to her. "You owe me," he said.

He reached out his hand and pushed it under the blanket and touched her long nightshirt, an old man's nightshirt, where one of her breasts strained against the fabric. At this he sucked in his breath. When he released it, it was a moan. "Oh, Char—"

He took her shirt and ripped it all the way down the front. He put his hands on her naked body and began to knead her breasts.

"No, no," he muttered. "You're not a girl." Then he brought his mouth to her nipples, sucking so hard it hurt her.

She could feel his rough lips moving across her skin. She felt her breath, her body, her will, snap into a paralyzed stillness. She felt herself watching it all from far away.

He lifted his head and met her eyes. "Oh, you're gonna get it now."

Holding her eyes he dropped his hands to his belt and began to undo the buckle and the buttons on his pants. "Gotta do it Char—gonna break your cherry."

He pushed himself between Charlotte's legs, slamming her against the stall door. She could feel the hardness of him pushing inside her. It was starting to hurt. But she didn't resist.

At that moment Beelzebub began to squeal and scream, trumpeting biblically on his hind legs. Then the whole stable was in an uproar—horses whinnying, neighing, thrashing. Beelzebub, king of them all, continued to rear and pound his feet on the ground. He lunged at the stall door with pinned ears, mouth open, head shaking and teeth glistening.

The sound was tremendous; the whole stable reverberated with it. Lee lost his grip and Charlotte fell to the ground. He scuttled backwards.

Pushing open the stable door in alarm, Jonas was shouting, "Charlotte…what the hell is going on?"

He covered the distance to her in a moment. She was pulling herself up from the hay-strewn floor. She pulled her torn night-shirt together as she stood up…breathing hard, her body, her breath, her will, crashing back into her. Lee had vanished.

"Are you alright Charlotte? What happened?"

But it had all been such a blur; Charlotte, not certain herself, could not say.

TWENTY

Charlotte sat next to Jonas on the wagon as they rode into town the following morning. He seemed distracted, lost in his own thoughts with a rare angry expression on his face. What was it he was feeling? She could not make it out. Something she had not felt from him before. His face was closed and his manner was stern. She wished he would talk to her now about the horses, the weather, or her chores. She wished he would scold her, though he seldom did that. She wished he would hum a little song to the horses or sing to her, like he always did. Anything. Anything to keep her mind off the events of last night.

Last night…she hadn't known what to say to Jonas. Thank God he hadn't pushed the matter. He had just made her some tea while she cleaned herself up. But this morning she felt embarrassed, sitting there next to him, still not knowing what to say.

Jonas flicked his wrist and the whip unfurled over the heads of the horses with a reverberating snap. As they approached a crossroad, he stopped the wagon. He turned his head toward Charlotte. In the sunlight, it somehow looked to her as though there had been tears in his eyes. She felt her heart make a jump in her chest that pained her. He must have seen this because he smiled at her, a spark of familiar mischief lighting up his face. She sighed with relief. She must have been mistaken; it was going to be alright—he was going to be playful.

They entered the crossroads and with little effort, Jonas played the four reins, guiding the team of horses into a perfect ninety degree left turn.

"Now how did I do that?"

"You didn't do anything," she teased. "The horses know the road, is all."

"That so?" He laughed.

He turned the team around in the middle of the road, then handed her the reins. "You do it, then."

"Sure." She gave a confident sidelong look at Jonas. This was not the first time he had asked her to do something new and when she did it well—and if it had to do with horses she just about always did it well—he would shake his head in mock amazement. "You beats all, missy," he'd say.

She took the four reins in her left hand, cracked Jonas' whip with her right and yelled out at the team just as he had. She gave the reins a confident shake. They were off. The team started to move back toward the crossroad. She glanced over at him. He sat there staring straight ahead, his face a mask. This she expected—it was part of the game—and she smiled to herself at the anticipation of his rueful praise: "Dang it Charlotte, can't nobody beat you as far as horses is concerned. What a girl."

She shuddered with a sudden recollection: Lee last night saying to her, "you're not a girl." Why would he say that then? She didn't understand him anymore. When they were younger, they knew each other always with a look, a smile, a whistle, without words. It was like they were the same person somehow. Now he was a stranger. Like he was....

She needed to focus. Which rein had Jonas used to turn the team around? They were tangled in her hand. The lead horses had already passed the midpoint, and she hadn't started the turn yet. Impulsively, she yanked on one of the reins hard and the left lead horse turned, crashing into its team mate. The right wheel horse, confused and frightened, began snorting, neighing and kicking at the lead horse in front of him. For one of the few times with the horses, she didn't know what to do. She yanked hard on the reins.

Jonas started to turn his head, about to say something to her, but the little wagon at that instant hit a jagged rut in the road. It lurched and teetered and, with a great gasp of wood, tipped over onto its side. Charlotte cried out. The horses came to an abrupt, confused halt. Charlotte and Jonas were dumped into the dust.

"You alright? You hurt yourself?" Jonas asked as he picked himself up.

Charlotte was already getting up on her feet. She was alright. The horses were all right. The wagon seemed alright too, even if out of commission—it's wooden wheels spinning in the air.

"Why didn't you help me?" she shouted. "You let it happen." Tears were coming to her eyes.

"Now you know this was your doing, Charlotte. I don't have to tell you that. You know you weren't concentrating. You weren't studying how I drove, like you usually do. Your mind was other places. When you're working with horses, you got to be thinking only of them. You got to be here with them, breathing with them…and tears is not going to help set this wagon straight."

Charlotte rubbed the tears hard from her face with her fist. He was right. She had let herself be distracted. She would never let that happen again.

Jonas walked over to the horses to check on them. He stopped and looked back at her.

"Life's going to do that to you missy. Gonna upset your wagon, not just once but many times. And you got to choose who's sitting next to you. Someone you can trust…or not."

Someone you can trust or not? He was talking about Lee, she thought with amazement. He knew her so well. He seemed to always know what she was thinking. Her eyes lighting with love and trust, she went to him. Together they moved among the horses, calming them. Then together they righted the little wagon.

When that night Lee came to her again, she would not let him touch her.

TWENTY-ONE

When people tell time by the sun and the seasons, time becomes irrelevant, foreign to one's everyday thoughts. If you have children and watch them grow, then you know time…every day you see it moving, right there in front of you. But if you are alone, then time moves in other people's world, not yours. And all you know or care about time is that your body awakens at the same instant, the hunger in your belly arises at the same moment, and the seasons and life move along, day in and day out, day in and day out, no different from any other. Then it happens one day that you look into the face of an acquaintance, or maybe into the face of a long lost friend, and you see something alarming, shocking, unacceptable. Time has left its decaying fingerprints on that face you used to know. And then you realize that it must be the same for you.

Providence, Rhode Island
1847

Charlotte's face was now tanned, her arms and shoulders muscular. There was no visible softness about her. Gone was the golden prettiness the other girls had envied, a lifetime ago in the orphanage. Not educated enough to be a teacher, not willing nor winsome enough to be a wife or a saloon girl, she'd scrabbled together over the many years a small independent livelihood. She'd cared for several elderly women and done heavy work in an institution.

Now she was working in the kitchen at Mrs. Bidwell's Boarding House for Women. It was work. It was a place to live. It was a kind of life. But it was empty. And she was disappearing.

On this dreary fall day, she was just another plainly-dressed, uncomfortable passenger in a rattling stagecoach on her way to Boston...a small valise in her lap, her hands twisting a handkerchief. What was it Jonas used to say? "This one mysterious life you got, what you gonna do with it?" Well, she had survived somehow. And she had turned thirty-five. That's what she did with it. Got old. That's what she had done with it.

As she sat watching the clouds change shape through the coach window, the wheezing, chattering man next to her continued talking. His mouth had been wheezing and chattering the whole trip. She hadn't paid attention to a word he had said, but now he was asking her a question...something about a state law that had been passed in South Carolina. Misinterpreting her blank look for interest, he continued on, "...you know that law that forbids Negroes and white cotton mill workers from looking out the same window."

Charlotte blanched.

"Are you okay?" he boomed out. "Okay... it's a new word, don't you know? Very in vogue. No one knows where it came from, maybe from the Indians. And no one knows what it stands for but anyone who is anyone is using it now."

Charlotte was about to beg the driver of the coach to stop and let her off as she would rather walk, when the Boston Society for Destitute Children came into view, looking the same as ever—on the verge of decrepitude and in dire need of a coat of paint. The fields surrounding the weathered building were brown and desolate.

And as always whenever she returned, her dark thoughts rose up. The most anguishing of all...the day Beelzebub had died. She'd cried and cried on Jonas' shoulder, and then, soon after, she packed up her few belongings.

"What will you do out there?" Jonas had said to her. "You're a woman. You can't tend horses. They won't let you. Here you got a job doin' what you love and what you're good at."

"I've been at this place since I was a baby Jonas. Don't know anything else. I don't want to work here the rest of my life and then die here too. You know how you always say you've got to put your arms around life? That's what I want to do. See what's out there. I'm scared... but I'll find a job somehow. I'm so sorry Jonas; I wish you could come with me. I'm going to miss you. But I need to do this. I'll visit you often. I promise."

The coach stopped, and Charlotte hopped down, hurrying toward the stables.

Miss Haden looked out her office window with her familiar disapproval. That woman. Here again. To visit Jonas.

A little while later, Charlotte loomed, unannounced, in her office doorway.

"It's too damn cold out there for a man of his age," Charlotte said. "He's shaking. And no one's been taking care of him. He's very sick. He's dying. Why the hell hasn't a doctor seen him?"

She advanced further into the room and leaned onto the desk, disturbing Miss Haden's neat piles of paper. It was the same bloody desk, the same bloody office—down to the leather strap hanging from the hook on the wall. Well over fifteen years had passed and how was it possible that nothing had changed except for the gray hair that now threaded through Miss Haden's head and her wire rimmed spectacles she was now wearing.

Miss Haden stood up in one quick movement. "Remove your hands from my desk. Sit down."

"I will not sit down until you explain to me why you've left an old man out in the stable to die. He has been nothing but faithful to you. You take better care of your livestock. You would call a doctor to attend to a sick horse. Why not Jonas?"

"I'm afraid there's nothing a doctor can do for him now," she said."I need to get back to work." She looked back down at her account book.

But Charlotte didn't budge. "How can you know that? How can you be so certain?"

"He's very old." Miss Haden looked up again from her book, her pale pink-rimmed eyes peering over her spectacle rims.

"Do you know how old he is?" said Charlotte. "Do you know anything about him?"

"Of course I do. I hired him. He's old. He's a darky. A man of low ambition. Do you understand? I'm running the orphanage now. Mr. Meade is no longer here. And I'm busy. You need to leave."

For a moment Charlotte stared at Miss Haden's pink rabbit eyes.

"You are a whore bitch. You always were. How could you treat another human being with such disregard? With such disdain. With no respect. Like a piece of garbage. You've damaged everyone who has ever been under your care. Me, Lee, and now Jonas. And all the children. Fuck you. Fuck you forever."

Charlotte turned and walked out the door, leaving Miss Haden standing there frozen over her desk, speechless, the pulsing blue vein in her neck the only sign of life in her body.

In Jonas' shack behind the stable, he lay resting on his cot. Charlotte sat down on a little box beside him and gently stroked his face.

How can it be that you could love somebody so much and still know so little about them? Jonas knew everything about her. He always seemed to understand things about her before she even knew them herself. But he never spoke of himself or of his feelings. He never spoke of the past. She had once asked him about his mama and papa and if he had ever been married and if he had any children. It was the first time she saw pain in his eyes; just a flash of it, then back to that mysterious little smile he always wore. "Past is past, missy. All that matters is this." And he took a deep breath. "Remember that Charlotte."

She held his frail body in her arms and spooned water over his cracked, dry lips. "Try to swallow this. I'm here. I'll be here. I'm so sorry I left you."

Jonas' hand grasped her wrist. She saw in his face that unexpected last strength she had seen before in the eyes of Beelzebub on the night he died as he lay panting his last breath.

Charlotte leaned down and kissed Jonas' forehead. She heard him whisper, "I seen you grow scared of life."

He was right. It was true. She knew it was true. She sat there holding him in her arms. She watched him struggle for breath. There was nothing she could do but hold him…help him through this. There was a long moment of silence. And then she felt the spirit leave Jonas with a small rattling sigh. The light in his once twinkling eyes fading away. It was over so fast.

Alone behind the stable, Charlotte dug the grave, venting her anger, her regrets, into the shovel; biting its metal edge into the fall earth. It was almost twilight when she tamped down a simple cross of wood she'd hand carved. *Jonas Parkhurst. Friend. Father. 1847.*

On her knees, exhausted, past pain and anger…she rested her chin for a moment on her hand atop the grave marker. She closed her eyes, and from the velvety darkness of her own inner spaces, felt a warm comforting hand on her shoulder pressing down. Startled, she looked up. No, no one was there.

She entered the stable one last time. It was eerie without the living presence of Jonas. His old whip hung on the hooks on the wall where he had always kept it. Charlotte reached up, took it down and placed her hand into the worn grooves of the handle. She raised it high above her head and then snapped it once. The sound reverberated in the silence.

In another moment she was ready. She scanned the stable and walked out, the whip under her arm. She would never return.

TWENTY-TWO

At the Bidwell Boardinghouse, breakfast was in progress. A half dozen or so women, ranging in age from their thirties to their fifties, surrounded a long table in the fussily-decorated dining room—a room swaged and bedecked with tatting and lace. Lined up against the wall were legions of diminutive overstuffed chairs, fetchingly bowlegged, useless. At the head of the table sat the owner of the boarding house, Mrs. Alice E. Bidwell, poured to capacity into a lace-trimmed dress.

The women gossiped with each other and pecked at their little plates of food.

"Girls," squealed a woman, entering the room with bits of paper waving in her hand.

She was coiffed and dressed in a ghastly fashion, a frock the color of dried blood, breast-plated with elaborate bugle-beads and braiding. The woman sat down on the edge of one of the little chairs and fanned herself for a moment with the papers, overcome it would seem, with the news. She regained her composure.

"Girls, I have clippings. From *Godey's Lady's Book*," she announced, "and *The Libertine.*"

An expectant silence descended as the woman started to read:

FAST WOMEN

One of our most promising lady writers, Mrs. R. B. Hicks, editress of the Kaleidoscope, thus deftly describes this new variety of womankind:

"This fast age, with its fast horses and faster men, has brought about that rather fashionable monstrosity, the fast woman. They

are a want of the age, these fast women, or the age would never have developed them. Fast young men wanted something to keep up with them, and, presto! We have the fast young woman.

Accordingly we see them with dresses décolleté and bare arms, with loud-ringing laugh and questionable wit, with polka and redowa, and a thousand other accomplishments peculiar to them-selves, attracting the blasé foplings, whose attention the true woman would instinctively shun. But, though they are so attended, and so applauded, and so exhilarated, there is no young fopling in their train who has not at least brains enough to sneer at them behind their backs. And thus it happens that these fast young women do not marry quite as fast as they dance. In the hymeneal race, we find them lagging behind; and, as their speed is all gotten up expressly for the hymeneal race, it must be exceedingly mortifying to them to find themselves beaten by dozens of quiet, genteel girls who never danced a polka in their lives. It is the old fable of the hare and the tortoise. We would advise them not to be quite so fast."

The women clucked their agreement.

"Another example ladies, of this wanton shamelessness, is this article I've clipped, entitled, *Lives of the Nymphs.*" She proceeded to read in ecstatic voice:

"We the Libertine newspaper, have pledged to keep a watchful eye on all brothels and their frail inmates. This sad tale is the story of a rich, successful courtesan, Amanda Green—the tall, full-formed daughter of a dressmaker, who was abducted by a man in a coach and plied with Champagne. At the crowing of the cock she was no more a maid. Abandoned by her gentleman abuser, she took up with a German piano tuner—after which there was no recourse but a life of open shame. May those who have not yet sinned, take warning by her example. She is very handsome. She resides at Mrs. Shannon's, No. 74 West Broadway."

Some of the women tittered. A few others began coughing behind their cloth napkins.

Charlotte was in the kitchen, pulling a baking sheet laden with golden brown biscuits out of the cast iron oven. The whole kitchen smelled of baking. It was toasty warm and inviting. A quiet peace prevailed. But then the silence was broken by the summoning ring of the dining room bell.

Charlotte sighed; she'd become, over the years, a sigher. In a moment she pushed through the door into the dining room carrying the platter of biscuits. The women were still prattling on about the newspaper clippings. She began to serve each of them.

"You see what happens when you polka," said a woman smirking.

"Bare arms. What is young womanhood coming to," said another. "Never catch a proper man that way."

The majority of the women again clucked their agreement. A few sat buttering their rolls, eyes averted.

Charlotte turned and took the empty serving platter back into the kitchen. She leaned against the frame of the kitchen back door—for she'd become, over the years, also a leaner against doorframes. She let the cool air bathe away the heat inside.

Lee came around the side of the house, moving toward her with a lanky stride and the same smoldering eyes, which at the moment were looking a bit sheepish.

Lee had lived some other places for six months or for a year or for two, and then was pulled by the gravitation of an unfinished fate, back to a shaggy orbit about Charlotte for six months or for a year or for two. Once he'd been gone much longer. When he came back, he mentioned a baby boy and a wife. But with no accompanying details or repeated mention of their existence, Charlotte was not altogether sure he was being truthful with her. She had also heard unsavory rumors that he had been living with another man.

Despite her misgivings about his character and intentions, she always took him back into her life. Not sexually of course.

She hadn't let Lee touch her since that night so many years ago in the stable. She had loved him. She had been drawn to him. But somehow she had never trusted him. Her instincts, with a little help from Jonas of course, told her no good would come of it. But, Lee was the only person who knew her past, and with whom she'd traveled through time. And of course, for better or for worse, she realized he was the closest to family she might ever have in this lifetime.

Referring to his feelings about her, Lee had once explained in a drunken ramble, "there's a hand ain't been played yet," and raised a glass to an uncomprehending bartender in some nameless saloon.

Charlotte watched him approach her now. He stood before her, head down, shifting his weight from foot to foot.

"Now what?" she asked.

"One of the horses is walking funny."

"I can't keep doing your job for you. I've got my own work to do."

"It's not for me, Char. For the horse. He's suffering. And you're so good at fixing 'em."

Charlotte glanced back at the pile of dirty dishes awaiting her. She let out a sigh, pushed past Lee and strode out towards the corral. Lee, behind her, smiled to himself.

In the corral, she tried to examine the hoof on the horse. She saw that there was a nail embedded deep within. The appaloosa began to nip at her. Calming him, she realized that she should not try to fix the hoof by herself. She would need to take him to the farrier. She'd probably get in trouble from Mrs. Bidwell for leaving the dirty dishes. But, nothing to be done. The horse needed tending.

TWENTY-THREE

Charlotte led the limping horse by the halter, Lee trailing behind. They wound through the narrow back streets of Providence and then entered a series of smaller unpaved alleys. They were at the edge of town now. Stretching ahead of them was salt marshland, punctuated by quaggy islands of tough spartina grass and isolated clusters of tall broken reeds. A few gulls cried.

There before them stood the blacksmith's shop, a crude construction of rough boards. In front hung a hand-lettered sign:

Byron Williams
Farrier / Blacksmith

"I hear this one's good," she said. "Better than the old farrier."

The horse snorted in pain. Charlotte stroked his side, whispering to him, "Sorry boy. It's alright. We're here now."

She handed the reins over to Lee and turned to leave. She should be back slicing beets for the boardinghouse supper. She should be shelling peas. But then she heard singing, a male voice accompanied by the rhythm of hammer on anvil. The sound rolled out of the shop on the still winter air. She had to see.

Peering through the open doorway, she saw the blacksmith at work. His back and arms sweating as he bent over the coals— a young Negro man. He hadn't noticed them arrive; he didn't know they were standing there staring at him, so deep was his concentration.

Lee yelled out. "Hey you. Byron Williams. Put a shirt on boy. There's a lady here."

The blacksmith looked up, bewildered for an instant, someone startled out of a trance. In a moment though, he'd taken them both in: a man with the eyes of a hungry coyote, a woman with tight guarded eyes the color of lavender.

"Got a horse out here with a limp," Lee continued. "He's got a nail in his hoof. Oh, and don't get no ideas about taking advantage on price, boy. My sister here knows all there is to know about horses."

Charlotte's face clouded with embarrassment. She stepped away from the door.

Byron, suppressing his anger, reached for his shirt and pulled it over his head. He grabbed some of his tools and went out to check on the horse. First thing he saw was Charlotte smiling at him in apology. Nodding his head, he accepted the apology. He knelt down next to the horse and turned the hoof up in his hands.

The horse began to snort and jerk his head.

Charlotte went around to the horse's other side and began to stroke and calm him.

In a moment Byron had spotted the problem.

"You see there?" she said as she continued to quiet the horse. "The nail's dug its way under the shoe. I didn't want to fool with it."

He released the hoof and stood up, dusting down his pants. She smiled at him over the back of the horse. He smiled back and something invisible spread through the air between the two of them.

Lee sensed it too, and it confused and enraged him. He had to stop it. Without thinking a moment longer he grabbed a pair of the blacksmith's pliers, hunched down, seized the horse's hoof, and clamped onto the head of the nail with the tool. In a fast abrupt motion he twisted and wrenched the nail out. The horse reared and screamed out in pain as Lee scrambled aside.

"Lee!" shouted Charlotte in distress, shocked by his cruelty.

Byron looked at him with undisguised disgust. He turned to the horse. "Easy, boy, easy," he said, comforting him. He looked at Charlotte. "You'll have to leave him for the day. You can come for him later." He wouldn't address the man at all. "I'll be wanting to check that shoe and his foot."

"Thank-you. And I'm so sorry," she said. Their eyes slid for a moment into contact. "I'll come back for him after dinner."

Charlotte walked home ignoring Lee. He followed a few paces behind her. So much was working through him. He tried to resolve it by grabbing her from behind, his hands encircling her waist. He turned her around.

"Come on Char. I didn't mean to hurt the horse." He leaned in to kiss her.

She shook him off. "What are you doing? Leave me alone."

She was furious, walking faster, refusing even to turn to look at him.

Lee let her go. He stopped in the dusty road, his face filling with shame and self-loathing. What the hell was wrong with him. He had to get a drink.

So much was working through Charlotte too, though back at work she tended to lunch. She tended to dinner. She dutifully attended to her beets. She attended to her peas. She punched down the risen dough, divided it up into rolls, and put them in a large pan for the oven. She set the table, served the meals, and cleaned it up. She finished the washing up. She untied her apron, put on her hat and coat, and walked out the kitchen door to collect Mrs. B's horse.

TWENTY-FOUR

B yron had finished work for the day. He sat in his cabin, next to an oil lamp, a book open in his lap. He got up as he heard someone approaching and opened the door to see Charlotte walking towards him.

"I came for the horse," she said.

He watched amused, as she strolled past him into the cabin. "Where's your brother?" he said.

"He's not my brother. And sorry about earlier…he doesn't understand how you treat horses."

"But you do?"

"Horses are easy. It's him I don't always understand."

He smiled and picked up his book, Emerson's *Essays*, from the table, turning several pages until he found what he was looking for. He began to read to her:

> *It seems as if heaven has sent its insane angels into our world as to an asylum, and here they will break out in their native music and utter at intervals the words they have heard in heaven; then the mad fit returns and they mope and wallow like dogs.*

"I guess he's right about the mad dog part," Charlotte said. "Lee's been run out of near every town he ever set foot in. But I've never heard him utter words heard in heaven. He's more one for words heard in hell."

Byron chuckled. "I'll get your horse, Miss…?"

"Parkhurst."

Outside in the shadows Lee stood alongside the blacksmith's shop. He watched Charlotte and Byron come out of the cabin and walk over to the small fenced-in area where the horses were kept.

Byron untied Mrs. Bidwell's appaloosa. "The foot will be fine. I put a special salve of wool fat oil on it. You'll need to continue putting it on his foot for about a week. So it doesn't get infected. Keep an eye on it, and go easy on him. Don't go ridin' him for a few weeks. Let it heal."

Charlotte nodded. She stood there next to Byron, stroking the horse, scuffling her feet in the dirt.

"You know I shouldn't have said that about Lee. He's as close as I come to having family in this world. There is good in him—at least there used to be. Guess it's kind of hard to see, sometimes."

Byron handed her the reins and a small tin of salve for the horse. He smiled, gazing at her. His smile was shy, warm, complicated.

She felt self-conscious, out of breath. "Oh, almost forgot. How much do we owe you for fixin' him up?"

"A quarter'll be fine."

She handed him the money. "Thank-you again...for fixin' him up...and I very much enjoyed the poem you read...and I... it was nice to talk to you." She couldn't think of anything else to say. "Good night, then."

"Good night, Miss Parkhurst."

Reins in hand, she hurried away.

Lee stayed in the shadows until Byron had gone inside; then he stepped out to track Charlotte safely home.

TWENTY-FIVE

The following afternoon, Charlotte came out of the general store, her arms laden with groceries. As she passed a tiny bookshop she saw, displayed in the front window, copies of Charles Dickens' newest serial novel, *Dealings with the Firm of Dombey & Son: Wholesale, Retail and for Exportation,* and also, copies of Emerson's *Essays,* volumes one and two. She took a few more steps then stopped, checked her coin purse, turned, and went into the bookshop.

Back at the boarding house she sat at the utility table in the kitchen, poring over Emerson's essays, lips moving to each word, finger moving slowly across the page. There were dirty dishes stacked all over the counter behind her. She heard a low melodious whistle but she ignored it and kept reading. Maybe he'd give up.

But in a moment Lee entered through the back door, dressed in dirty work clothes. She continued to ignore him.

He hovered near the door. "Hey, I know I did wrong by that horse yesterday," he said. "Doing wrong by it, I did wrong by you, and I apologize."

She looked up from her book, her eyes softening.

He continued, "I don't know what I can say for myself, except, the way that Negro was looking at you—well it set me on fire and I didn't know what I was doing till it was done." He contrived to look both apologetic and outraged.

She glared at him, then rose from the table and tried to leave the room.

Lee blocked her way, his rough hands grabbing her.

"I don't understand you Char. You took that darky's name back at the orphanage, too. What the fucks the matter with you?"

"Go to hell, Lee."

"You listen to me. This town don't take kindly to mixing of the races. Maybe that would work in Boston, but not here. As your brother, I'm obliged to warn you."

"You're not my brother."

Her words stung, and his grasp loosened. She took advantage of the moment to shake free. She lunged and ran through the door into the dining room, disappearing into the interior of the house.

Lee stood by the kitchen door, full of familiar hurt and anger. He turned and walked out, slamming the door hard behind him.

That evening, Charlotte still fuming over her altercation with Lee, made the decision. She grabbed her new copy of Emerson and marched her way over to Byron's cabin.

TWENTY-SIX

The shopkeeper held the door open for Charlotte. She smiled her thanks.

"Now you have a wonderful afternoon, Miss Parkhurst. And keep yourself warm. It's chilly outside," he said.

"Thank-you, Mr. Bronson. I'll see you tomorrow."

How nice everyone was she thought. How blue the sky. How crisp the air felt on her face. Even the run-down buildings seemed to sparkle. It was a grand day. Days in general had been grand. She let out a long easy sigh and headed back to Mrs. Bidwell's to prepare dinner. Even that didn't seem like a chore today.

It had been almost a week since she had gone to his cabin. She couldn't stop thinking of him. It was the first time in her life she'd ever felt this way. God, the sweet way he looked at her.

It was time to go and surprise him again. As soon as she was done with the dishes she would leave…maybe take him some leftovers as well.

He'd been surprised at her spur of the moment visit last week but welcomed her in anyways. They'd sat and read together till dawn. He'd explained his love of Emerson to her…that the poet's words gave him courage and inspiration to not only live the life that had been given to him, but also to find a way to sculpt something good from it.

It had been hard to leave. Harder still to go an entire week without going back. Tonight could not come soon enough.

Twenty-Seven

Charlotte and Byron were sitting at his rickety little table. By the light of the lantern, she read aloud from Emerson:

Be true to your own act, and congratulate yourself if you have done something strange and extravagant, and broken the monotony of a decorous age. It was a high counsel that I once heard given to a young person, "Always do what you are afraid to do." A simple manly character need never make an a-po-lo-gy...

She paused, stumbling over the word. Byron reached over to find her place on the page, his hand brushing hers as she pointed it out. In that moment an electric shadow passed over them. He moved his hand away from hers.

She blushed. "Oh Lord…"

"What is it?"

"It's…it's late," Charlotte said.

She jumped up knocking over the chair as she pulled on her coat. Embarrassed, she picked it up. As she was fumbling with her hat and gloves, Byron stood up.

"Charlotte," he paused for a moment, struggling with his words. "I've been thinking a lot…since the last time. Please don't come here again."

"What? What do you mean? What are you talking about?"

"I've been thinking about our friendship. You don't know what people can do. I have found the strength to be here and make a life for myself. But I don't know if I have strength enough for the ugliness that could happen to you. Please Charlotte...don't come here again."

She listened, dumbfounded, trying to absorb his words. "I don't care what other people think. I have to go now, but we'll talk about this later."

She picked up her copy of Emerson from the table and hurried out.

TWENTY-EIGHT

L ate the following evening, Charlotte stood at her bedroom window watching the snow fall. She exhaled against the pane, her breath condensing in a cloud against the glass. She turned from the window and glanced into the small mirror above her bureau, stopping for a moment to straighten the frizz of curls on her forehead. Over and over she hummed a maddening fragment of song.

After what seemed like forever, she heard Mrs. Bidwell move down the hallway and disappear into her room. Charlotte opened her bedroom door a crack. Already dressed in her coat and hat, she looked down the hall toward Mrs. Bidwell's room. Light shone under the closed door and then was extinguished, leaving the hallway in darkness.

A short time later, carrying a small parcel, she slipped out the back door leaving it unlocked. From her window Mrs. Bidwell, in her nightdress, stood looking down at the street and Charlotte's departing footsteps in the snow.

Byron was sitting at his wooden table, whiskey in hand, staring out into nothing. There was a knock at the door, followed by a familiar voice. He hesitated but let her in. Charlotte smiled at him as she removed her hat and gloves, setting the parcel down on the table.

"Did you eat? I brought you some supper."

She hung up her coat, and began to unwrap the parcel of food. "I hope you like dumplings. And pumpkin cake. Old Biddie Bidwell would wring my neck if she knew. She's so proper and respectable she puts stockings on her piano legs."

She looked up at Byron's solemn face. "She really does."

"Charlotte, I told you not to come here again. What words can I use? How can I say this so you will understand?"

She put her fingertip close to his lips. "Don't," she said. "Just don't."

"Damn it, Charlotte. You're like a child. You don't know what the world is like. You don't know the viciousness. You act as though our friendship is just an ordinary thing. It's not. It's dangerous. I don't think you understand that."

"My God, do you think I'm stupid? You're a Negro man and I'm a white woman. I know that. To hell with what people think. The person I loved most in this world was a Negro man. He was my father. Well, like my father. He taught me everything. He used to say, 'This one mysterious life you got, what you gonna do with it?' I wasted a lot of years…not doing anything with it. So I figure you either put your arms around it and be free or you don't and you live feeling like you missed something but you don't know what it was. It's like you're afraid of…"

"Stop it. Stop talking gibberish, damn it. You aren't listening to me. You really think life is that simple? You think that all you have to do is to put your arms around it and people will let you be free? The world can be cruel and wicked and ignorant."

"I know that. I grew up with wickedness all around me in the orphanage. Children…Lee…were tied to trees with rope… beaten. I was beaten. But I also remember butterflies and Lee by my side. And when I got older, I had Jonas and the horses. I was lucky. Until I went out into the world…it wasn't easy to be a woman on my own. Men get to have dreams. Women don't. I couldn't depend on anyone but myself. I know I'm rambling. What I'm trying to say is…I know you're right. The world is harsh. I don't understand how some people can do the things they do. But we've found something here. I'm not going to let go of it because it's hard."

Byron sat down at the table. He took a long swig of whiskey. "I want to tell you something."

"All right." She sat down across the table from him. "Just don't tell me to leave."

"Please be still, Charlotte. Just listen to me. Alright? I've always thought the reason people act the way they do is because way down deep most people are afraid of anything different than themselves. I saw it in the eyes of the white folk in the big house that my mama worked in. They looked at me like I was a small black animal to be petted and fed, so I could grow up strong to tend their crops. You know how I learned to read? In a tool shed. At night. My mama, because she was smart, was secretly taught to read by her missus, so she could help the white children with their studies. After working hard for sixteen hours, she would sit there with me late at night on the dirt floor of that little shed, by the light of a bit of candle she had 'borrowed'; and when the candle burned out, the lesson was over. In Mississippi it is against the law to learn to read if you are a Negro. If they'd ever caught her, she would have been horsewhipped within an inch of her life. Or cat-hauled. You know what cat-haulin' is? It's a form of punishment where a tomcat is used to claw at the back of the slave. I was ten the first time I saw cat-haulin. My mama wanted her son to be free. She always said she'd rather be whipped to death than allow her son to grow up to be the property of another man. When I was twelve, she told me to run away...helped me run away. I'm one of the fortunate ones. I'm no man's chattel. Life gave her that much. Course, she never knew it. I don't even know what happened to her."

Seeing the pain on his face, Charlotte didn't know what to do. She sat there with tears in her eyes. She was so moved by this man. She would take his demons and his fears.

"I'm so sorry, Byron. I don't know what to say. If you want me to go I will. But I want to stay here with you."

Byron just stared into the fire. "Charlotte, I don't want you to go, but you need to go. And don't come back."

Without another word, she pulled on her hat and coat and walked out. The white snow and the black sky with its tossed handful of star points glittered. She wept her way home, tears freezing on her face, her head down against the snow all stirred up by the night wind skittering around in powdery curlicues and tendrils, sifting through her clothing and down her neck.

TWENTY-NINE

It was a bad surprise when Charlotte stepped up to the back kitchen door and turned the knob. The door was bolted. She tried it a second time. Surely this was just someone's oversight. Then she noticed her packed carpetbag was lying to the side of the door. There was an envelope with her name scrawled across it in Mrs. Bidwell's flowery script. It was pinned to the side of the bag. Her hands shaking, she tore off the envelope and read the note enclosed; "You are not welcome here anymore... Mrs. Flora S. Bidwell."

Charlotte stood there for a long stunned moment, shivering. She was panting. Every time she took a breath, the cold hurt deep inside.

She grabbed her bag and ran out to the barn. Her nose was freezing. She tried to whistle, but her mouth was too cold. She rubbed her lips hard with her gloved hand and tried again. A sharp whistle—whit, whit, whoo. No answer. She whistled again.

Charlotte heard Lee's whistle back. She pulled open the barn door, starting inside. Something was thrashing by lantern light under the dark blanket on Lee's cot. There was an empty liquor bottle discarded in the hay nearby. Lee's head poked out from under the blanket. Another fair-haired head appeared beside him. She could not make out the face. Christ, Lee was up to it again.

"Come on in Char," Lee said. "I got room for one more. It's been a long time."

Embarrassed, she turned and walked out of the barn.

100

Karen Kondazian

At Byron's cabin it was quiet. She knocked on the door. There was no answer. She knocked again, harder, and called out his name. Eyes full of sleep, he opened the door. His face was stern but he let her in. The interior of the shack was lit by the glow of the fire. It was warm.

"I'm sorry, I'm so sorry," Charlotte said, her teeth chattering. "I know you told me not to come back, but I've been turned out. I had nowhere else to go."

"You're freezing. You'd better go warm yourself by the fire."

She walked over to the fireplace and took off her gloves, rubbing her hands over the flames until warmth returned to her body.

"Well...you were right," she said. "People are ugly."

As she turned her head away from him, he reached out and took her hand surprising even himself. And that first deliberate touch went through both of them like lightning to the bone.

He pulled her towards him. She could feel his warm hands touching her, moving her. He covered her mouth with his, and Charlotte, who'd imagined this much, had the odd sensation of weightlessness.

Then his hands seemed to be pushing her far away for a moment; no, he was removing her coat, sliding her blouse and her chemise off her shoulders. Her breasts swung free and he caught his breath. "God in heaven," he whispered.

He lay her down on the mattress and brought his mouth to her breasts. What she felt then was something she had never experienced...surrender. Byron removed the rest of her clothing. Then his own. She could see his body in the firelight. Looking at Byron standing there, she almost laughed out loud. His flesh had the kind of beauty that perhaps even death might pass by.

He lowered his body over hers. Her eyes snapped open as he entered her. He moved inside her. And then there was a tearing, a ripping. He saw her pain, slowed down and restrained himself with difficulty.

"It will get better. I promise. Follow me," he whispered.

Ignoring the pain, she let her breath, her body, follow his. She was being tap rooted to the center of the earth.

Afterwards, she lay awake, staring at the ceiling as he fell asleep beside her. She listened to him breathe until she too slept.

The next morning, she slid her bare legs from beneath the blanket, pausing for a moment when she saw a trace of her blood on the sheet. Byron's hand reached from the covers. He closed his hand round her wrist, holding her there.

He kissed her little by little, all over her body. There were parts of her body she did not even know could be kissed. Parts that caused her to bite her lips...that made her feel helpless, insatiable. He moved her and rocked her and within the safety of his body she let herself go. She arched her body to him and felt his body answer. She felt him dive to the very pit of her, and felt the acute pleasure and wonder of it. Unexpected tears came, then laughter—his and then hers—bodies rolling and slapping together into a breathless one.

And so for a few days, Charlotte never even left his cabin. They had their time of sweetness. They had blushes and self-berating retreats. Spirited conversations on the steps of the cabin. They had some false starts and awkward hesitations. The yearning to touch, the reticence beneath. When neither felt the need to talk, so replete was the silence...gazing out at the countryside, their senses addled by each other's presence.

THIRTY

M rs. Bidwell wasn't the only one who had gotten wind of Charlotte and Byron's relationship. Charlotte walked through town a few days later and the townspeople drew back from her and whispered among themselves. But she didn't notice.

Layered upon the streets and businesses and people around her were transparent images of her rich and unspeakable nights with Byron. There he was, his body in the warm light of the fire. She watched herself. She watched him. From the front and from the back and from the side. And she watched too, over and over, the scene of their breakfasting—dining? What time had it been?—on old bread and black coffee with sweet honey, sitting knee to knee at the table. And afterwards they'd return to his mattress. When exhaustion took over their bodies, against the firelight, they made crazy shadow figures on the wall with their fingers and their toes. Who'd have thought they were such geniuses?

Charlotte went into Bronson's General Store. She moved among the cramped, packed aisles gathering supplies. A little girl stood there watching her. Charlotte smiled at her, squeezing past as she moved out of the aisle. Another scene was opening in her brain: Byron standing behind her, bending her forward, holding her by the hip bones.

But then the image of Byron was replaced by a quick movement. The little girl's mother had appeared.

"Filth. Garbage," said the mother.

The attack was so unexpected that it froze Charlotte for a moment. She stood there clutching her canned goods to her chest. In a daze, she made her way toward the front of the store.

One of Mr. Bronson's cronies was leaning against the counter talking to him as she approached. She set the canned goods among the other supplies she had piled in a neat stack on one side of the counter.

"Excuse me, Mr. Bronson," she said. "I need three pounds of flour and a cake of yeast."

He ignored her. As if she didn't exist, he nodded to his shop boy, who began to pick up her goods and replace them one by one on the shelves.

"Well now," continued the other man. "You see your Negro's got enough problems on his own, what with insanity and idiocy by birth on account of his brain size, which God saw fit to make smaller than a white man's. So you got your good Negro, and your uppity Negro. A good Negro don't mate against God and the Good Book."

Charlotte heard herself screaming. It took her a minute to realize that the voice was coming from inside her head. The voice told her that she had to walk away from this place. Now. But she could not move her feet. She could not catch her breath.

The man looked straight at her. "An uppity Negro who mates against God cannot be tolerated in a town of decent folk. Not to mention you know, amalgamation is unnatural and against the law in our good state of Rhode Island."

Charlotte's fear turned into rage, which saved her. Now she could move. She spat at the man's feet and ran out of the store, letting the door slam hard behind her.

She stormed back to Byron's and stuck her head in the door of his shop. "I'm taking the wagon and riding to Pawtucket for supplies."

By the time he put his tools down and stepped outside, she was already hitching up the wagon.

"Charlotte. What's the matter?"

Ignoring him, she climbed up top and took hold of the reins. He reached up to grab her wrist and saw her troubled face, figuring out what must have happened. An expression of resolve came into his eyes.

"I want to show you something, something maybe for us," he said. "Just hold on."

He grabbed his coat, secured the door to the shop and jumped into the wagon next to her. She handed him the reins. He gave the horses a soft slap.

THIRTY-ONE

They sat in the wagon atop a hill, looking down. From a distance it was idyllic—a quaint, tiny farmhouse in need of paint. A picturesque, tumbled-down barn surrounded by a patchwork of snow-covered fields.

"Do you like it?" he asked. "What do you think?"

"Like it? What is this place?" she replied. "What are we doing here?"

"I have a crazy idea. I want to show it to you first." He started the wagon down the road toward the farm.

The place seemed on the verge of collapse. Byron pushed open the front door to the farmhouse. The door creaked and sagged on its hinges. Inside, everything was dust and cobwebs. Piles of autumn leaves moldered in the corners. There was a big old rusty stove. Charlotte lifted a burner from the top. A squeal: a family of mice were living inside.

He grabbed her hand and led her back outside. He led her past a now roof-less outhouse, past an old well clogged up with years of overgrowth, and then to the barn. There was a sizable hole in the side. They gazed in; there was a rusty plow, some moldering stable gear, and a few bales of wet hay. Across the ceiling were great beams. As they looked, an enormous rat ran across. And then a disorganized army of squealing rats ran every which way across the barn floor.

Charlotte was inclined to run away from this decrepit place, but she held her tongue.

"Look Charlotte. I've been thinking about us. I want to be with you. But you know I think it's a bad idea. It's dangerous. The only way I think it could work…us being together…is if we live as far out of Providence as possible. Away from people's eyes, away from their judgments."

"Yes, yes. I want us to be together. But live here? In this place? What are you talking about? How? With what?"

He took her hand and walked her to an old swing that hung from the big tree in the front yard. The wooden swing was bobbing in the breeze like a lonely child waiting to play. They brushed the snow off and tested it. It held their weight.

"A good sign," he said.

Then he spoke to her with a kind of excitement she had never seen from him.

"A Mister Wendell Phillips owns this land. He's an abolition-ist and a lawyer from Boston. His daddy was the first mayor of Boston. When I was a boy, he was the one that helped me run away through the Underground Railroad. He took me under his wing…he and his group; they helped me be a free man. We kept in touch and when I moved to Providence, he made me a job of-fer. He said I was a strong man and a good man and that I could fix this place up and live here. I'd be doing him a favor…no one has lived here since his grandparents passed on. The rest of the family is in Boston, but he doesn't want to sell the land. I think he has a mind to retire here someday. I would be the caretaker. That's what all the town folk will think. That's what Mister Phillips said he would tell them. I didn't take him up on it. I didn't want to do it alone. But I'm not alone no more. And being so far out of town, people should let us be. What do you say? I know it's a lot of work."

By now, he was squeezing Charlotte's hand so hard with an-ticipation, it almost hurt. She studied this man whose eyes she'd somehow recognized the moment they'd met.

"I think it's—I think the farm is beautiful," said Charlotte. Tears were welling up in her.

Byron enfolded her in a bear hug, lifting her off the ground. Already, though neither had any inkling of course—their love was that young—the cells of their child were multiplying within her.

 THIRTY-TWO

I t was late in the spring of 1848. Byron had made the deal. The farm had become theirs to watch over, theirs to call home.

He knelt on the earth, measuring a tiny seedling against his finger. The farm was beginning to blossom under their hard work and care.

Charlotte, her belly now round, moved across the field toward him carrying a covered basket of food.

Nearby, Emerson, the stray dog they'd taken in, was protecting his new master and mistress. He sniffed out a rabbit and chased it away from the field.

The surrounding hillside was knee-deep in Indian grass and wildflowers. At the top of the hill a horse tugged at the grass near a break of trees. Lee Colton watched Charlotte and Byron eat their lunch in the field. It had not taken him long to track her down—plenty of people in town were more than happy to share the details of this "loathsome and unnatural relationship."

It was summer. Lee watched from the hillside as Charlotte sat in the shade of the porch sewing. Byron was hammering something on the other side of the barn—repairing the hole in the side no doubt. Lee knew their property well. Sometimes in the daytime, when he was sure they were gone, he'd scout around noting this change and that.

Autumn. Byron sat on the chopping stump outside the door of the farmhouse, nervously smoking a pipe, Emerson lying at his feet. Lantern light spilled out the window over him.

Lee on the hillside awaited the 'blessed' event.

Inside, Charlotte cried out.

Emerson whimpered, looking at Byron. Byron's face wore the same doleful concern as that of the dog. How many hours had they been waiting out here?

Charlotte was half up on the bed, her nightgown twisted in her hands, legs wide, face red with exertion and pain. An elderly black midwife leaned over her with calm intensity.

Charlotte bore down with a subterranean cry of release and the child, at last, red and mewling, entered the world. At the sound of the thin cry undulating out through the pores of the house, tears sprang into Byron's eyes. On the hillside Lee could see him leap up. Emerson gave a quick bark of attention. Byron stood just outside the farmhouse door, every part of him ready to bolt inside as soon as he was permitted.

Lee—he was crying up there, alone on the hillside. He wiped his face angrily with his sleeve, leaving a streak of dirt across his cheek.

The midwife, after cutting the cord and daubing away the last of the vernix, unsmiling, offered the child to Charlotte, who was herself sobbing with powerful, indescribable feelings. Charlotte held the baby to her breast and it began to suckle.

"Oh my God, look. Look," she exclaimed in awe. "Call Byron."

The midwife walked to the front door and stuck her head out.

"You have a healthy daughter," she said. "You're lucky. It was a very hard delivery—her havin' a baby at that age. Now get yourself inside. She wants you."

Byron squeezed past her through the doorway.

The midwife walked outside, staring with deep concern into the moonless night. After a moment, she turned and went back in.

Byron was sitting next to Charlotte on the bed, his arm around her, her head on his chest and the baby at her breast. He looked down at the child.

"My God. She's beautiful. She's so beautiful," he said. He paused, looking over them both. "Thank you." He had a wild kind of grin on his face.

The midwife pulled her coat around her, picked up her bag, and went out without a word.

Lee on the hillside watched her go. He was raging inside with a brew of unspeakable emotions. He'd lost Charlotte, lost her for good now. Lost her to a nigger. He was devastated. He was humiliated. He would—this is how his thoughts went—he would kill them all.

Thirty-Three

It was a crisp, clear fall morning, punctuated by the rhythmic fall of Byron's axe as he chopped wood. Inside the farmhouse, the baby was asleep in a fluffy white sea of blankets. Emerson went up and sniffed at the baby, touching her with his wet nose.

"That's enough now, Emerson," said Charlotte. "Go outside."

The dog trotted out and across the front porch as Charlotte followed carrying a basket of laundry. She slung it into the wagon, already hitched to the team.

She went back inside and brought out the baby in her basket, and placed her in the shade on the porch. She waited for Byron to put his axe down, then walked over to him and leaned in for a quick kiss.

"I'm going to the river to do the wash. The baby's asleep. I'll be back soon to feed her. Keep an eye on her. And don't let Emerson wake her up."

Byron started to protest her leaving, but she cut him off, "I'm fine. I'm feeling strong. And there's a lot of work to be done."

"I'd rather wear dirty clothes than have something happen to you. You just had a baby. Get yourself back in bed."

"I promise I'll take it easy. I just need to stretch myself. Watch the baby. Don't worry. I'll be back before she wakes up."

He paused for a moment, leaning on his axe, "All right, I'll let you go if you finally pick her a name. What about Bess? Or Clara?"

Charlotte, getting into the wagon, made a small, noncommittal sound.

"She deserves to have a name," he said. "If you won't name her, I will."

Charlotte smiled down at him. "I know, I know. You're right. I need to make a decision…I'm sorry. There's so many names in my head. I want it to be perfect. When I come back. I promise."

"No ifs or ands about it, we are going to name that baby today," he said. "I think Bess, my mama's name; and that's that."

"Maybe," said Charlotte winking at him. She lifted the reins and drove off. Byron shook his head with amused exasperation.

THIRTY-FOUR

Charlotte had finished washing the baby's things and was now pounding Byron's clothes over a rock on the riverbank. Her hands were red and stiff from the icy cold water. The basket rested nearby filled with wet laundry. This was hard work. She'd much prefer to swing an axe, at least when her body was back to itself in a few weeks. Actually, she'd prefer to do nothing but nurse the child. Just lie there and feed the baby. What bliss. How strange that somehow, that empty place inside her had seemed to vanish. She wouldn't change her life these days for any other.

As she started scrubbing Byron's shirt on the rock, she felt the engorgement of her breasts ease. Her breasts, enormous these days, straining her dress to its utmost, were leaking their milk. Looking down she could see the stain of it rise on the front of her bodice. She should be back at home feeding her child now.

There was a sound: the crack of a single gunshot.

Charlotte looked up. What the hell was that? Her heart stopped in her chest. Her cold fingers released the shirt. The swift river current carried it away. She was appalled by her carelessness. But this was something she couldn't ignore.

She got up, her knees aching with stiffness, and stood still for a moment, listening hard. Then, heeding the alarm in her heart, she began to move. She dragged the heavy laundry basket over to the wagon. She lugged it over the side, spilling most of the clothing onto the dirty wagon bed. It couldn't be helped. They'd laugh about it later: her over-reaction, her protectiveness of her baby.

She ran around the side of the wagon, climbed on in a great flurry of skirts, and whipped the horses. They bolted. She whipped them again. "Sorry," she whispered to the horses, as the wagon jolted forward at great rackety speed over the rock and dirt road. "I'm a mother now." It's true; that's what she said; it wasn't Byron she was thinking of.

Charlotte whipped the horses again, urging the rough wagon faster than it could go. Her heart felt like it was skipping beats. She had started crying; tears were coursing down her cheeks. She rounded a curve and the wagon skidded out, one wheel hitting a boulder. The spokes crushed inward like toothpicks and the small wagon overturned. She fell onto the hard ground and rolled across the road. In an instant, she was up on her feet, not even pausing to check the horses or her bruised body. Frantic, she ran ahead on foot.

She reached the crest of the road where in a moment she would be able to see the farm. Her breath was deep and frayed. She came round the break of trees. The cabin looked peaceful and serene, wood smoke curling from the chimney. She felt a tremendous wave of relief. She imagined herself weeping in Byron's arms, laughing a little: I was so scared. He would be baffled and would shake his head but would pet her hair and kiss her and laugh too. Still, she needed to see her baby.

She lifted her skirts and started down the road toward the cabin. Chickens pecked in the yard around the coop; a pair of staked goats bleated as she passed by—the usual sights and sounds.

But then she heard a rumble of hooves. Her face drained itself of color.

"Byron? Byron," she called. She ran toward the farmhouse.

What she couldn't see: on the far side of the farm, Byron was running, hurling himself up the hill. The baby was clutched in a bundle of white against his chest. His breath was desperate. Right behind him was a pack of horses and riders. One of them was trying to lasso him. It was a game to them; they were rounding him up.

The riders were hooded, their faces concealed under flour sacks with rude round openings for eyes and gashes for mouths. "Over that way," one of them shouted.

Two riders broke away to take Byron's other side. They had him surrounded. He stood frozen in the center, panting huge gasps, hugging the baby closer. The baby was screaming.

"Little one," he whispered between gasps for air. "Don't worry. I'll take care of you." She didn't even have a name. So crazy at a time like this it crossed his mind. She should have been named. Damn Charlotte's obstinance. He knew that they were about to die. She should have had a name. She should have had a name. The thought ran through his head over and over.

The men raggedly dismounted their horses. They approached him.

Charlotte stumbled as she neared the house.

Emerson was lying unmoving on the ground in front of the porch, a gaping wound in his side, the packed earth soaked with his blood. Her face opened wide with horror.

At the top of the hill the men were gathered around a tree. A branch dipped as a rope went taut with the drop of Byron's weight.

The hooded men were hovering, watching the body struggle and convulse. His legs drawn up, his chest heaving, the baby silent now, clenched in a death grip in her father's arms.

"That's enough, now," said one of the hooded men. "We done what we came for. Scared the shit out of him. Taught him a lesson. Let him down."

"Let him down now," another man repeated. But the man who had tied the rope to the tree ignored them.

"Hell, I ain't no murderer," said the first man. He grabbed his reins and swung himself back onto his saddle. The other hooded men began to scatter toward their horses.

Charlotte was running. Her dress was gathered in bunches in her hand. She panted up the hill. She crested the hill.

It was the last moment already. She saw it end.

Byron's body rocked in the air. The baby slipped from his grasp and fell to the hard ground. The body on the rope was still. The branch creaked with the weight. She stopped short, paralyzed, unable to move.

The hooded men were wheeling on their horses, kicking the horses' sides hard with their heels. They vanished.

Piteous cries were bubbling from Charlotte's mouth. Her legs crumpled beneath her as she reached the tree. The world swam before her eyes and then for a moment ceased to be. Except, the last hooded man stepped out from behind the tree next to her, raising a liquor bottle to his lips under the hood. He tossed the bottle aside and fumbled with his pants. He hunched down over her and in a single movement ripped her dress apart like someone tearing open a package.

She came back to consciousness, struggling, clawing at him as he held her down. He was at her underclothes now. Her hands scratched his hood and pulled it half-over his head. It was Lee.

His hands grabbed her face, forcing her to look at him. His face was wild with pain. "I love you," he gasped. "I love you."
A roaring sound came from her mouth, and she spat in his face. A sudden look of surprise, and then he slapped her hard, bearing down on her.

"You whore," he said. "You nigger fucker." He frantically kissed her mouth and neck. "Whore. Whore," he screamed as he plunged himself into her. But he was limp with drink.

By then Charlotte had fainted, or died.

In a rage Lee bit into her breast, leaving a double arc of tooth marks. Her unresponsiveness spurred his rage; he used his elbows against the dirt to hoist his way up her body until he'd positioned his groin over her face, his own forehead braced against the needle-covered loam. He was screaming again. "I know you suck on that nigger. I know you do it."

But the will had left him by then. He got up to his feet, swaying. He managed to pull his pants back up. He didn't feel so good. His mouth tasted like blood and milk. He wobbled to his horse, struggling to mount and, after retching, rode off.

THIRTY-FIVE

Charlotte lay motionless in a streaked and dirty heap on the grass, her face vacant. The branches swayed in the darkness, their leaves soughing. Byron's body hung there, twisting with the movement of the wind. Somewhere far, far away, she could hear the bobbing of the little wooden swing, back and forth, back and forth. It was cold. The moon was rising. Then Charlotte's body shifted on the ground. Consciousness and everything else all at once drifted back to her. She awoke to herself vomiting.

It was full, that moon, and hid nothing. It shone down over the tree where Byron's body hung. Charlotte was dragging a wooden chair up the hillside. She was weeping…the baby, the beautiful broken thing. She'd already lifted from where it was splayed in the dirt and carried her, shrieking with the anguish of it all, down to the house. She'd washed the baby's body and kissed it all over. Then she'd wrapped the little body in her shawl and placed it in its cradle. She kissed and kissed its little brow.

She couldn't let her mind turn to the baby now. She stood on the chair behind Byron's body. For a moment she laid her head against his legs, and then she reached her arms around him. She tried to hoist him up a bit; if she could lift him, she thought she might be able to loosen the knot around his neck. But he was too heavy; what had she been thinking? She got down from the chair and went to where the other end of the rope was tied around the trunk of the tree. She tried to unknot it there. If she cut the rope with a knife, the body would crash to the ground. She couldn't bear that thought.

At last she was able to undo the knot. She started to release the rope. For the first moment the bark of the tree branch from which he hung dragged on the rope enough that she could slow the speed of it. But then the weight was too much; the rope slid, burning through her hand. She couldn't stop it and his body thudded hard onto the ground.

The sound of the body falling was terrible. She'd never forget that sound. With a cry of apology she went to him. "I'm so sorry," she bawled. "I'm so sorry, Byron."

She straightened his body out on the ground, averting her eyes as much as possible from his empty face. Where had he gone to, that man she'd loved? That man who'd loved her.

She wouldn't be able to move his body tonight. She was beyond exhaustion…no strength left in her. She forced herself back down to the house, took the baby from the cradle, and the warm winter blanket from their big shared bed, and returned to the hilltop. That night they slept all together for the last time.

THIRTY-SIX

It was dawn. Charlotte lay asleep on Byron's chest, her arm enfolding the baby at her breast. Her eyes opened. She grimaced, her face in agony, and closed her eyes, willing herself to die.

She opened her eyes again; she had a grave to dig.

She worked all day at it. She felt her mind go numb with the work, and this was good…disappearing into the rhythm of the shoveling. The earth here was rocky and difficult, and she wanted to make the grave deep, deep as she could. She spoke to Byron as she worked, and to the baby. She said everything she could think to say: a lifetime's worth of thoughts and regrets. Finally she'd said it all.

It's time, Byron, she said to him then. She bent down over his head and took him under his arms, dragging the body onto the blanket and then tugging the blanket to the long hole in the ground. She laid him alongside the opening and lowered him, feet and legs first, as best she could. It was complicated, getting him down there. She'd left room for herself, too, there in the grave; she could crouch alongside him to untumble him, to arrange him as if he were sleeping.

Then she lifted the baby, tiny, swaddled in white, so sweet. She made soothing sounds to the little one as she laid the bundle on Byron's chest, folding his arms around her. She placed the warm winter blanket over them, tucking them in. Then she placed Emerson at Byron's feet.

It did not feel right to climb out of the grave, leaving them there; in the dark shadow, amongst the hairy ends of tree roots, the rocks and yellowish clay layered in with the dark softer dirt and the worms and millipedes and pill bugs.

And horrible it was then to lift a shovelful of the soil and drop it down upon them. Yet another pain went through her, so deep that all she could do was stand at the edge of the grave, looking away, pretending it wasn't there, throwing dirt from her shovel onto their bodies.

Once they were under a layer of earth and she couldn't make out their lineation any longer, all that remained was filling the hole. It was a faint degree easier now. She worked shovel by shovel, filling it up and then raising it round, like a featherbed, above the level of the ground. She finished just before dusk. It was done.

Then she remembered the horses. She found the two poor creatures still tied to the tipped wagon near the river, scared but unharmed. They had dragged the broken wagon until it had lodged itself between two large rocks. She unhitched them and took them back home. It was already dark as she walked them into the barn, so they could eat and rest.

THIRTY-SEVEN

By candlelight Charlotte laid out on the farmhouse bed…a little red homespun baby dress, a pair of tiny crocheted shoes, Byron's worn copy of Emerson and one of his shirts, his old hat, coins in a tin box, Jonas' whip. She stood there for a moment, then gathered the clothes into her arms, embracing them, inhaling them. Enough. She bundled everything together into a saddlebag with some food and a canteen of water. From Byron's bed table, she took his five shot Colt Baby Dragoon pistol and holster that Weldon Phillips had given him as a gift after they took over the farm. Byron had, with care and patience, taught her how to shoot it and how to load it with its .31 caliber balls and powder. Now as she fed its chamber, she intoned Lee's name with each click. She snapped it shut.

She would shoot a hole deep into his heart. She could not turn the other cheek. She would not turn the other cheek. Not in this lifetime.

She'd already made the final preparations. She'd played them over and over in her mind. What she would do. How she would do it.

Outside it was quiet and dark and cold. A small flame appeared from the curtains of the bedroom window. The flame turned into fire. It moved around the house, faster and higher, reaching, stretching its arms, consuming and purifying all. Chickens and goats scattered, released from their pens. As she watched it burn, she had a fleeting moment of peace. The house looked so serene against the darkness, its burning face turned toward the comforting coolness of that constant sky.

She went out to the barn and released all but one of the horses. She placed Byron's pistol in its holster on the saddle, along with her small bundle of possessions. There was nothing left for her. Lee had swallowed her whole.

She rode off into the night.

THIRTY-EIGHT

It was almost sunrise as Charlotte reached town. She headed towards the stagecoach stop to inquire if anyone had seen Lee. Knowing him, he'd be skipping town as soon as possible. She had all night to envision how she would kill him. All night to imagine it over and over and over. She would move her finger against the curved metal of the trigger. She would pull with all her strength. She had no idea when or how this thing would happen. But, in fact, her future was already seamlessly in place.

As she turned down the street toward the stagecoach stop, there was Lee. He was grinning, having a smoke with a couple of gals. There he was. It was shocking to see him. It was almost as though she had dreamed him there. All she wanted to do now was turn and run. She took a deep breath. It wasn't enough. She took another, deeper. And another. Even deeper. Still not enough. She felt dizzy, faint…as though she were suffocating.

Somewhere in the distance she heard the driver yell at Lee to get in. She heard the stagecoach start off in her direction. It clattered by on the narrow street. She was compelled to look up. For an instant, Lee's face was framed in the coach window staring straight ahead. Her head jerked away. He hadn't seen her. The coach rattled on. She turned in her saddle to watch it disappear down the street. It rounded the corner and was gone.

The coach was gone. Lee was gone. And she was doing nothing. Just sitting there. Trying to catch her breath. She was rooted in place…staring glazed-eyed at the plume of coach dust still floating in the street. She must follow him, kill him, not lose him. But why had all will seeped from her? Her mind could not focus to command her body to move…her hands to lift the reins. Too

many nights without sleep. Tears were rolling down her face…
no sobs, just tears flooding her eyes so that she could not see.

She sat alone for a long while, wet eyes wide open, the morning
sun glaring down on her.

If she died this second, no one except Lee would even know
that she had ever existed. How strange to think that there was
no one. They were all sleeping under the earth…their beautiful
flesh turning to mulch.

Then an odd thing. Dampness, wetness on her saddle beneath
her. She looked down. Blood. Whose blood? For a long moment
she stared…feeling that her mind was slipping from her. Blood.
It must be, yes, her blood. That was it. Was she sick? She remembered the mid-wife saying she might bleed after. That must be it.
Or could it be her monthly curse? More than nine months she
had been without it, and she had forgotten of its existence.

She returned to their farm. The embers were still hot; there
was the sooty smell of burnt wood. She washed herself from
the horse's water trough. She took Byron's work shirt from her
wrapped bundle, ripping it to shreds and using it as a pad to stop
the blood.

She slept in the warm sweet straw in their barn, which was
still standing…the only thing left still standing. No house or life
existed. The fire had frightened away the animals. All life and
sound was gone. Through closed lids, all she could hear that night
was her own shallow breath and the sound of the little swing,
dancing in the wind.

The night seemed so long. Dark and light behind her lids. She
could not open her eyes; she did not want to open them.

She lay in the hay, curled in a tight ball, hour after hour, not
moving. Beneath her skin she felt a sharp pain in her throat, in
her stomach…hunger…thirst. She tried to open her eyes but they
were glued shut with sleep. Threading itself between the layers of

darkness was the comforting blanket of cricket voices clicking. More long hours behind lids of dark and light.

At last she moved, stretching her full length on the ground, an animal waking from winter's hibernation. She made a whimper. She took a breath. She was still alive.

THIRTY-NINE

Returning to the stagecoach stop, Charlotte reined in her horse. She called out to the station keeper who was just disappearing into the doorway.

"Sir, I'm a friend of Lee Colton. Yesterday, I was told he left here by coach. Can you please tell me his destination?"

The station keeper looked curiously at the disheveled woman before him. Not quite Lee's usual taste in women.

"No ma'am. Misinformed. Not yesterday. Colton left two days ago for Boston. Then 'round the horn' to Frisco, or so he said."

Two days? How was that possible? She slept that long?

She thanked the man and wheeled her horse around; there were plans to make, passage to calculate, monies to earn.

Something caught her eye. Next to a wanted poster of the notorious gang, the Daybreak Boys, was a large printed sign tacked to the side of the ticket window:

BE A WHIP!
JAMES E. BIRCH
STAGE COMPANY
STAGECOACH DRIVERS NEEDED
IN
SACRAMENTO, CALIFORNIA
(TRANSPORTATION EXPENSES PAID!)
ONLY FOR THE HARDY AND COURAGEOUS!!!
TRIALS EVERY SATURDAY THIS MONTH
INQUIRE WITHIN

It didn't take even a moment. She made up her mind.

She returned once more to what was left of the farm. She went and found the broken wagon with their laundry that she had abandoned four days earlier. She found some shears in the barn. She knew what she had to do.

She was now unrecognizable...haggard and drawn, dressed in Byron's clothes. She had wrapped tight strips of cloth around her breasts, a scarf around her neck, a long shirt to hide the rest of her woman's figure and gloves that concealed her small hands. Her hair was cropped short just as Lee had cut it so many years ago... the irony of which was not lost on her. He had wanted Charley. Then fucking Charley is who he'd get. She would get the whip job, follow him to California and kill him there.

FORTY

Charlotte rode down the main street of Providence, Byron's old hat pulled low over her forehead. She rode past Mrs. Bidwell's boarding house and the bookshop. She rode past Bronson's General Store. Mr. Bronson was opening the shutters. Of the horse and its rider he noticed nothing out of the ordinary. He glanced up at the click-clocking and then his eyes slid back down to his hands fastening the shutters on the pesky hooks under the clapboards. The horse had looked inconsequential. The rider had looked inconsequential. The hooves clopped in the usual way.

She tried to take all this in. That the woman in her had died in anguish and a vengeful man had been born in her place apparently brooked no notice of the universe. Nor had the universe even blinked in the absorption into itself of her tragedy.

It was astonishing to her that the sun had re-risen and shone down on them all in the same way as always before. That the townspeople weren't transfixed in shock, dumbfounded—changed outright at the death of the old world and the hollow, hopeless replacement offered in exchange. But no, their lives seemed to be moving on as usual. Charlotte looked around her in dismay. The townspeople were, all of them, just the same as any other day. How could that be?

She rode on, past the crumbling brick buildings and the peeling white houses. Everything was temporary; she understood that now. All of this was temporary. It would all be snatched away. It was all on loan. Even the people we love. They were all on loan. One day you see their face across a rickety table or you pass them hurrying from here to there, or you see them leave you in

your bed; and their profile passes you by...and you don't know...
your thoughts somewhere else. And then they are snatched away
forever and you did not know to say goodbye. You did not know.

It was going to be a bracing autumn day. The leaves were glim-
mering in the early light; they'd been turning crisp in the cold
nights and rattled now with the breeze. They were orange, gold,
and red. In her old life she might have called it glorious. But now
she knew the truth about all this beauty.

FORTY-ONE

A course had been set up on the outskirts of town for the stagecoaching trials. Seated in a wagon hitched to a six-team was a young driver. His whip unfurled against a transparent sky with a resounding snap, urging the team onto the course at a hard gallop. A group of men were gathered nearby watching him, calling out encouragement.

The Birch Stage Company scout, distinguished by his dark suit and derby hat, stood at the roadside. He was holding an official-looking notebook, shaking his head, unimpressed. He glanced over at Charlotte, standing diffidently off to one side, her hands in her pants pockets. Intense whooping from the onlookers drew the scout's attention away from Charlotte toward the approaching driver, who was now whipping the team back towards the finish. It was clear that the driver didn't have control. The lead team stopped short. The middle team whinnied as the leads tangled and the wagon lurched up for a moment on two wheels, then fell back with a crash.

The driver got down from the wagon. He gave an awkward smile as he approached the scout.

"Gotta work on your reining," said the scout. "It's shit. You know damn well your control of the horses depends on it."

The young man's face fell.

The scout turned to Charlotte. "Now you, boy. You're next. What's your name?"

Making sure to push her voice down low she answered, "Charley, sir."

"Charley what?"

"Charley Parkhurst."

"You know Yank-style reining Parkhurst?"

She nodded. There were two styles of reining horses, the old British way, and the Yankee improvement. The Brits ran their horse teams yoked in tight with no room to move. Yank-style reining took longer to learn, but was a hell of a lot easier on the horses.

"Ever driven stage?"

"Yep."

"How long?"

"Two years down in Georgia," lied Charlotte, knowing full well her skill would back up her words.

"Okay, so how near could you drive to the edge of a bluff with a sheer drop of a thousand feet with perfect safety to yourself, team and passengers?"

When asked the same question, Charlotte had overheard several other prospective whips bragging about how close they could get to the edge. One fella even said he would drive with 'one-half the wheel over the cliff'.

Charlotte took a different route. "The truth is sir, I might not suit your company. For I would keep as far from that cliff as the horses would let me."

"Good man. That's a damn good answer. Now let's see what you're made of Parkhurst."

Taking her time, she walked over to the horses. She checked the teams, running her hand over some of the horses' flanks, whispering to them. The horses whickered back.

Then Charley climbed up and settled into the wagon. She grabbed hold of the reins with her left hand and tucked her whip into the crook between right thumb and forefinger. The horses' ears flickered in anticipation of the reining to come. Charlotte was back in her element. She played the reins over her fingers perfectly, just as Jonas had taught her, and the wagon moved flawlessly through the course.

The men watched with grudging admiration as she turned the team a full and graceful 180 degrees and then started back again.

The previous driver standing next to the scout said, "Damn. Who the fuck is that? He's got good hands"

The scout turned to him, notebook in hand. "That…" he stopped, looked down, and made a notation in his book ending it with a grand flourish of the pen. "That, my dear boy is a whip."

BOOK TWO

There's no respect for youth or age.
Aboard the California stage.
And drivers often stop and yell,
Get out all hands and push like hell.

They promise when your fare you pay.
You'll have to walk but half the way.
Then add, aside, with cunning laugh,
You'll push and pull the other half.

The bandit grins like it's a joke.
He stops the stage and lifts your poke.
You want to scrap, but man alive,
That bad man totes a forty-five.

—A CALIFORNIA FOLK SONG

ONE

And so Charlotte began her all-expense paid trip from Boston to California. She took the steamer R. B. Forbes south down the Atlantic to Aspinwall, Panama. Then she had to fight the heat and the mosquitoes when crossing, by mule, the Yankee strip across the Isthmus to the Pacific.

At last, she sailed north up the coast towards San Francisco on a smaller steamer, the Dreadnaught. About a hundred miles out, one of the ship's pumps began to break down and they were forced to disembark in the nearest port city of Santa Cruz, California.

Up until then they had been making record time...four months of travelling, attributable to fair weather, no deaths, nor thank God, any pirate encounters.

During her voyage, Charlotte became acquainted with one John Morton of Morton Draying and Warehouse Company of San Francisco and a European traveler John Charles Duchow.

She studied these two men...their behavior, their mien. Dominance, control, self assurance, mastery...that's what Charlotte observed made up the mask of a man. That, plus a confident swagger. She also noticed that men never stared strangers in the eye. They tended to look anywhere but at each other.

She learned to swear, spit, chew tobacco, smoke a cigar, gamble and swig a shot of whiskey from her two new friends, who treated her as a son. They kept saying, to Charlotte's great chagrin, that if only there was a whore around, that they would teach him a few "special tricks" as well.

One of the masculine habits that she found difficult to acquire was keeping her legs spread apart, as men were wont to do. She

remembered how Miss Haden used to warn all the girls at the
orphanage that if they didn't keep their legs tight together, the
devil would jump in between them. But she realized with some
astonishment, that when she kept her legs tight together, or when
the pitch of her voice quite by accident became her own female
voice, or when an effeminate behavior over-took her, no one at
all seemed to notice. How could that be?

After much cogitating on the subject, she decided that it
seemed that one could reinvent oneself in this new mysterious,
musky world she was invading—and who that new self was,
people did not question. Perhaps it was the men's clothes, the
short hair, the pungent smell of sweat she allowed. Or perhaps it
was just that people were too involved with their own person to
really look, observe and give a damn.

During her long journey, Charlotte, when she wasn't seasick
or carousing with her two friends, had endless hours of daytime
daydreams and nighttime nightmares to conjure up the how, the
where, the when of finding and killing Lee.

How this would be accomplished, this feat...or even if she
could pull the trigger, when and given the moment...or if she
herself would be dead sooner than later; she did not know. She
had frozen once before. She also did not know if Lee had vanished
into the largeness of California or disappeared into another state.
Perhaps it might be years before she found him or perhaps never.

But there was nothing else she could think about. Her thoughts
were unrelenting. They were persistent. She had to obliterate him
from the face of the earth.

As the months on the sea drifted on however, her initial re-
vengeful rage subsided somewhat. And all she seemed to feel
was the old familiar emptiness, the bleakness, the loneliness. It
seemed to hide itself from her whenever she was with her friends
though, playing their men's games. So she stayed close to the two

men, not leaving their side until the sun came up, reflecting itself on the glinting waves, hurting her drunken red eyes. She would stagger to her bunk after vomiting up the night's liquid refreshments and sleep until the sun began to set.

Two

California
1849

A stagecoach, heading from Santa Cruz to Sacramento, made its way along a rutted road, the horses kicking up clouds of brume-like dust. Uninhabited terrain stretched as far as the eye could see. Perched on the box next to the driver, her face, hat, and clothes covered by a layer of dirt and grit, sat Charley Parkhurst…four months and a few weeks later already a pretty damn good man.

She was surprised at how easy her physical transformation had been. As a man, she now spoke, whereas as a woman, she would have been silent; as a man, she would take what she desired, whereas as a woman, she would have acquiesced. She must now push forward into this new world she was discovering and this new person she was becoming…a world of freedom and reprisal—an eye for an eye.

Charley pulled a can of snuff from her vest pocket and offered it to the driver.

"Thankee kindly," he said, plucking some from the can with his thumb and forefinger. He stuffed it under his lip. She made a mental note: thankee kindly.

The driver leaned over his side of the coach, hawked up liquid, pursed—in an almost delicate way—his lips, and then in a moment of fierce concentrated precision aimed at a branch on a passing bush and spat. That he missed that branch and hit another mattered to him not a whit. He settled back, a bemused smile dancing across his lips.

A moment later, Charley sloshed the tobacco around her mouth and spat out the brown juice, after which she, too, sat back. She did the smile as well, looking around in that same god-like benevolent way. She could get used to this: sitting up high, controlling the horses, spitting, man-smiling, everything.

As they neared their destination, she could see a scattering of cloud-like canvas and frame dwellings spreading out from the greenbelt that marked the confluence of the American and Sacramento Rivers. "That's it?" she said.

"Yep. That's Sacramento. Beating heart of the Mother lode."

"Don't look like much."

"Well," said the stagecoach driver, glancing over at Charley with a smile, "it ain't in some ways. In other ways you might say it is. Depends what you want it to be."

The coach and six-team trotted alongside the riverbank. In a short time the reaching arms of Sacramento surrounded them, and then, with an escalation of sights and sounds and voices, Sacramento itself—the clamoring, kaleidoscopic scene that had now become part of the fantasy of every man and boy in America. Charley leaned over the side of the coach, enthralled.

The stagecoach driver saw the direction of her gaze. "That's the Embarcadero," he said. "And that's the San Francisco steamer over there, carrying all the gold hungry men bound for Sutter's Mill."

She was taken aback by the dozens of barks, brigs, and schooners moored along the docks. They created a forest of masts... their cables looped around tree trunks and roots. The street was choked with stagecoaches and wagons, disgorging passengers, the passengers running for the boats. Men of every shape, color, and constitution—swearing, spitting, sweating, shoving.

Later, Charley would learn their names: Mexicans, Indians, Chinese, Australians, Basques, Croats. She noticed that there were no women of any shape or color.

The stagecoach driver was thinking the same thing. "Not a woman in sight," he said, sighing.

Charley forced a sigh, following suit.

The driver looked over at her. "Oh hell, don't worry. You can find tarts pretty easy though. If you got the cash."

"Thanks for the tip," she said.

The coach came to a halt at the Whistman Stagecoach stop.

"You can find Birch's Stage Company that-away," the driver pointed. "About a hundred yards down the street. Big sign. Can't miss it. Good luck on the new job."

"Thankee kindly."

Charley reached under her seat to pick up the grip containing her few belongings. She stepped down off the coach, placing boot leather into the dusty street, and at once was swept up in the inexorable river of men. Men with the glint of gold in their eyes, men striking up deals, men tugging on horses, mules, asses, and oxen. She had not realized before her long journey began just how many different types of men existed in the world.

She found herself intoxicated by the new possibilities of who she could become. In this land of dreams and digging for gold, the past could disappear. She could imagine that some would find this kind of amnesia worth almost as much as the golden dust they bled for.

Charley was pulled along in the torrent of men, herself indistinguishable from all the others...being moved along like a scrubby calf in the middle of a cattle drive on some endless trail. She was pushed up onto a storefront porch. Surprised by the sudden stillness around her, she caught her breath, then plunged back into the street and the moving course of men flowing around island-stacks of barrels, boxes, lumber, and supplies, to fight her way to her destination.

As she was struggling through the crowd, she saw auctioneers, dressed in wild colors, bedecked with ruffles. Some of them standing on wooden boxes, hawking their wares—gold mining equipment, sacks of flour, raw pork, dangling chickens, apples. There was one hawking old clothing and locked suitcases.

Charley was pushed onward. Over here was a cluster of gaming tables manned by sharp-eyed fellows with clever fox-faces. They were clean-shaven or pointy-bearded; they were all well-dressed. One of these professionals sat at each of the tables, shuffling over and over his deck of cards: Flip, flip, slap. Flip, flip, slap.

She noticed one of them looking over at her, sizing her up. The gambler wore fine boots and fancy clothes and had pomaded hair. He looked good to Charley, probably because he was clean and groomed. Then she noticed his fingers. They were long and graceful, toying with the faro deck. Once she'd let herself look hard she couldn't take her eyes away. They were beautiful, those fingers, the hands of an artist. They executed a dazzling display of shuffling.

The gambler took Charley in.

"I see that you're interested in the game of faro, my man." He looked down at the table and shuffled. "What brings you to the West? Come to seek your fortune in gold?"

Charley looked up now at green calculating eyes, an aristocratic nose and forehead. His voice was refined.

"No, sir," said Charley. "Got me a job as a whip over at the Birch Stage Company."

The gambler raised his head, cocked an eyebrow. "A whip? Mr...."

She nodded. "Charley Parkhurst."

The gambler extended a manicured hand. "Edmund. Edmund Bennett."

She shook his hand.

"Kind of small to handle a six-team, aren't you?" he said.

"Reining is a matter of skill, not of size. But then I expect you know about as much about my profession as I know about yours."

"Meant no offense. Why don't you come back when you get your paycheck and I'll give you a lesson. We'll double your money by the end of the day."

"I'm not a gambling man, Mr. Bennett."

Edmund looked out over the chaos around them. "This is wide open territory, Charley. Step one foot out of town and there's no law, no church, no social order of any kind. We are all of us gambling men."

A trio of drunken miners paused near Edmund's table. He gestured for them to approach.

"Step right up, gentlemen."

They crowded close around him.

"Good day, Charley," Edmund said. "Pleased to make your acquaintance. And good luck on the job."

As he was dismissing her though, his eyes caught something. He stared at her, fascinated.

Charley, willing herself to hold still, to not give away more than this man already somehow knew, felt herself deeply read. It was not a pleasant sensation.

Still, in a moment he had turned his attention back to his potential customers. He smiled at them with patent falseness—all that anyone expected was falseness—anything more than that was strange, was suspect. His fingers were doing something dizzifying. The men watched, their mouths open with concentration.

As he shuffled and dealt, Charley backed off and disappeared into the crowd.

Edmund flicked his eyes up once to monitor her departure.

THREE

C harley hesitated for a moment before she entered the office of the Birch Stage Company. She reminded herself...keep the voice low. No need to give herself away first day on the job.

"You shouldn't trouble yourself to find a permanent room here in Sacramento," advised Jake, the sandy haired fellow at the front desk. "You won't be using it much."

He eyed Charley, as if estimating the stamina of this new recruit from back east. "You'll sleep on the road. We got way stations from here to Santa Cruz. Eat there too. You better like beans and stale johnnycake and shit coffee. Other times you sleep wherever you can find a place. In the stagecoach, under a tree even."

Charley nodded her understanding. She wasn't in Sacramento to indulge in creature comforts.

"You know how to shoot a gun?" he asked.

"Yeah. I'm a pretty good shot," she said.

"You could get killed. You know that?"

Again Charley nodded. She knew about getting killed.

"Pay's good, though. And if you last it out six months, Mr. Birch pays for room and board. And get yourself a pair of good driving boots...with high, small heels to catch the brake at the foot-hold. Now come on out back. I'll show you the horses."

Charley followed him. At the stable she went right over to one of the horses, a beautiful Morgan stallion that resembled Beelzebub. She began to stroke his neck, murmuring soft sounds to him.

"Good thing you love horses. That's important," Jake said. "Oh and I almost forgot...we lost a whip real sudden and his run up to Nicolaus needs a new driver right away. Think you can start right off Wednesday?"

"Sure, no problem, but I was hoping to do runs to San Francisco. Is that possible?"

"Nope. Not in the near future. Only the experienced whips get the longer routes. Why? You got a gal in Frisco?"

"No reason. Just always wanted to go. Do have an old friend that's supposed to be there now though. Lee Colton. You haven't met anyone by that name passing through here have you?"

"Not that I know of. Course, I don't know everybody who passes through town either. Now…as to Wednesday. Be here by dawn. Any other questions?"

"No. I'll see you then."

Charley left and headed straight to the nearest saloon.

Once there, she pounded back a few shots of whiskey. How was she going to find Lee if she was stuck on runs out in the middle of nowhere? Would she ever find him?

Fuck. Here she was, dressed as a goddamned man in this godforsaken place. What the hell had she been thinking? What had she done? Thousands of miles away from anything she ever knew. What could she do?

Well, she sure as hell wasn't making a return trip on the Dreadnaught. That she knew. Christ almighty. She needed to sleep. She also needed to pee.

Charley slid off the barstool and stumbled outside. She found a secluded cluster of bushes behind the bar and relieved herself. Then she headed next door to a flophouse.

The Empire was a flimsy canvas-and-frame affair with a tattered petticoat for a door. She paid and entered. Inside, the dirt floor was strewn with straw. Board and barrel tables were clustered along one wall. Her dusty boots stepped over sleeping bodies of snoring, scratching, odorous, coughing men. Almost every inch of floor space was taken up. She picked one of the few free spots under one of the tables, dropped her pack to the floor, and crawled under, pulling the pack in with her. It would work as a pillow. She turned to find a somewhat comfortable position. In a moment the cool night air set in. She closed her eyes and tried to settle in to sleep, such sleep as she could sieve from her dreams.

FOUR

adn't even been three weeks and Charley was already becoming a familiar face along the Sacramento/Nicolaus route. Now alone on the driver's box, she was grinning on high as the horses bolted forward. In the stiff wind of the escalating speed, she leaned back on her throne, as the coach and six galloped on.

Up ahead, to the side of the road, a miner waved his hat to Charley from where he and some cronies stood at their diggings.

"Hey, Charley," shouted the miner. His clothes were extraordinarily patched—patches patching the patches.

Charley waved back. The miner flipped a coin, a California gold dollar, down on to the road. Charley watched the coin fall in a glittering arc onto the road ahead. She adjusted the reins and the coin disappeared under one narrow wheel rim of the stagecoach; it was exposed for a split second, then disappeared under the next wheel.

The miner shot his fist into the air.

"Goddamnit. Told you," he whooped to the others. He waved his hat at the departing coach, and then extended it upside down to the men. "Pay up you pieces of shit."

"Damn you. Never thought he could do it," said one of the other miners with grudging admiration as he explored his pocket for cash.

As the months went on, Charley began to pick up more and more runs. Jim Birch started to turn to her every time he needed a last minute replacement.

And this particular run to Hangtown was no exception.

Charley stopped the coach outside a ramshackle swing station, one of an eclectic collection of buildings along the stagecoach routes constructed of whatever could be scrounged from scrap heaps and the rough countryside.

The exhausted passengers climbed out of the coach, some having arrived at their destination, others to stretch their legs or relieve themselves. A young stock tender came out of the station to switch out the horses for the next leg of the journey.

Two prairie nymphs, heavily painted, sashayed up to the coach and handed Charley their tickets. They each tried to flirt with Charley—two variations on the theme of coquetry. It was no good. They ran through their repertoire of looks; they positioned their breasts, one pouted her lips, the other pulled up her skirt to reveal a flash of plump calf.

Charley avoided their gaze.

Puzzled, the girls each worked him even a little harder. It was like flirting with a plank or with a rock.

"Where's Ben?" asked one of the gals.

Charley shrugged. "My run now."

"What's your name?" asked the second gal.

"What's yours?" said Charley.

"Ben always lets one of us ride up top in the plum seat. And it's my turn."

"Well, I'm not Ben."

"You sure ain't."

"Whatever you say, Miss." Charley looked away. She was still getting accustomed to this part of the job.

"Aw, c'mon. When we get to Hangtown, I know how to treat you real nice."

She put a high-button boot on the wheel lug, intending to climb up, but the first gal pulled her down.

"What are you doing, you bitch? It's my turn," said the second gal.

"Shut your damned mouth. It don't matter. He ain't Ben."

At that moment, a well-dressed man climbed up behind them, taking the coveted seat. He grinned over at Charley as he handed over his ticket. It took her a moment and then she remembered the green eyes and the artist hands. It was that gambler, Edmund Bennett, looking impeccable. Charley found herself grinning back hard. She glanced down with relief at the two bickering gals who'd noticed that the plum place they were fighting over was now occupied.

"Edmund," both gals squealed in unison.

Edmund tipped his hat to them in a courtly manner.

"You sly devil. Headin' home to Hangtown?" said the first gal, jutting out one hip and then the other, pouting, touching her oily curls.

Charley lost no time; she raised the whip and called out, "Clear the road."

With a final squeak the gals dove into the stagecoach, the second gal just squeezing through the doorway before the coach jolted off…the sudden lunge forward swinging the door closed on her last hopeless flounce.

Inside the coach, the gals were still giggling. "Edmund Bennett, you rat." They adored him; he had manners of a certain sort; he had money; it was the expedient thing to do, to adore him.

Charley settled the horses first into a sweet trot and then into a sweeter lope. Edmund lit a cigar and offered it to her. She nodded her thanks and took it. She puffed on it, looking everywhere but at the man riding next to her. She wished that she weren't so aware that Edmund, for his part, was studying her, a slight knowing smile on his face. It was as though he knew her secret. No one else had looked at her the way this man did. But did he know? And if he did, what was giving her away?

They went on for some time in silence except for the hypnotic sound of hooves on packed soil. Their silence was soon broken.

Up ahead, swaying from a branch of a great old oak tree, was a dead body.

Charley involuntarily slowed the coach; the sight of the hanging body paralyzing her for a moment, the image releasing a sudden rush of memories. She tried to stop her legs and hands from shaking but couldn't. The horses, confused, stuttered to a stop.

Edmund, puzzled by Charley's agitation and obvious unease, waited. He could wait. Wait and the hand will be shown. Maybe it was the driver's first time seeing a hanging. Or, maybe, the driver had seen too many. He puffed on his cigar—even more intrigued by this whip than he had been before.

Charley took a deep breath.

"Guess they don't call it Hangtown for nothing," she said, doing her best to keep her voice steady and nonchalant.

"This is not the work of Hangtown boys," said Edmund. "They've got their hanging tree right smack dab in the middle of town—you know, where folks can have a necktie social, bring the kids, make a day of it." He gave a cynical smile and then gestured for Charley to bring the coach a little closer to the tree.

She walked the horses forward. Some of the passengers were sticking their heads out the windows, straining for a closer look. She forced herself to look at the man swinging from the tree. It was a white man. He didn't look like Byron at all.

Edmund continued. "No, this is range detective's work. Look there, the fellow has a "t" carved into his face. That's the sentence in these parts for equine abduction. Horse thievery. Brutal, but effective…usually."

"Seems this fella never learned that lesson," she said. "Sure as hell hope for his sake, his face was carved up after he was hung."

"Isn't it Emerson who says you can read the whole history of a man in his face?" Edmund asked.

Without hesitation, Charley answered. "'Faces never lie…' is what he said. 'A man passes for that he is worth. What he is engraves itself on his face, on his form, on his fortunes, in letters of light which all men may read but himself.'"

"Why, Charley, my man," said Edmund. "I'm impressed. A whip and a scholar."

"Nah. Only damn book I own."

Edmund laughed. He pulled a silver flask from his pocket and took a nip. He held it out to Charley.

"Don't mind if I do." She took a strong swig.

"Another cigar as well?" he said.

Charley thanked him and took the cigar, lit it and took a long draw. She found her eyes darting back up to the body.

"See the feet?" said Edmund. "See how they're tied up tight? That's a signature. They all have their signatures. My guess is Love."

"Who?"

"Harry Love. One of the best damn range detectives in the mother lode, or so they say. They say he ties the feet because he hates to see them dance."

"Poor bastard," said Charley.

"Yes," said Edmund. "Poor bastard."

Charley drew in a few deep calming draws. Thank God for cigars. They had become one of her new passions. If she were ever a woman again, she'd not easily drop cigars. You could hide all your feelings in the smoking of a cigar.

She could glance at the corpse for a longer instant now; it was getting easier and easier. She took her time, taking it all in. She watched the body sway for another moment.

She twitched the reins and the coach moved forward, continuing on towards Hangtown. But again her thoughts drifted back to Byron.

And then there were three of them—Lee's image had just slid out of its hiding place.

It had started again…Christ almighty.

That hanging corpse—it had all come flooding back again.
She tried her hardest to fight it—to push it back out of her mind.
But she had day after day driving the coach with nothing to do
but seethe and drink and remember.

Revenge seemed to be her only salvation. But now that seemed
impossible. The thought of letting go of that revenge was abhor-
rent to her. But what else was there.

Life had been glorious these last few months. Her job, the
horses, the independence she had found living as a man.

She would not let Lee take anything more from her.

She had to have the courage to jab a needle into the heart of
her wound...and with a single breath, release the rot inside. She
would try to take that breath. She would try to untie Lee from
her rage...but to give him her forgiveness? Never.

FIVE

Charley was making a name for herself. She was working more hours than any of the other whips in Birch's Sacramento operations. She had developed a reputation for always being on time, with zero accidents to boot. Helped no doubt by her decision to quit drinking on the job.

She had found her freedom.

Her eyes still searched for Lee in the faces she passed. But that was okay. Somehow, this journey of hers…she could never have imagined would bring her to where she was.

Saving up enough money, she bought herself a few acres of land on the outskirts of Sacramento. The cabin on it was crude but homey and serviceable, a big improvement from soiled rooming houses or the cold ground where she'd laid her tired head when she first arrived in California.

It was more than a life.

Sacramento seemed to be changing so fast—right before Charley's eyes. In January, 1850, a major flood had hit the city when the American and Sacramento rivers crested at the same time. Since the rebuild, there were fewer canvas-and-frame structures and more brick buildings, more Yankee-style wooden stores painted white with green trim, and covered top to bottom with enormous signs. There was more of an air of permanence about the city now.

Charley, who did not most days have the time nor the inclination to read a newspaper, did read, along with everybody else in California, an article that stated that on the auspicious day, September 9, 1850, President Millard Filmore had just signed his signature, decreeing that California was now the 31st state in the Union—and it had joined as a free state, safe from slavery. Since that day, there had been an unprecedented orgy of drinking, bonfires, processions, serenades, speeches, suppers, and cannon salutes—but mostly drinking. In fact, the word seemed to have been passed around that it was the duty of every patriot in California to get howling drunk. And Charley, of course, was happy to oblige.

Everywhere wild crowds were wobbling about shouting and cheering. A veteran reporter remarked, "One thing is certain; every face I meet is very happy."

Newspaper reporters from the east, now wanting any excuse to come out west, swarmed over the crags and peaks with their notepads and pencils, writing their confabulatory tales—*Wild Stagecoach Drivers of the Wild, Wild West.*

All of the whips put on a show for them.

There was a thundering sound—someone driving a coach and six, careening down a treacherous mountain road. There atop the driver's box, whip cracking, obscenities and tobacco juice flying, sat Charley Parkhurst, putting on one terrific spectacle for John Ross Browne—who was white-knuckling it in the seat of honor by Charley's side, trying to hold onto pad and pencil, flapping hat, and guard rail all at the same time. At Jim Birch's request, Charley was giving the famous writer a private demonstration of stagecoaching expertise. Charley was forgetting that it was a performance though, so convincing she was in her taciturnity, her stoicism, her spitting of tobacco juice.

There was a scrabbling sound of scree under the horses' pounding hooves; a thick cloud of dust rose up for a moment obscuring the road. The dust cleared. They were coming up on a curve ahead.

"We going to make that?" shouted Browne.

"Yeah," shouted back Charley. "I been over this road so many times I can do it with my eyes closed."

Browne looked over to see Charley driving with her eyes closed. "Mr. Parkhurst!"

Charley grinned wide and opened her eyes. She spat to the side and slowed the coach down to a brisk walk in order to make the curve.

"Truth is, I listen to the wheels. When they rattle, I'm on hard ground. When they don't rattle, I figure it's too late anyways."

Browne looked over the edge of the coach down the cliff. The wheels seemed awfully close. He cleared his throat. "Uh…do many people get killed on this route?"

"Nary a kill that I know of. Some of the drivers mashes 'em once in a while, but that's whiskey or bad driving. Last summer a few stages went over the grade, but nobody was hurt bad—just a few legs and arms broken. Them was opposition stages. You know a stage is worth more than two thousand dollars, and legs costs heavy besides. Our company's very strict though. They won't keep drivers, as a general thing, that get drunk and mash up stages."

Browne was not comforted.

Charley pulled a couple cigars out of her pocket and offered him one.

"A smoke to calm your nerves?"

"Don't mind if I do."

Browne lit both cigars and handed one to Charley. The coach continued on.

"Exhilarating ride," Browne said. He took a few draws and let out a deep sigh. "Most excitement I've had since watching Hyer beat Sullivan in '49."

Charley had no idea what the hell he was referring to so she just kept puffing away on her cigar.

Ahead on a ledge overhanging the road, a mountain lion was crouching at the same level as the driver's box—its colors were the colors of the rock, tawny and buff.

The horses were sensing danger. Charley noticed their agitation but was unsure of the cause. Something was out there—a
spot of intense stillness somewhere very nearby. She could feel
it. Then she spotted the cat, the powerful focused trance of
predation, the golden eyes flaring at her. The creature, all flank
and claws, drew back in a tight ball to spring. Charley snapped
the whip out to the side. She was so quick at it that her gloved
hands were a blur. Browne didn't know what was happening.
The mountain lion flinched, snarled, and backed off from the
overhang as the stagecoach passed.

At that exact moment, Browne met eyes with the fanged,
snarling creature on the ledge. He let out a blood curdling scream.
The horses, still very much on edge, panicked. And then like the
speeding shock waves following an eruption of dynamite, they
bolted out of control.

"Damn you," swore Charley, not at Browne—she expected
that sort of behavior from writers—but at the horses, who were
Westerners who should've known better.

She tried to regain control of the team, swearing steadily at
them. The abusive words were a soothing flow, an even flow, and
in a moment would have worked to quiet them. Already they were
contemplating allowing themselves to be calmed—but then, the
stagecoach grazed a rock, lurched to one side, and Charley was
thrown off the box.

Still clutching tightly onto the reins, she was dragged a good
ten yards over hard-packed dirt, her body bouncing and twisting.
It was a few agonizing seconds until the confused horses started
to slow down at the unusual pull on the reins.

Browne's mouth dropped open in horror—he couldn't even
scream this time. The befuddled team came to a full stop, snorting.

Browne stared back at Charley who was stretched out on
the road. Was the blasted man dead? Charley wasn't moving,
not at all.

"Okay, boys, okay," Browne said to the horses. He made an unconvincing gesture that suggested he was about to descend from the driver's box, but somehow his limbs weren't moving. He heard a cough. He turned to look.

Charley was folding her knees below her and pushing herself up with her arms, in obvious pain.

"Oh, my God. I thought you were dead," Browne yelled out.

A long minute more as Charley untangled the reins, reassured the horses, and then with her crooked smile, she climbed back up onto the driver's box.

Browne stared at her, scratched and bloody and covered with road dust. "You okay? Can I do anything?"

"Nope. I'm fine. Thank God I didn't get dragged under the damn wheels. If we'd been going any faster, you would've been scraping me up and pouring me in a hole."

She took her seat and adjusted the reins. It was costing her a lot to move without groaning in pain—but Browne's look of shock and awe was gratifying.

"Shit," she said. "Guess the whip's life depends on the temper of a horse or the strength of a screw. I hear we got a position opening up if you're interested."

Grimacing, Browne shook his head and said nothing. As they drove towards town, he kept stealing quick looks at Charley.

In the pressure of the writers attention, Charley forced herself not to cry out in pain as she was sure she'd busted some ribs in her little tumble to the ground.

They continued on, albeit slower than usual, and at last trotted up Front Street in Sacramento. Charley stopped the coach in front of the headquarters of the Birch Stage Company.

Browne, still shaky, held out his hand. "It's been a pleasure, Mr. Parkhurst, of the variety I hope never to experience again in my life."

As Browne walked away, pain creased Charley's face and she doubled over, holding onto the side of the coach for support. With difficulty she made her way through the business of checking in the coach and team. Every breath and step she took was like the stab of a knife in her lungs. She needed to find a doctor.

Six

D r. Tom Jarvis, MD and DVM, seemed to be a bit of a
loner for a doctor, judging by his office—an unprepos-
sessing shack on the outskirts of town. All the better
for Charley, of course. She stopped in the dirt road out front and
slumped over to one side on her horse, pausing there for a long
time trying to catch her breath and calculate the odds of the thing.
She couldn't see any way around it. She reluctantly got down from
her horse, gasping with pain, and went inside.

Dr. Jarvis was a round man in his fifties with the pink, spidery
veins of a confirmed drinker. Charley stood next to the wooden
examining table as the doctor made some notes.

"Now, take off your shirt, sit down and let's have a look," he
said.

She was expecting this. "I told you what it is," she said. "I got
drug by a six-team and busted my sides in. Give me some tape
and something for the pain, and I'll be on my way."

"I'm the doctor here. You need help. Would you be letting
me drive that stagecoach of yours, Mister"—he looked down at
his notes—"Parkhurst? You stick to your job and allow me to do
mine."

He held Charley's gaze unflinching, until with a deep sigh she
unbuttoned her shirt, exposing the dirty bindings that covered
her breasts.

Dr. Jarvis stared. "What the hell is that?"

She removed her shirt and almost defiantly began to loosen
the strips of cloth from around her breasts. She winced in pain.

The doctor offered a brown bottle, "Here. Take a couple of
slugs of this."

She took a grateful drink. Then she took another and handed back the bottle. The pain was making her nauseous.

Dr. Jarvis lifted the bottle up for a slug of his own.

She resumed unwrapping herself, prepared for the doctor's shocked expression, the crude exclamation that would ensue, the joke maybe, and then, worst of all, questions. The idea of someone wanting to know the whys and wherefores about her history frightened her, and she almost lost courage.

But when she arrived at the inmost layer and revealed the contours of her breasts, the doctor made no visible reaction.

"Okay," he said. He placed his hands on her rib cage and palpated, causing her to groan.

"One…two…and three. You busted three. You're damn lucky though Mr. Parkhurst…your own bandages helped you from breaking more. Now, you want me to tape you up, or you still want to do it yourself?"

"Go ahead," she said.

Afterward, her ribs taped, strips of cloth back in place over her breasts, her shirt back on, she began, "Uh…Doc, I'd appreciate it if —"

"I respect your privacy. Not a word to anyone. But you're not the only one, you know."

She looked up. "Who? Here? In these parts?"

"Yep…in these parts, and other parts as well. Nothing to worry about…nothing unusual. Hell, most people wouldn't see a grasshopper if it landed on their nose. Sure, I guess a few folks might surmise the truth about you fellas but I guess they figure it's live and let live…You must know what I mean yourself."

Dr. Jarvis took another swig of his brown bottle and then seeing Charley's incredulous eyes, offered her some as well. "Finish it up. You've had a hard day."

She took the bottle in a kind of haze and downed the liquid without even tasting it. It was stunning, this revelation.

Dr. Jarvis handed her a bottle of laudanum. "Not more than four times a day."

She paid her bill. Starting towards the door, she turned and said, "Thanks Doc. For...everything."

As she rode home, her thoughts were drifting...hard to focus. Damn...there were others like her. All that hiding. Fear of being discovered. And is it possible that some folks might know? How the hell could they know? Smell us out like an animal or maybe they actually looked at another human being. Unbelievable. She was not alone...there were others. For some strange reason this was comforting, soothing and also very funny. If she was not hurting so much she would be laughing out loud. Was that why Edmund kept staring at her? Maybe he knew. She was going to drive herself crazy thinking about all this...one hinge short of a nuthouse door if she wasn't careful. And what could she do about it anyway. What she needed to do was just get into her bed and mend.

SEVEN

Shingle Springs, California on yet another Saturday night—the wingding night the miners were in from their diggings, milling about the streets half-drunk and more often than not, drunken in full. They were alone, each and every soul. And like every soul had, or once had, immortal longings— rare and high and strange and intense. Each man's longings distinct from the immortal longings of all others. But it was hard to see this about them if you were to look from the outside at the milling men in all their jagged humanness, as they migrated through the streets in great accidental throngs—their personal edges now furry and hapless and animal. Disorganized so hopelessly with the desperate single-mindedness of their week's hard work and now filled with prodigious sloshings of drink.

Charley, migrating with the rest, passed a huckster trying to persuade the passer-by inside a saloon for the blood sport of ratting.

"Live rats in a ring with a weasel. Place your bets. How long will your rat live? Win big!"

Charley shook her head in disbelief and pushed her way out of the swarming throng of drunken men and crossed the road.

She saw a big canvas-and-frame tent festooned with a vivid banner:

**Vivaldi & Co. Presents
A selection from William Shakespeare's
Tragedy of Antony and Cleopatra.
2 Live Females Inside!**

It must have sprung up overnight like some kind of giant mush-room, a huge flapping one, appendaged here and there with canvas vestibules.

Inside the tent, behind a curtain, sat Anna. She stared at herself in a broken bit of mirror. She was liquid-eyed, raven-haired, a genuine Italian beauty. She knew it. She had once had immortal longings in her. In her dreams since early childhood, she'd soar bodiless from one glorious theatrical role to another—a dove of unusual spirit lighting upon and entering and waking up the great dead characters of the stage so that they'd move and speak and inspire and in all the important matters, transform mankind once and for all.

Anna frowned into the mirror. She could hear Luigi, the bark-er, through the canvas of the tent. He'd be standing on the barrel, a slight Italian man with a voice three times his size, hawking the night's entertainment.

"Vivaldi and Company—under the artistic direction of famoso impresario Luigi Vivaldi—who is none other than myself…"

He'd be bowing now, waving his hat.

"We present for your pleasure this evening—a selection from Shakespeare's *Antony and Cleopatra*. The famous death scene. The bard at his most sensual. A story of passion and intrigue. A deli-cious repast for the hungry soul and a feast, a feast for the eyes."

Building the volume of his voice, he added, "Gentlemen, I bring you not one, but two—two members of the fair and gentle sex in the classic roles of Egypt's queen and her lovely young handmaiden."

Anna muttered into the mirror: "Pigs and goats." She was wasted in this rude land of sex-craved men.

Her daughter Tonia plopped on a tatty Egyptian wig and made a face into the mirror over her mother's shoulder. She was a sturdy looking girl of eleven—the kind of child whose cheeks, much to her distaste, were always being pinched.

"Don't call them pigs and goats Mama," she said. "I like pigs and goats; they're nice."

Outside, a pair of drunken miners supported each other as they wove their way out of the general crowd over towards the barker. "You sayin' you got real live women in there?" one of them shouted.

"I got not one but, two—two members of the female classification."

"Well then goddamnit, I want them to sing *Sweet Betsy From Pike* and shake their titties."

A group of half-crazed men surged past Charley en masse and crowded around Luigi in their haste to buy tickets for the show. Coins and pouches of gold dust flew.

Charley, curious to see these two members of the female classification, bought a ticket for herself as well.

"Take it off, Cleo," shouted one of the men as he entered the tent.

Anna heard it and grimaced. Tonia gave a short laugh. Others in the growing crowd had picked up the cry, "Come on out Cleo. Take it off. Take it all off."

"Pigs," muttered Anna. She began swearing dark words in Italian.

This, Tonia knew to be a very bad sign. Tonight she would have to be extra careful. Times like this her mother was known to skip most of the words and scream things at the men, curses that made Tonia blush. Those were the terrible nights Luigi refused to pay them and they had to beg for food. Not to mention, that when her mother misbehaved, she incited the audience and sometimes they had to run for their lives.

The crude stage was fashioned from crates, boards, and barrels. Anna entered as Cleopatra, head held high. She was dressed in a long golden dress, trim bodice cut low showing her full cleavage. The men roared, some of them throwing coins up onto the stage. Anna's hair, curly and long, flowed around her shoulders. She moved her arm. The men roared. She began to smile. The men roared. Then she touched her fingers to her bodice in the general vicinity of her breasts. Roar upon roar. The men were beside themselves. Candles serving as footlights cast her body into relief. Her gestures got larger and larger.

Luigi, at the side of the stage made a signal that in Luigi talk meant: remember the bosoms. She tightened her lips for a moment but then recovered…pouted, pointed her toes and arched her back. Luigi responded with a big smile, nodding his head up and down, then rubbing his fingers together in the universal sign: money.

Anna tossed her hair back with disdain. This was not what she dreamed her life to be…but she continued.

Tonia, as Charmian the handmaiden, brought a basket of figs onstage and handed them to Anna. Anna flounced and preened.

She turned to her handmaiden, "Charmian, give me my robe, put on my crown…" She was hammering out the words, "…I have immortal longings in me."

Tonia clumsily draped a worn velvet robe around Anna's shoulders. She placed a painted crown, with several of the jewels missing, on Anna's head.

Charley, who had been standing near the back of the crowd watching, thought, mother and daughter no doubt. Mother and daughter. A stab in her heart at the sight of the lovely pair, alive to one another. Charley was grateful for the darkness and the crowd. No one could see her face.

Anna reached into the basket and pulled out a pathetic-looking homemade snake. A miner gave a sharp whisper. "Here comes the titty part." He threw a few coins onto the stage.

Anna then bent down to kiss her handmaiden, her eyes flickering warning to Tonia: don't laugh. Sometimes Tonia would start to shake at this point, trying to hold in her laughter.

"Farewell, kind Charmian," Anna proclaimed.

She raised up the sad looking snake, turned round in a kind of odd pirouette, and then writhed the snake around her. Despite herself, she became involved in her performance. She loved to die on stage. She held the snake in front of her face and narrowed her eyes.

"Come, thou mortal wretch..." she hissed. "With thy sharp teeth this knot intrinsicate of life at once untie. Poor venomous fool, be angry, and dispatch!" The words of the Bard were drowning beneath her thick accent but no one cared.

With a grand gesture Anna plunged the snake inside her bodice. The miners in the front row strained to see.

"Titty," shouted a man. A few more coins were thrown.

Tonia pulled a snake from the basket and applied it to her pale upper arm, made a face and fell to the floor.

"No. Titty," shouted another. "Titty."

"O eastern star..." cried Anna.

She swayed and also dropped to the floor. It still wasn't over. She spoke.

"Peace, peace..." she intoned. "Dost thou not see my baby at my breast, that sucks the nurse asleep?"

A miner shouted, "Breast? I don't see no breast."
Anna moaned, "O Antony."

She reached out to the last snake, spilled from the basket to the floor at her side, and applied it to the inside of her wrist. She shuddered on the floor in agony, rolled her eyes, sighed. She then died.

Pretty good tonight, Anna thought.

A hush descended over the crowd.

Then a single voice threaded itself through the silence. "We've been had."

Another voice. "Take it off. Goddamn it, take it all the hell off."

A chorus of drunken voices. "Take it off. Take it off." Stomping in rhythm. Fists punching the air. "Take it off."

Anna, still lying dead on the stage floor, the candles rattling before her, was seething. Her eyes were closed, but under the heavy Egyptian-style greasepaint, her skin was flushing red.

She sprang to her feet, rising from the dead, swearing a blue streak in Italian.

Charley, who'd been inching her way to leave, stopped and looked back in interest at the cursing woman.

Anna reached down with both hands grabbing the clay figs from the basket, and started to hurl them into the crowd, screaming now in Italian and English. Tonia, still lying on the stage, watched wide-eyed.

"That fucking whore hit me," shouted a miner near Charley.

He picked up what remained of the offending fig and hurled it back towards the stage. The flight of the fig happened towards Tonia, who rolled away, dodging it. It smacked onto the floor and shattered into powdery pieces.

Tonia was laughing, noted Anna with disapproval.

"Leave. Go," Anna shouted at her. Tonia was still laughing, but obediently rose and left the stage.

The drunken miners were yelling obscenities. A few had started fighting amongst themselves. A full-on brawl was about to begin. Left weaponless, Anna had an instinct. With great flaming eyes, she grabbed the top of her bodice and with both hands pulled it down and then slowly back up again, revealing her lavish breasts to the men for a brilliant moment.

There was a breathless silence.

Anna, with calculated imperiousness, strode off the stage. She knew that her insolence had shut them up. Knocked them into a cocked hat.

Now that the stage was empty, the herd of men began to dissipate, in grumbling, cursing clumps. In one of those clumps was Charley.

Outside, extricated from the sour smell of male sweat, she could breathe the cool night air again. She looked round at the moonlit tent with the last of the subdued men stumbling out and disappearing into the shadows. She had seen something memorable tonight. In her defiant act, that lone woman against a crowd of drunken men, had gambled and had somehow won. That woman had won her applause.

EIGHT

E arly the next morning as Charley was collecting the last tickets for the trip back to Sacramento from several miners boarding the stagecoach, Anna and Tonia, carrying a bag between them, ran up behind the coach.

"Wait driver. Wait for us," shouted Anna.

Charley turned and saw Anna and the heat of a blush suffused her neck and rose to her face.

Anna saw the man turn lobster red. Ahh, one of the pigs and goats, she thought. He saw my play last night and he's embarrassed in his behavior. Perfect. She was going to try to entice her way to a free ticket anyway...this would just make it easier. Anna smiled the smile that always got her her way.

"We're running late and I'm full up," Charley muttered. "Only passenger space left is up top with the baggage. If you want to get on, jingle your spurs lady."

Nodding to Tonia to climb up top, Anna followed. How odd. Why was he being brusque with her? That was usually not the case with men who saw her acting. He must just be in a bad mood...he had not yet asked for their tickets either. Thank God.

Her voluminous petticoats made for a difficult ascent, and at one point she looked hard at Charley and Charley knew she'd have to give her a hand up. That was the manly thing to do. Charley held out her gloved hand, frowning.

What's this sour look? Anna thought. What's this? She wouldn't have it. She paused to gather her skirts, revealing to Charley an eyeful of well-turned ankle. A miner inside the stagecoach caught the show, too. He leaned out through the open window and gaped.

Anna saw him see. She threatened him with her parasol as she ascended to the top.

Charley looked up at her. "Tickets?"

Anna said, "I—I don't have a ticket. We don't have any money. Nothing."

"Damnit woman. Why didn't you say so before you climbed up top? You're making us even more late than we already are."

Taking on the most helpless tone she could muster, she whispered, "Can we...work something out?"

Fuck it, Charley thought. She'd deal with this woman later. She hopped up onto the driver's box and grabbed the reins. She cracked the whip.

Anna, who thought perhaps he didn't understand, began again—but her words were drowned out by the rattling rumble of the coach. She turned and smiled at Tonia and settled down into the least uncomfortable position she could find, her skirts spread like a puddle around her. She had gotten them a free ride, once again.

Soon after the horses started to move, a second stagecoach pulled up alongside Charley's. The driver yelled out, "Hey, Parkie. You low down dirty thief. You stole my run. Now I'm stuck driving the fucking Mokelumne Hill route."

"Naw, you lost your run 'cuz you were soused again Ben," Charley hooted. "Why else do I always get your runs? Don't give me your bullshit."

"Bullshit? You don't know dung from wild honey."

The two coaches were moving at a slow pace abreast each other—the two drivers joking back and forth.

"Ben, your brain cavity wouldn't make a drinkin' cup for a canary."

"Oh yeah? Well your face looks like a dime's worth of dog meat."

Both drivers were laughing almost uncontrollably now.

"Hey Parkie. I'm doing the coaching competition. What about you? The prize money is pretty good."

"Maybe, but you ain't no competition in my book."

"You're so full of shit. Let's see what you're made of. How 'bout a practice run?"

"We got passengers Ben. Otherwise, I'd catawamptiously chaw you up."

"You scared? You turnin' into a nancy-boy?"

Charley laughed. "Who you callin' a nancy-boy? Fuck you. Let's go. When I'm done with you pretty-boy, there won't be enough of your face left for you to snore."

"You're on."

"Hang on up top!" Charley yelled out. "Clear the way."

The two whips cracked and the six-teams tore into a gallop. The roadway before them cleared, miners and livestock fleeing before the racing coaches. Charley let out a wordless shout of exaltation.

Wind tore through the hair of the mother and daughter, the black tendrils whipping across their cheeks. This was fun, Tonia thought, as she and Anna clung to the baggage rails.

Ben was laughing like a madman and so was Charley. They whipped in unison, and in unison each turned and glanced at each other for a moment with glowing faces, grinning.

But then the two drivers each looked ahead and saw the same alarming sight—something that each of them in their brainless buckery had known but forgotten. The road was narrowing, heading into a hairpin turn.

"Holy shit," muttered Charley.

Anna turned forward, saw the road ahead, and shrieked. "Stop this coach this instant," she shouted over the rushing wind. "Stop!"

At the sight of the narrow curve, Ben lost his nerve. He pulled back, dropping speed.

Worried she could not stop the coach in time, Charley screamed over her shoulder: "All passengers to the left of the coach when I give the word. Get ready."

Anna and Tonia crouched to their knees, ready to move... Anna crying to God to save them.

The coach was starting to lift off the road onto one side. Charley bellowed: "Everybody left. Now."

Inside the coach, the passengers followed the order. Up top, Anna and Tonia threw themselves over the bags to the left side of the coach, holding on for dear life to the rails. The sudden shift of weight balanced the coach just enough that the wheels steadied out, taking the turn.

"Madonna mia, mama protect us," prayed Anna.

The coach finished the turn and then started to slow down.

Tonia's face was filled with joy. She let go of the railing and raised her arms up to the sky, squealing with pleasure.

"Tonia, behave yourself," shouted Anna.

The passengers all together released their desperately-held breaths.

Charley, heart pounding in her chest, was taking in great gulps of air. What in hell had gotten into her? She had never taken risks like this before with her passengers. It was as though she was behaving like some damn man.

The team was now trotting. The world was moving past the coach at a normal pace. Anna let go of her iron grip on the railing and dusted herself off. She moved back to her former position and arranged her skirts. She glared at the back of Charley's head.

"Men," she mumbled. "They're such idiots."

But Tonia looked over at Charley with the bright-eyed, dreamy expression of a young girl who has just found her hero.

NINE

The coach arrived later that afternoon in Sacramento. As soon as Anna and Tonia's feet touched the ground, Anna grabbed Tonia's hand and tried to slip away before the driver could ask them for their fare again.

But Charley cornered her. "Ma'am, your fare...for you and the child?"

"I told you on the coach I have no money. I'm so sorry. The monster that runs our theatre company let us go without pay or food last night. Are you sure we can't...work out some other kind of payment?"

Charley balked at the implication. "Thankee kindly, ma'am, but that's quite alright." She looked down at the bright eyed girl staring up at her. "Guess your mama got lucky this time." She smiled at the girl, reached into her pocket and handed her several candies.

Tonia blushed. "Thank-you, sir." She wasted no time unwrapping one of them and popping it into her mouth.

Charley turned back to Anna. "Alright ma'am, we'll consider last night's entertainment as payment. Next time though, you might not be so lucky."

"Oh, thank-you. Thank-you," Anna said. "Aren't you nice. And you saw my performance? Well that horrible little man, Luigi, left us with nothing. We have no place to live. I thought maybe I could find work here in Sacramento."

"To be honest, ma'am, there isn't much standing-up-vertical-type work for a woman in these parts." Charley chuckled but then regretted what she'd said.

Anna, feigning incomprehension, gave a blank look.

Charley rushed to add, "Unless you want to take in laundry. There's never no shortage of dirty shirts."

"I have two talents. I can act, and I can cook, Mr. ...what is your name?"

"Charley Parkhurst, ma'am."

"Well I'm Anna Schiavelli and this is my daughter Antonia." She gave Charley a stunning smile. "Mr. Parkhurst, you are a kindly soul. Could I ask another favor of you? You don't by any chance know of any family that we could perhaps stay with?"

Charley looked at her bewildered.

"I'm a wonderful cook and housekeeper. Tonia is good at chores. I need to settle down for awhile. I must admit to you, sir, that I'm a little desperate. As I said, we have no place to sleep tonight. If I were alone it wouldn't matter so much. You yourself don't by any chance have an extra bed for Tonia and me?" She lifted her big eyes and gave a look that was sorrowful, modest, and grand, all at the same time.

The small hairs on Charley's arms rose at the strong brown gaze. She had to give her credit. This woman had grit.

Since arriving in California, Charley had remained distant and taciturn with most folks she met...for obvious reasons. But in spite of herself and her apprehension, she found herself moved by the mother and daughter's plight and mettle. She decided to take the risk and give them temporary lodging. She could handle sleeping in the barn for a few days until the mother and girl were settled.

Charley's place was a homey old two-room cabin on River Road, just outside of Sacramento. There was a fenced-in garden in the front, with potatoes, carrots, tomatoes, and a little strawberry patch. To the side was a small barn and corral and next to that a well and a tiny shed with a few chickens and a goat. In the back was an outhouse.

The two horses in the corral were looking round just now, snorting as if in disbelief at the procession making its way across the straggly grass. First came Charley, the sun beating down on her sweating face, carrying a large, overstuffed cloth valise. Behind her came Anna holding her head up with pride. She had once again found a way to provide for Tonia. She always made her own opportunities.

Behind Anna, came Tonia—she was looking at everything, smiling, skipping. "Oh, a goat," she said. "I love goats." Anna turned around to give her one of her warning looks. Tonia blatantly ignored her. "Oh, horses," she said. "What pretty horses. I love horses."

Charley pushed open the cabin door and entered.

Anna and Tonia stopped at the doorway and looked in. They could see a table and chairs, a fireplace, some cooking pots, a small iron stove. There was also a door to another room.

Charley dropped the valise on the floor. "You can stay here while you look for something. You both take the bed in the other room. I'll sleep in the barn."

With a brush of her skirt and a flirtatious thank-you, Anna swept past Charley through the bedroom doorway to take possession of the room.

Ten

T he following evening when Charley came back from town she could smell dinner even before she dismounted. She'd never smelled anything this good, this rich. What could it be? What on earth could there have been to cook? She opened the door in a kind of trance of anticipation. Inside, on the stove, was a large pot of rich-looking soup, beads of golden fat swimming in pools on the surface. The table was set for three. In the center of the table was a bowl of pasta and a roasted chicken, plump, golden-brown and juicy, sprinkled with herbs. For a moment Charley stood in awed silence, and in that silence she heard a tiny sound. It was the fragile crust of the bread, pulled from the oven just an instant earlier, crackling as it started to cool. Simple tears sprang to her eyes and she blinked them back.

Anna saw it and gave Charley a sweet smile. Her face was flushed with the heat of cooking, and wisps of her black hair curled around her face.

"My God, where did you find all this food to cook with?" Charley asked.

Tonia, who was so excited she was gulping air, blurted out, "Well, mama stole Luigi's food before we left, some bread and pasta and she took some lard, oh, and some cheese, my favorite. Mama always does that when we get fired. That's how we eat until some nice person takes us in."

Anna, her face turning from flush to horror, pinched Tonia hard on the arm. "No, no, no, Tonia, you're mistaken."

Tonia giggled, as her mother gave her a dark look.

Charley didn't even notice, so hypnotized she was by the feast on the table.

She washed up and they all sat down, Charley at the head of the table and Anna and Tonia on either side. They all grabbed their napkins, which to Charley, looked oddly like torn pieces of her bed linen.

"I do hope that you like soup?" said Anna.

"Yes, ma'am," said Charley. She picked up her spoon and dipped it into the broth. The fat bubbles shimmered as she lifted the spoon to her mouth.

The three of them ate in silence by candlelight. Charley kept her head down; the soup commanded total commitment.

"Is it good, Mr. Parkhurst?"

"Yes, ma'am. Sure is good."

Anna served the pasta. Swirls of aromatic steam rose above each plate. She must have picked wild herbs for the flavoring, Charley thought. Or did she carry them in that perpetually bestowing valise as well?

Just as she was about to say thank-you, a wave of unexpected melancholy came over her. She realized for the first time how much she had needed this...to be taken care of. But Anna was bestowing this miracle on her because she believed Charley a man...a man very much in need of Anna's special mothering.

As if reading Charley's thoughts, Anna asked, "Where is your wife, Mr. Parkhurst?"

"My wife?" Charley looked away. "I'm a single man, ma'am."

Tonia sucked a long noisy strand of pasta up through her lips.

"Spaghetti, don't do that," Anna said. "Wrap it with your fork inside your spoon, like I taught you."

"Spaghetti?" laughed Charley.

"I call her 'Spaghetti' because when she was little, it was the only food she would eat. Not just any spaghetti. Spaghetti her mama would make. Isn't that right, my little noodle?"

Tonia hated this. "Oh, mama," she said in anguish, twisting her body in the rough wooden chair.

"And she still loves my spaghetti. Maybe a little too much."

Now Tonia out-and-out glared at her. "Mother!" She got up, knocking the chair down behind her. She covered the distance of the room in a moment, stamping out the front door of the cabin and slamming it behind her.

Anna was embarrassed. She looked at Charley. "Excuse her. It's the age. I will speak to her." She started to rise from her chair.

Charley got up and gestured for Anna to stay. "I'll go talk to her." She was relieved not to have to explain further her lack of a wife.

Tonia was outside leaning on the corral fence. She was watching the horses in the twilight, her fingers drumming on the wooden slats. Charley approached and stood next to her without speaking. The horses noticed them and ambled over.

After a few moments Tonia said, "I don't know why my mother says such stupid things to me."

"I'm sure she doesn't mean to hurt you," Charley said. "But you know, sometimes grown-ups don't always think before they speak."

Charley began to stroke one of the horses.

Tonia copied Charley's movement.

"You know my mother used to never criticize me," Tonia said. "We used to live in this big house with all these nice ladies who were actresses. I was just a little girl then. I had so much fun there. And Agnes, who ran the house, was always so nice to me and she always gave me cake. Anyway, I know my mama loved me, but she was always so busy with all her boyfriends that she never paid much attention to me. But now all she does is criticize me."

Tonia was talking so fast she had to stop to catch her breath.

"Oh, my goodness," Charley said. "So…were you born in Italy or America?"

"Oh I was born in New York City. I'm an American. My mama came over from Italy when she was sixteen. My daddy brought her over and then my mama said he died. And that's when I was born. There was this other man, Frank, she said…who taught her to be an actress. And then there was Alfred, and we all toured in a funny play but then Luigi discovered us, and we went with him. And he let me be an actress."

Tonia stopped petting the horse. She turned and looked up into Charley's face.

"You know, I don't think I will be an actress when I grow up."

"No?" said Charley.

"I wanted to be, but mama says I don't have the artist temperament."

"What do you want to do then?"

"I didn't know until yesterday." She paused. "Now I know I want to be a stagecoach driver."

"Well now. A stagecoach driver." Charley turned that one over in her mind. "That's no occupation for a young lady."

"I don't want to be a young lady."

"Wait a few years until you meet a handsome boy. You'll change your mind."

Tonia looked straight at Charley. "No, I won't."

"Well, maybe you won't at that."

The girl was awkward and honest and spunky Charley thought—reminded her of herself. "Maybe you will be a woman stagecoach driver. Shock everyone. Shock your mother. It wouldn't shock me much. In fact, it wouldn't shock me at all." Charley winked at her. "You know…while you're here, if your momma gives us permission, I'll give you some coaching lessons."

Tonia's eyes lit up with excitement.

"And I have another idea. Have you ever seen one of those Concord stages?"

Tonia shook her head no.

"Well, how about you come to work with me tomorrow to see a brand new one?"

"Yes," she squealed.

"Good. Now come inside. Finish your dinner. Pinky deserves to be enjoyed."

"Pinky?"

"The chicken."

"Oh, no. It had a name?"

"No matter," chuckled Charley. "Your mother has a great talent for cooking."

Walking back in the darkness towards the cabin, she added, "Don't be too hard on her, Tonia. Everything she does is because she loves you. It may be that your path, growing into a woman, ends up different from hers. If that's so, that's because you live in more modern times."

Tonia, flattered at Charley's serious attention, took her hand.

Anna was waiting in the doorway.

"I'm sorry, mama," Tonia said. She felt sorry for her mother now, not privileged to have grown up in modern times.

Anna touched her arm. "It's all right my baby." She was aware of Charley standing there. It would go easier for them with a man in the picture: two strong women. They needed someone to keep them at arm's length. He would do that for them.

And at that moment, Anna made up her mind; someway, somehow, she would find a way to make them a family.

ELEVEN

A brand new Concord stagecoach stood before them. It had bright yellow wheels with a vermilion body and black trim. The side panels were decorated with a hand-painted landscape, and fine oiled leather curtains hung from the windows. Jim Birch, president of the stage company, stood with some of his top drivers, Hank Monk and Charley among them. At Charley's side was an excited Tonia.

"Here she is," said Birch, "tidy and graceful as a lady, and—like a lady—barely a straight line in her body." He ran his hands over the coach. "But that's not why I love her. That's not why I had her brought round the Cape. The Concord is the best. It's as smooth a ride as you're ever going to get. You're going to feel like a baby rocking in its cradle. The Concord Company is sending over three more just like her. Sacramento is now the busiest stage hub in the country. We need the best because we are the best. We've got the best horses, the best runs, and by far the best whips. I'm proud of you boys. You are nickel-plated and don't you forget it. That's why I chose you and that's why you work for us. Now to cap the climax, I have some important news. In a few months our company will be merging with Wells Fargo & Company. We will be known as the Wells Fargo & Company Overland Stage. For those who are willing, there will be more frequent and longer runs with pay to match. All coaches will be outfitted with new green mailboxes. You will note the new middle bench inside the coach as well, with the hanging leather straps to hold on to. This is the new second class travel. Up top is now third class, the hangers-on. And this here is a poster of the Wells Fargo Stagecoach rules."

He held one up to show the group. "Each swing-station will have one posted."

WELLS FARGO RULES FOR RIDING THE STAGECOACH
Adherence to the Following Rules Will Insure a Pleasant Trip for All

1. Abstinence from liquor is requested, but if you must drink, share the bottle. To do otherwise makes you appear selfish and un-neighborly.
2. Abstain entirely in cold weather—you'll freeze twice as fast under the influence.
3. If ladies are present, gentlemen are urged to forego smoking cigars and pipes as the odor of same is repugnant to the Gentle Sex. Chewing tobacco is permitted, but spit with the wind, not against it.
4. Gentlemen must refrain from the use of rough language in the presence of ladies and children.
5. Buffalo robes are provided for your comfort during cold weather. Hogging robes will not be tolerated and the offender will be made to ride with the driver.
6. Don't snore loudly or lop over your neighbors while sleeping or use your fellow passenger's shoulder for a pillow; he or she may not understand and friction may result.
7. Firearms may be kept on your person for use in emergencies. Do not fire them for pleasure or shoot at wild animals as the sound riles the horses.
8. In the event of runaway horses, remain calm. Leaping from the coach in panic will leave you injured, at the mercy of the elements, hostile Indians and hungry wolves. If the team runs away, sit still and take your chances.
9. Forbidden topics of discussion are stagecoach robberies and Indi-

an uprisings. Also, don't discuss politics or religion, nor point out places on the road where horrible murders have been committed.

10.	Gents guilty of unchivalrous behavior toward lady passengers will be put off the stage. It's a long walk back. A word to the wise is sufficient.

11.	Expect annoyance, discomfort and some hardships. If you are disappointed, thank heaven.

Birch continued on, "Please make sure all passengers are familiar with these rules."

He then turned to look down at an enthralled Tonia.

"Hey Tonia, what do you say? You and Charley want to take the Concord on her first ride? Make sure she's all in good working order?"

Tonia squeezed her eyes shut at the utter joy of it and nodded her head up and down.

It wasn't long before the bright red Concord, with its dazzling yellow wheels, was on the road. Tonia was riding shotgun alongside her handsome Charley. They grinned at each other, their eyes narrowed against the bleaching sunlight, the wind sanding their faces. Tonia thought how like a god Charley looked. With such ease he flicked a finger coiled with the reins, and the horses, like something so powerful, rippled this way or that in response to his bidding. She would be just like him someday.

Tonia ran pell-mell through the cabin door later that afternoon as drunk as can be on happiness. Of course, Anna was displeased when she learned the cause of it, but at that point it was too late to matter much—Tonia was smitten.

And from then on, from time to time, they would sneak off and Charley would take her along on a real run.

When they'd return home, Anna would, of course, scold them both. Charley would then say to her, "Aw, shucks ma'am, I clear forgot your feeling about these matters." And then she'd wink at Tonia.

Somehow those few days that Charley thought Anna and Tonia would stay, turned into something much longer. Anna was taking care of the cooking and the upkeep of the place, which suited Charley just fine. Tonia was in charge of feeding all the animals. And she had also started attending school in town.

It worked well enough, satisfying all their needs to belong to a family. With pleasure now outweighing loneliness, Charley's fear of being discovered subsided.

Charley behaved towards Anna like a little boy, somewhat irresponsible and mischievous, and Anna in turn, had no choice but to respond somewhat like a half-exasperated mother with a second, albeit extra-big, child.

As much as Charley was son of sorts to Anna, he was also an indulgent father of sorts to Tonia—and this in turn, as well as the fact that Charley provided for the two of them, made him in Anna's eyes man enough to husband her.

Anna began to work on Charley with deliberation, opening those top buttons, leaning enticingly in the serving of dinner, touching Charley's arm in conversation. "Don't you think so?" she'd say, bending in, her lips moist.

"Yes, ma'am," Charley would say and then change the subject.

And Anna would think: Doesn't he see that I'm willing?

Tonia, of course, saw it all, coming and going.

TWELVE

I t was an unusually warm, muggy day and Charley with Tonia beside her were taking a run to Stockton. As usual, they were having a wonderful time together, sharing private thoughts, telling funny stories and finding solutions to all of Tonia's predicaments, particularly surrounding her mother.

"Now Tonia, when you grow up to be a famous whip and need to handle any unruly ladies aboard, perhaps like your dear mama, all you have to do is yell 'Indians!' It will quiet them down quicker than 40 Rod Whiskey does a man."

Tonia giggled.

The Concord went around a curve, slowing as it approached the steep grade outside of town.

Charley brought the team to a stop. "First class passengers, stay where you are," she yelled. "Second class, get out and walk. Third class, get down and push." And as always, the second and third class passengers, grumbling and mumbling, got out and milled around beside the coach waiting for further instructions.

There was the sound of snapping twigs. In the bushes next to the road someone was lying in wait. The barrel of a sawed-off shotgun snaked out from between the leaves. The hammer cocked with a loud click. A shot rang out. There was pandemonium— screaming passengers diving for cover.

Charley's mind was racing. The first hold-up of her career, and of course, Tonia had to be with her. She pushed her into a flattened position down by her feet. There was no way to hide her, but at least she was out of the range of any random flying bullets.

"Everybody out of the coach and hands high in the air. Now. Including you driver. And the kid," shouted the bandit.

The first-class passengers exited the coach and joined the frightened group, hands raised high. They all looked over at the bizarre figure standing before them.

The bandit's entire face was covered with a sugar sack, slits for his eyes, nose and mouth. His feet were covered with a pair of burlap sugar sacks as well, tied around the ankles.

"Damn it," said Charley under her breath. "It's Sugarfoot."

Although Charley had never had the pleasure of Sugarfoot's company, she knew, as everyone knew, about his peculiar signature—his face and boots always wrapped in sugar sacks. No one could understand why he covered his boots. Charley also observed that the well-armed bandit was toting a pair of low-slung revolvers in addition to his shotgun. He wore an elegant brown duster and leather gloves. The duster looked somehow fresh, laundered.

She looked around to see if there was anyone else hiding in the bushes. Sugarfoot appeared to be alone, but she had heard rumors that he worked with a gang.

"Gentlemen...and ladies...this is a hold-up," said the bandit. He was now courteous and soft-spoken. "Stay calm and no one will get hurt." He looked them over, his wrapped feet planted in shooting position, his gun trained on the lot of them. "I want you gentleman one by one to reach for your guns nice and slow. Place them on the ground. Then I would appreciate you kicking them towards me. If any of you decide to challenge me, I guarantee you, my men hiding in the bush will send you speedily to your maker. You driver, let's begin with you."

He braced himself behind his shotgun as each man complied.

"Thank-you gentlemen. Now driver, would you be so kind as to climb up and throw down the box."

He had a peculiar kind of English accent Charley noted, even with his voice somewhat muffled behind the sack. That was something she never knew about Sugarfoot—he's a damn Britisher.

Charley looked at him straight on. "I got nothing but mail."

"Indeed," said Sugarfoot. "But that's what they all say. You don't mind if I ascertain that fact with my very own eyes, do you, sir? It's not that I don't trust you. Now, please throw down the box."

As Charley climbed up to the driver's seat, she felt her legs shaking. She reached under into the strongbox hold. She tugged the box forward and with difficulty toppled it down to the ground. She then returned to her place next to Tonia and the rest of the passengers.

The box lay there on the dirt for a moment while all of them stared at it.

Sugarfoot aimed, shot off the lock, and advanced towards it, kicking off the last remnants of the twisted metal. He then kicked it open. White paper spilled out. Mail. Just mail.

"Ah, a man of his word, for once," said Sugarfoot. "I salute you, driver." He sighed, looking at the row of pale-faced passengers. "Oh dear. What to do?"

He paced up and down the row. "I do apologize. You look like a kindly lot. You wouldn't send me away empty-handed now, would you?"

He trained his gun on the first passenger in line, and threw an empty sugar sack at him. "You," his voice turned cold and threatening.

The man jumped and plunged his hand in his pocket for his coin purse. He placed the purse into the sack, "Here. Take it."

"Your watch too."

The man quivering, opened his waist coat, removed his gold pocket watch and dropped it into the sack.

"Thank-you my good man," said Sugarfoot. "Now please pass the sack along to our next friend."

He pointed the gun at the next passenger. "I'm afraid it's your turn, sir."

The next passenger made no move for a long moment. Instead he chewed on his tobacco. Then keeping his eyes fixed on Sugarfoot, spat on the ground.

Sugarfoot stepped forward. "Tut, tut," he said scolding, cocking his gun. "The goddess Hygeia, my dear sir, begs observance. It's plain prudence to display good manners to the chap with the gun."

The man kept his eyes on Sugarfoot and continued to chew, but now his hand was reaching into his pocket. He pulled out his wallet and dropped it into the waiting sack.

"Wise man," said Sugarfoot. "Next."

One by one, the passengers relieved themselves of the contents of their pockets: their gold dust, money, watches, and jewelry.

Charley, who was the last to receive the sack, emptied all the coins from her pockets. She dropped them inside and held it out to Sugarfoot.

"Please young lady," said Sugarfoot pointing to Tonia. "Would you be a little angel and deliver the goods to me?"

"Hell, don't involve the girl," said Charley.

"I must insist. But don't fret. I would never hurt a child."

Tonia stepped forward, her eyes bright with excitement, "Don't worry, Charley. I'm not afraid."

Charley hesitated but then handed the sack over to Tonia.

Tonia's little feet began to move towards Sugarfoot and everyone held their breath.

Charley felt her whole body trembling. She wanted to leap at Sugarfoot and defend the child. But she knew that to act would put Tonia in even greater danger.

Tonia reached Sugarfoot and held up the sack, her face defiant and feisty.

He studied her for a long moment. "You're quite the brave little girl, aren't you?" He reached down with his free hand and pinched her chubby cheek. "Thank-you my dear child."

Sugarfoot removed the sack from her hands. He then surprised them all by reaching into it and lifting out a silver dollar. "Here sweetheart," he said, handing it to Tonia.

She took the coin and stared at it, stared at him.

He said, "They've all been so good, haven't they?"

Fascinated, Tonia nodded.

"Tell you what," continued Sugarfoot with loud stagy intimacy. "I want you to buy them each a cup of coffee when you reach your destination. Will you do that for me, my little sweetheart?"

She nodded again.

Sugarfoot regarded the others.

"Oh and by the way, my friends, now that you have made your charitable contribution for the day, don't forget your civic duty… remember to vote when you get to Stockton. And with that, I bid you farewell."

"Who are you going to vote for sir?" squeaked Tonia.

Charley gave an infuriated look. It was not the occasion for chitchat.

"I don't mind telling you," said Sugarfoot, continuing his loud but confidential tones to Tonia. "It will not be for Mr. Franklin Pierce. I cast my vote with the thinking minority of this country, for old General Scott.

A distraught portly woman shouted, "I knew it. A Whig. A Democrat would never rob a woman."

Sugarfoot addressed her, the shotgun still trained forward. "A Democrat, madam, would not have left you with the price of a cup of coffee, and would have taken your bloomers as well."

He gave a jaunty wave of his shotgun.

"Everyone face down on the road, if you please. And I'm ever so sorry, my little sweetheart," he said to Tonia, "but you must take this undignified posture along with the others.

As they all lay face down on the ground Sugarfoot approached Charley. His burlap-clad feet stepped close to her head, the shotgun coming close to her temple.

Fuck, thought Charley.

But then the bandit bent down and placed a cigar on the ground by her hand. "No hard feelings, I trust?"

Charley was not amused. "Next time I'll break even with you," she said looking up at him.

Sugarfoot laughed. "Break even with me?"

"I'll be ready for you. I promise," she said.

"And the time after that?"

"There won't be another time after that."

Sugarfoot let out another laugh and then vanished into the tall brush.

The passengers, still on the ground, heard the sound of a horse galloping away into the distance. They sat up in the dust...angry, relieved and bewildered.

THIRTEEN

Anna forbade Tonia from ever riding the coach again. Tonia was not daunted. One morning, after the incident, she set up an imitation of a driver's box and team, with four lengths of rope attached to pieces of wood that were meant to be the horses' heads. She sat up on a little box, calling out words she'd heard Charley say. She was commanding the imaginary horses to gallop faster and faster and to turn at the same time.

Charley was nearby repairing the corral fence…amused at watching Tonia play her game of make-believe.

Tonia saw Charley watching her. "Don't laugh at me."

"I would never ever laugh at you. You're doing a good job. But we're both going to get in trouble when your mother sees what you're doing."

"I don't care. Do you really think I'm doing a good job?"

"Yes, I do. Your reining is improving. I can tell you've been paying attention on our coach runs. Did you know though, that a horse can sense what you want even without the reins?"

"What do you mean?"

"Once they trust you, they respond to your energy—what it is you want from them."

"They can read my mind? Like a fortune teller?"

Charley laughed. "Not quite. But you can't hide anything from a horse. They know if you care about them, respect them. And after a while there's a strong connection that can happen between you and them. They're smart and wise creatures. And you know what? I've heard that the Indians even believe that horses are spiritual teachers, that they are a bridge between heaven and earth."

"Really?" said Tonia, not quite understanding but captivated by Charley's words. "How did you learn so much about horses?"

"I had a great teacher...a man who was like my father. His name was Jonas. He taught me everything I know about horses. And about people as well. I miss him. I wish he could see me sometimes...up on the driver's box."

Just then, Anna appeared, stepping out on the porch. "Charley. Get in here."

"See," Charley said to Tonia. "I told you we're in trouble." She smiled a henpecked smile and shrugged.

Tonia shrugged back; it was a little thing they did.

Anna turned and went back inside. Charley followed.

Kneading bread with a vengeance, Anna did not bother to look up. "I don't like what you're doing with Tonia. I want it to stop."

"What?"

"All this nonsense with the horses and the stagecoach driving. She could have been killed the other day. And besides, it's not proper."

"Look, I agreed to not ever take her on the coach runs again, but I don't see any harm in her having some fun and playing her pretend games. Besides, I don't see as it hurts a woman to know her way around a horse."

Charley picked at a little piece of the dough.

Anna swatted her hand away. "It is all she talks about, all she thinks about. She dreams about it at night."

"Well, I was the same way at her age—"

"But you're a man. It's cruel to encourage her to have a dream that will never come true."

"I won't encourage her, then."

"It's not just that. She admires you. She looks up to you, as if you were some kind of god. She loves you. I'm afraid of how she will be hurt when—"

"When what?"

"When you ask us to leave."

"My God, who said I would want you to leave? I know we haven't talked about it…but I'm very happy with the way things are. I love having you and Tonia here."

"But that will change. I've known men like you. Maybe not tomorrow or the next day—"

"Anna."

Charley moved toward her wanting to embrace her, to assure her. Not knowing if she should dare. What was this thing between them? Not the love of a woman for a man, as Anna believed. Not exactly love between two women, either. It was something else, made up of equal parts gratitude, need, and fear.

Anna held herself very still.

"I'm not going anywhere—and neither are you," Charley said.

Anna looked up, brushing away her tears with a floury hand.

Charley, not knowing what the hell to do, turned and walked out the door.

FOURTEEN

It was the following summer that Charley, Ben and Hank with several other whips were finishing up a new, one room cabin adjacent to Charley's original structure. The men, sweating hard under a hot sun, were pounding in their last nails before lunch.

"Anyone want a nip before we eat?" Ben asked, offering up a flask.

"Are you crazy?" laughed Hank, "You'll pound a nail through your fucking drunk hand if you're not careful."

"And if you're not careful Hank, I'm going to force feed you some of my Indian whiskey."

"What the hell is that? Or should I ask?" said Charley.

Ben took a long swig from his flask. "Well, you take one barrel of river water, and two gallons of alcohol. Then you add two ounces of strychnine to make the Indians crazy, cuz strychnine is a fucking great stimulant. Add three plugs of tobacco to make 'em sick; an Indian wouldn't figure it was whiskey unless it made him sick. Then add five bars of soap to give it a bead, and a half-pound of red pepper. And then you put in some sage brush and boil it until it's brown. You strain this into a barrel and hell, you got yourself some delicious Indian whiskey."

Charley let out a high-pitched hoot, "Remind me never to ask you for a drink. No wonder you can't get yourself a woman... drinkin' shit like that."

"I just make it...I don't drink it. And you're not one to talk about the ladies."

"Yeah," joked Hank. "Whenever any marriage-minded spinster pursues Parkie, he solves the problem by switching routes.

So then Charley, why the hell you building this sage hen a cabin right next door?"

"Shit," slurred Ben. "With the price of lumber these days, wouldn't it a been cheaper just to marry her?"

Everyone laughed.

"Come on, Parkie. We all know you're a little peculiar, but tell it to us straight. That Anna is one damn fine lookin' woman. Don't the two of you ever do it?"

"I'm a man as likes my privacy, Ben. That's all."

Charley gave Ben a dirty look, then turned her attention to hammering in a nail. Around her now, the men were trading sly, suggestive glances. She pretended not to notice.

By evening, most of the cabin had been finished—orange-yellow lantern light spilled out through its open window. There was still a sound of hammering; alone, Charley was putting up the shutter on the window frame.

Anna walked through the front door. She was carrying a tray with a covered plate of food, a large jar of homemade wine, and two tin cups. She set the tray down on the floor.

"I brought you some supper."

"Smells good, Anna. Thank-you."

Charley finished the hammering and sat down on the floor while Anna knelt and poured the purplish red liquid into the cups.

She then sank down next to Charley, spreading her skirt around her. "Tonia's in bed asleep."

She caught Charley's eye. She smiled and handed Charley the wine. The two clinked cups, raising the wine to their lips to drink.

Something was happening or about to happen. Charley could feel it moving through the night air. She took a swig of her wine.

"The place isn't much, but it'll keep the rain off your head." She looked up at the roof and laughed. "I hope."

Anna looked around the cabin. "It's nice. I can see it's going to be nice. Thank-you." She refilled Charley's cup. "And, you won't have to stay in the barn anymore. You can sleep in your own bed now."

"Oh, I haven't minded. Spent most of my growing up years sleeping in a stable."

There was a long moment of uncomfortable silence.

"Charley?" said Anna. "Can I ask you something? Do you like me?"

Oh shit, thought Charley. She felt a wave of nausea. She knew what was coming. What the hell was she going to say to Anna?

"Well...sure. Of course I like you fine."

"Charley, it's been a year that we've been living here with you. You never speak of yourself. You hardly speak at all to me. And you have never once spoken of...that is..." She looked right at Charley. "How is it that you think of me?"

"How do I think of you?"

"I'm like a wife to you, Charley, in every way but one."

"I think of you as...as my friend."

"But why have you never touched me? Why have you never tried to make love? Is there something wrong with me?"

"Of course there's nothing wrong with you."

Fuck. Had she deluded herself into thinking that this moment would not come, or had she just ignored all the signs because she didn't want to face the inevitable questions. Hell, she barely remembered she was a woman most days. But then the words were at the tip of her tongue...I'm not who you think I am. Dear God yes—the relief of being known. She wanted to shout it—to show her. She caught her breath, slowed her thoughts. If she revealed her secret, she risked losing everything—the daily, comforting presence of Anna and Tonia, not to mention her job. She risked losing who she had fought so hard to become. Far safer, far surer to continue to be whom people thought she was. She opted for the noblest-sounding lie.

"It's just...I have far too much respect for you."

"Oh?" said Anna. She shifted a little closer to Charley, leaning forward on her hands so that Charley was facing her formidable cleavage of flesh. "I'm not so respectable."

Suddenly her lips were on Charley's.

And Charley was kissing back. She felt hazy and drunk and Anna's mouth tasted like new made wine, heady and sweet. The kiss went on and on, and Charley was part of it going on.

Anna took Charley's hand and laid it on her chest. Charley did not resist. She then slid Charley's hand down the great slope of her breast. The hairs on Charley's arm prickeled...it was a stunning sensation to touch another woman's flesh in such a manner. Ever since Byron, Charley had been somehow able to deny that desire to be held, to be filled, to be overwhelmed. Not that she had had much choice—living her life the way she was. But now...that long dormant need was returning with a vengeance. Anna was whispering in Italian...her hand inching up Charley's leg—mouth following, tongue tracing, etching the wet path. Then far away a soft whisper from below—"Charley...please take me."

Charley's eyes snapped open. Summoning all of herself, all of her will, she broke away, scrambling to her feet. For an instant she teetered in her resolve; she could so easily fall back to the floor with this woman. Enough. Enough. She could pretend to herself that she had re-invented herself. But the truth was something else. Just keep the mask locked in place. That was the only protection she had. Anna would put her hand low on Charley's body to feel the expected hardness there, and all she would find was a soft pillow of round flesh. And then there would be Anna's expected scream. And after that—the end of everything that meant anything in this world.

"I'm—I'm sorry. I'm so sorry." Charley stammered.

"What?" said Anna. "What?"

But Charley was gone in a blur, leaving her stunned and half undressed on the floor. A few moments passed. She looked down at her rejected body. She tucked her flesh back into her bodice. More moments passed. Longer ones. The sound of Charley's horse galloping away. Anna reached for her wine and drank it down. She finished Charley's, and then poured a third.

Sometime later in the night, Tonia wandered in from the other cabin, barefoot, in her nightdress.

"Mama? Where are you? Are you there?"

In a glance, Tonia took in the situation—not what had happened of course, but as only a daughter could understand her mother. There was pain and the pain had been caused by yet another man.

"Oh, my little mama," she said. She knelt down and put her arms around Anna who was lying in a heap on the floor. She helped her up and guided her back to their bed. Anna for once allowed herself to be led.

FIFTEEN

I t was Hangtown that Charley rode to that night.
   She had started riding just to get away. Anywhere.
   Somewhere. But she found herself heading towards
Hangtown. And Edmund...drawn towards him in some inex-
plicable way. She didn't even know anything about him. This
was craziness. What did she expect to happen tonight? What
could happen? But here she was riding through the darkness.
Not knowing if Edmund would even be there. Nor what she'd
do if he was.

Would she ever again be known as she had been with Byron?
That was her deepest fear—that she was nothing. A woman growing old alone, who would always be alone. A woman dressed as
a man.

Froth poured from the horse's mouth and its neck was soaked
and salted. Charley was running the horse too fast, kicking too
hard the sore flanks. But she needed to vanish. She needed to run.

As she rode, the great dead appeared beside her, immense and
slow and distant; moving in the shadows and broken flickers of
moonlight like giant Byzantine mosaics in the night. Uneven
patterns cast on rock face, flickering, stretching along the dry
ground as she moved past them. They were all there: Byron, Jonas,
Beelzebub. And everywhere her soft silent baby cast large upon
the landscape, still bearing that immaculate expression passed
through time from the ancients to the very newest born. She felt
the look of her child emanating from every rock and tree bark
glittering back through the moonlight. All of them were now
moving in the direction from which she'd come. So big, so slow,
so grand. And oh, they seemed not to know her, seemed not to

care—the slow traffic of the complex dead and she, human fool, racing feverishly in the other direction.

She kicked the horse again, hard.

The figures were vanishing, blinking away. They were gone. The lights of Hangtown were appearing. It was too bright here for enchantments.

The horse was slowing and Charley, whose body had out-sped itself, slowed enough that the soul caught up, entered it. She grunted as soul clicked back into place; the loneliness now was just the usual loneliness and she could bear it; it was not unfamiliar.

She was panting, catching her breath. Her heart was pounding. She could hear it.

The horse was walking now, snorting. Charley was pierced through with feelings of remorse and shame at her ill-treatment of the creature. She stroked the horse's neck, uttering apology after apology. "I'm sorry. I am so sorry."

And then, before them was Kittle Farley's Hangtown Saloon with its shroud of clamor and odor of drink. The horse halted and for several minutes they just stood there. Charley swung down from the horse and led him over to a watering trough to drink. She tied him to the hitching post. She used her dirty sleeve to scrub the tears from her face, composed an expression of sorts, and plunged inside…stagecoach driver goes to saloon, raises glass, laughs raucously, eyes the painted gals.

Little tables were scattered everywhere; a piano was angled against one wall, replete with piano player with rolled up sleeves, his fingers moving up and down the tinny-sounding keys. A polished wood bar stretched the length of another wall. The bar was lined three deep tonight with boisterous drinking men. Hung in the place of honor behind the bar was a picture of a voluptuous reclining woman, dark eyes and hair, Mediterranean in seasoning—with a satyr hovering over her, leering down at her near-nakedness.

The barkeep paused in his dispensing of drinks and reached under the picture. There was a small rubber bulb there and the barkeeps' hand closed around it, pumping it a few times. The painted woman's belly undulated, and her breasts bulged outwards, balloon-like, as the barkeep continued to pump.

"Keep at it, Kittle!" shouted the men. "Go! Go! Go!"

Kittle pumped and pumped, a foolish grin pasted on his face, and the breasts bulged and bulged, until at last the tips of them, daubed with red and purple and pink, dawned like pointy heavenly bodies. Orgasmic whooping and hooting filled the room.

A young miner stood next to Charley doing a double take, his eyes popping. "Oh, baby," he shouted, crossing his eyes in simulated ecstasy. "Give me some of that, barkeep."

The men laughed and raised a grateful toast to the naked lady.

Charley blanched—Edmund was there, standing at the bar, looking rather unsteady. What the hell did she think she was doing? She should leave. And yet she felt herself move through the crowd until she was standing at his side.

"Hey. Charley, my friend," warbled Edmund. He was in an advanced stage of drunkenness. He hooked an arm around Charley's elbow and allowed himself to be steered back to a chair where he landed with a thump. She slid into the chair next to him.

Edmund narrowed his eyes. "I hope you won't take it amiss," he said, "if I tell you that something about you has always puzzled me Charley Parkhurst."

So it's now, the unveiling, she thought. Shit. She had been hiding from this moment. Protecting her goddamned secret. Good. It's over.

But then Edmund saw a stray deck of cards lying on the table and lost his train of thought. He picked them up and attempted to shuffle them. His fingers were too drunk. Laughing at himself, he gave up, pushing the cards away with a resigned sigh.

"There are two things, my friend, in which a man should never attempt to engage beyond a certain point of inebriation," he slurred. "Cards and…"

As if on cue, a saloon gal interrupted him. She was very young, with a face that might have been pretty had it not been ruined with too much rouge and dissipation. She sidled up next to him and ran her hand through his hair.

"Edmund," she said simpering. "I got something special for you." She had a bright expression, a sing-song voice.

He swung her down into his lap, almost dropping her. "Oh you darling soiled dove. Haven't I already sampled what you've got?"

Charley watched as Edmund cupped the gal's chin in his hand and turned her head to face his. She pouted at him. Then stunningly, she relaxed her face for an instant into a real smile, a smile of sudden girlish sweetness—and then, just as quick, tightened her mouth and eyes…back into an appearance of false coyness.

It was a shocking moment; as if a mask had been dropped for an instant, confirming lest you weren't sure, that indeed there were masks. Had it really happened? Was everyone—including herself—playing a role here? But by then the girl had already disappeared back inside the gal.

"Why, yes, I believe I have sampled you my dear," Edmund said, rolling his eyes at Charley. He turned back to the hard whore on his lap and Charley watched as Edmund's hand snaked under her arm and squeezed her breast.

"Aren't you Mimi?" he said.

The gal slapped his hand away with a playful sulk. "What a bad boy you are." She wanted to punch him in the face, but she had her bread to earn. Instead she said, "You know the rules, Mr. Bennett." She made her dimples appear.

Edmund's other hand sneaked along the gal's leg, disappearing up her skirt.

"You are so naughty!" she squeaked. She turned and gave him a quick sloppy kiss. Then she sprang up off his lap, trailing her fingers through his hair as she started to move away. She looked back, batting her eyes and puckering her lips.

He reached up and grabbed her by the wrist, bringing her hand to his face.

"Come with me to San Francisco, my darling girl. I'll show you things you never dreamt of. And you'll get to see the head of the famous bandit Joaquin Murieta."

He turned and winked at Charley. "You should come too my boy—The Stockton House Saloon on Stockton Street. It's going to be on display for just one night, August 12th; supposed to draw a big crowd."

Still holding the gal's hand, Edmund turned it over and kissed it in such a gentle and sweet way that it took Charley's breath away. She suspected—she couldn't say why—that he was engaging the gal not for the gal's benefit, but for hers.

The gal of course, was oblivious to it all. She giggled. "Oh, Mr. Bennett, you rascal, you. You know I can't go. I'd lose my job."

She turned her back on him, remembering to twitch her hips in an exaggerated manner as she walked away.

Edmund turned his glazed eyes to Charley and smiled. For an almost imperceptible second, she saw in that smile a profound and moving sadness.

"I'm fractured with drink," he said. His eyes rolled up and his head fell forward onto the table with a loud painful-sounding clunk.

SIXTEEN

Kittle, the ever-cheerful barkeep, told Charley the way to Edmund's lodgings. With difficulty, she dragged a semi-conscious Edmund down the street into the Hangtown Hotel. The proprietor at the front desk glanced up at the sight of the staggering man with his arm draped over a smaller man's shoulder and looked back down to his work without a word.

"Key, Edmund?" said Charley.

Edmund plunged his right hand into his pocket and pulled out a key, dropping it to the floor in the process.

"Room six," said the proprietor with disdain. He lit a lantern and handed it to Charley.

The room was first class for Hangtown: it had a lock to begin with, plus it had a window and just enough space around the bed for a narrow bureau and a chair.

The strong moon glow filtered through the window. Charley lowered Edmund down onto the bed as he mumbled something unintelligible, his eyes closed. She pulled off his fine boots and stood them up next to the chair. As she turned to the door there was a voice from the bed.

"Charley, be a good lad and help me with these damned fancy pants," he slurred. "Damned buttons."

He was lying prostrate on the bed, his eyes still closed. Charley took a deep breath, then took a step from the door to the bed. She removed her gloves, leaned over him and began to unbutton the trousers. She pulled them down over the front of his hips and over his bulge. A shiver coursed through her body. She turned her eyes away, then went to Edmund's feet and pulled the trousers over the foot of the bed. She glanced at the long muscular legs noticing a couple of white scars. They looked liked old gunshot wounds.

"Looks like you've been in a gunfight or two?"

Edmund mumbled, "Cards can be a dangerous game my boy."

As she lifted his trousers to drape over the back of the chair something fell from the pocket. It was some sort of large coin. No, a large metal token. She picked it up.

DORA'S
12 Dupont Street. San Francisco
GAMING * WHISKEY * WOMEN

She flipped it over...

GOOD FOR TWO DRINKS OR ONE SCREW

Those are either expensive drinks or hideous whores, she thought.

She tucked the token back into his pants pocket. Undressed down to his undergarments, Edmund looked peaceful and handsome, now asleep on top of the blanket. She stood over him, looking down. She reached her fingertips like a curious child, toward the smooth skin of his cheek, touching him. She was startled by her gesture.

She put her gloves back on and stole out of the room.

Edmund opened his eyes briefly. Then shut them.

So, Charley left a sleeping Edmund and Hangtown in the dead of night, stopping at a swing station for a few hours sleep. When she awoke from her rest, she was filled with a kind of lightness that she didn't know she had been missing. It was as though the care-free Charlotte had somehow emerged out of last night's nightmare ride to Hangtown...and as after the cleansing throes of a fever, that playful girl had now burst through every pore. She felt her old Charlotte self again—full of hell, full of mischief. She would take a daring chance, make a dangerous adventure. Why the hell not. She had been holding her loneliness and her secret so tight that it had been suffocating her.

She rode towards home as the cool clear morning arched overhead—a pale pristine summer blue just before sunrise. She could not stop thinking about him.

On her way home she stopped off at the Wells Fargo office just long enough to tell her friend and boss Jim Birch that she needed to leave town for a few days on some personal business.

She arrived back at the cabins that afternoon. She called out, "Anna! You there?"

The door to the new cabin opened and Tonia appeared. "Hey, Charley."

"Hey, Tonia. Tell your mama I'll be gone a couple of days. Leaving first thing in the morning."

"Where to?"

"San Francisco."

"Oh I love San Francisco. Mama and I were there once with Luigi. Can we come?"

"I'm sorry Tonia. Not this time. I'll take you and your mama another time."

Anna appeared behind her daughter in the doorway. A stricken expression crossed her face for an instant, and then something else that Charley recognized. She played it over; she took the look apart until she was sure…it was already the beginning of not caring. She'd not be hurt for long, that woman.

Anna was summoning the pieces of a feeling to nest together like strong black birds in her heart. The feeling was righteous anger, and with that feeling protecting her she was invincible. We will be all right, Tonia and I. We don't need you. She was putting her hand on Tonia's shoulder. She was starting to close the door.

"I'll be back soon," Charley said. She wheeled the horse around and headed toward the barn.

SEVENTEEN

If Sacramento was the beating heart of the Mother lode, San
Francisco, flashy city, was its flesh. Women and men met
in the streets and looked each other over in front of elegant
shop windows glittering with merchandise. With a pocketful of
gold dust you could buy this and that and this. You could clothe
yourself all new. You could reinvent yourself fresh, no questions
asked. Especially if you were lucky to have the exchange rate of
man's, not woman's work.

Despite her hard-earned success as a whip, Charley was still
unused to having so much money. Now she would let herself
spend some of it. So here she was, Charlotte Parkhurst, peering
inside an expensive shop window. It made her think of Charles
Dickens—one of his poor orphan boys pushing his nose against
the bakery window dreaming of bread.

The difference was that she was able to enter that shop behind
the window and would matter-of-fact, buy the thing that she was
dreaming of. That it was to be a whore's wardrobe, she hastened
to remind herself, mattered not at all. She'd not be any more of
a whore than any usual wife. She had once read about a woman
that had been put in jail for refusing her husband's connubial
wishes, so what was the difference—wife or whore? Since a wife
wouldn't walk into a bar, a whore it would be.

She had stumbled upon the most amazing and wondrous
thought; she had the rare and exquisite freedom to choose—to
move between the world of man and woman, just like that.

With the shop clerk's help, it didn't take long to pile up the
counter with boxes filled with all the accoutrements of flashy
feminine ready-made fashion of the day—chemise, stockings,

garters, boots, corset, hoop skirt, dress, gloves, and a feathered hat. He's buying everything, thought the clerk in amazement. He must be dressing his gal from scratch. Even combs and rats for her hair. What's this all about? But the clerk said nothing of course, thrilled with the size of the purchase.

In a short while, Charley staggered out under the bulky stack of boxes and headed for the Oriental Hotel. She couldn't wait to tear them open and lift out the garments that had been wrapped in crisp frail tissue.

She had taken a second floor room in the elegant hotel. There was a good long mirror in the room…she had insisted on that to the hotelkeeper. She needed a room which would proffer her a proper view of her new person.

Taking a deep breath, she set about the complex task of dressing. It had been a long time since last she put on a dress, and it felt strange, almost indecent, this act of hers.

Nonetheless, she cast off her whip clothes—her Texas hat, embroidered gauntlet gloves, coat of buffalo skin, worn leather boots, pleated shirt. She then removed her blue jean overalls that had been turned up at the bottom, worn over a pair of good pants with a wide leather belt. And lastly, her undergarments and the sweaty strips of binding around her breasts.

She poured a standing pitcher of water into a basin and began to wash herself. The cool water felt reinvigorating on her grimy face. She then scrubbed away the darkness of the dirt branded on her body to reveal beneath, fine white skin.

After drying off, she pulled on ruffled pantalettes, and then a long white chemise with bodice trimmed with delicate lace. Gazing at her reflection in the mirror, she stopped to touch herself gently…like the man she had become, courting the woman she once was and was now to become again.

Snapping herself out of the daydream, she continued the course of her transformation. The rest would not be as easy.

She pulled a pair of silk stockings up over her muscular calves. Next, the corset with all the hooks and ties in the back. She wrestled with it, trying to hold the thing on in front with one hand while fastening it in back. She tried to use the boot buttoner to hook the corset. It didn't work. She tried hooking the corset on backwards, and then attempted to twist it around. It wouldn't budge. She took the corset off, hooked it up, and tried to pull the pre-hooked corset over her head. She was stuck, and it took a few long life-threatening moments before she extricated herself. In disgust, she threw it out of the open window. The muslin curtains flew apart as the corset shot past and then closed again behind it.

She pulled out a small bottle of whiskey from her belongings and downed a good long slug.

Continuing to dress, she managed to hook a hoop skirt, fitting it around her now thickened waist. And then came the yards of dress, pretty polished-violet satin with fashionable leg-of-mutton sleeves and a deep bosom-revealing neckline. There were about forty tiny pearl buttons from top to bottom, mercifully located in the front. She fortified herself with another slug of whiskey and began to button. Her strong calloused fingers felt uncoordinated; the little buttons kept slipping from her before she could slide them through the delicate corded eyelets. Worse yet, she had to breathe shallow the whole time, keeping her stomach well in without benefit of a corset. She performed much of the operation by feel and then checked it in the mirror.

She maneuvered a boot buttoner, doing up the many tiny buttons that fastened a pair of dainty boots. She then folded down her unsecured silk stockings over the top of the boots…a makeshift plan as the garters had been attached to the corset. The boots were tight. She'd not estimated the size well—her feet, like her waist, must have broadened since she last wore woman's clothes.

The room was getting dark. She lit the lantern by the bed. This was turning out to be much more difficult than she thought it would be. Did women do all this all the time? She could no longer imagine being such a creature. Tonight though, she was willing to go to the trouble.

The irony of this moment, plus the image of herself in the mirror, made her laugh out loud, and the buttons on her dress seemed on the edge of explosion. God, another thing she had to keep in her mind...she had to remember not to laugh out loud this evening, or she would be standing there revealing herself in her undergarments.

And this image that kept flitting and disappearing...of being pushed hard into a bed, or a wall, or the floor...with those green eyes above her. Enough. If she didn't stop this day dreaming, it would be morning and she still would not have finished this damn dressing.

Alright, now the hair. This wasn't going to be easy either. She pinned a coiled rat into place at the nape of the neck with the jeweled combs. Good enough, she thought. And the color did seem to almost match her sun-streaked blonde; at least it did by lantern light. Next she wound her own length of hair around the rat to pin it in place. The rat fell out. She started again...nearly weeping in frustration. Then after much maneuvering, it stuck.

Exhausted, she evaluated herself in the mirror. Holding the lantern in one hand, she leaned in close to examine her face, her fingers touching her sunburned cheeks with concern. She took some powder she'd bought and tried to cover her tanned, dry skin into a more fashionable feminine paleness. She accentuated her cheeks and lips with a little more rouge than was necessary. She then placed a black velvet bonnet trimmed with black ribbon and a black feather onto her head.

In the dim light, if she didn't look too close, she looked the part, she thought. She wondered if Edmund would think the same. She wondered if he'd even recognize her. Hell, she was actually wondering if she had misinterpreted his invitation. Did he even know that she was a woman or was this fantasy all in her head? She'd gone to a lot of trouble if that was the case.

Next to her on the dresser, the small bottle of whiskey was almost empty. She finished it off. She sprinkled on a liberal dose of the rose-water that the sales clerk had thrown in as a present for "the lady." Then, putting the bottle to her lips, Charley gargled some for good measure.

She pulled on her fancy gloves, picked up her black satin reticule, and tottered toward the door. She tried to walk through the narrow doorway, but her voluminous skirts prevented her. With an impatient sigh, she yanked them clear and stumbled out.

EIGHTEEN

C harley turned onto Stockton Street. Her boot caught in the hem of her underslip. She would need to be careful in this monstrosity of a dress. She remembered Ben telling her about some poor girl who had been dragged two miles by runaway horses—her hoop skirt entangled in the steps of the coach, with her head and shoulders dragging on the ground to a ghastly end.

As she walked toward the saloon, she noticed a tall man in front of her whose familiar walk took her breath away. Lee. Fuck. The shoulders, the back, they were the same. The color of his hair the same. He was drunk. She heard him speak to the gal beside him. His voice was rough and loud…it wasn't Lee's voice. It wasn't him at all. She caught her breath. Enough. Enough.

Some single men were eyeing her, a few made rude comments and one even grabbed her arm and offered her money. She resisted hard the impulse to spit in his face. She had to calm herself. What she needed was a cigar. She automatically reached for her coat pocket and instead, felt satin. Shit. Fucking dress. She should have remembered to put a cigar in her reticule. She'd have to get one from Edmund…if he was even there.

At last she saw the sign.

THE STOCKTON HOUSE SALOON
14 STOCKTON STREET
A FINE ESTABLISHMENT

Beneath the sign was a hand-printed poster.

The outside door to the establishment was open to the street, exposing a line of patrons waiting to see the famous head in the back room. Charley hesitated at the portal. She looked down at herself. As far as she could tell she looked every inch a woman— elegantly dressed, maybe even a little cheap. She gathered up the courage to proceed, at least to get through the front door. She must remind herself to sound the part as well.

She entered and, as she had hoped, she saw Edmund there. He was sitting at a gaming table playing cards, a cigar clenched between his teeth. He noted the mysterious lady's entrance. She panicked at the sight of him, losing her nerve. She turned back toward the door, then stopped in her tracks, steeling herself. She turned and strode back. He'd just won the hand and was now raking in his winnings, standing up from the table.

She was moving a little too quick for her command of feminine garb. The heel of her dainty boot caught in a floorboard and she tripped, falling headlong into a drunken miner's arms. The miner caught her, breaking her fall.

"Well, look what Providence sent me," he said, licking his lips.

Edmund stepped forward. "Thank you, sir, for your valiant rescue. But I believe the lady had another destination in mind."

Begrudging, the miner spat onto the sawdust floor and released her.

Charley's face was flushed. Edmund's gaze met hers and the two sets of eyes slid into place, so that she could not look away without effort.

"Well, well, well...look what a bath and a low-cut dress can do. It is you isn't it?" Edmund gave a small smile and a wink.

"I think it's me. I wasn't so sure when I looked in the mirror. Next time you can be the one who dresses up like a whore."

"Unlike you my dear, I'm afraid I don't have the cleavage to titivate that dress. Come, my boy," he whispered in her ear. "Let us peruse the famous head shall we?"

He maneuvered her past the waiting line of patrons and to the man collecting the money. He whispered something in his ear and slipped a large bill into his hand. The man waved them both into the back room.

Once inside, they approached a high table with observers gathered around it. On top of the table, in the place of honor, sat two liquid filled glass jars with peaked lid tops. The smaller one had the floating shriveled hand of Three-fingered Jack. In the larger one, sitting on the bottom of the jar, was the handsome head of Joaquin Murrieta—eyes staring out, mouth slightly agape, mustache intact.

Edmund leaned over, peering closely at the head. "Lucky bugger. Drowning in gin. What a tribute. They pickled the Robin Hood of El Dorado in gin. He's now and forever drunk and famous, traveling the countryside. You know they say success is the size of the hole a man leaves after he dies."

Charley could not take her eyes away from that face. Imagine ending up, head in a bottle, traveling across California.

"Well, I don't know about you, my dear," Edmund said, "but the sight of all that gin has made me thirsty. Let's get a drink." He took her elbow and guided her out of the room.

They went straight to the bar. Edmund ordered a bottle of whiskey and they downed several shots.

"Shit, at least we know the old bugger is actually dead," he said. "I once saw a miraculous revival. The corpse woke up during the funeral, much to the dismay of his friends and family."

"What the hell are you talking about?" asked Charley, laughing.

"You didn't read about that? It was in all the local papers. You know how many people are pronounced dead prematurely? Just this year the old Duke of Wellington died and wasn't buried until two months after his death…just in case. Hell, there's even a group of concerned citizens called the Society for the Prevention of People Being Buried Alive. You haven't heard of them?"

Charley shook her head in disbelief.

"The members place crowbars and shovels in the casket so the dead can dig their way out if they revive. Or sometimes they use a pipe that goes through the ground and into the casket for emergency communication. Then they hire servants to wait by the pipes and listen for calls for help. On the other hand, I've been told that wealthy families who want their dead to stay that way have a different option: coffins fitted with special nails that when hit, puncture capsules of poisoned gas."

Edmund grabbed the whiskey bottle and filled both their glasses again. He kept rambling on with great gusto.

"It's all true. I swear it. I myself prefer the Bateson Revival Device—you know, Bateson's Belfry? It's an iron bell mounted on the lid of the casket just above the dead man's head. The bell's connected to a cord placed in the dead man's hand so that the least tremor will sound the alarm. I have no idea if it's saved anyone's neck, but it's made old man Bateson a rich man. My hand to God, I wish I could come up with something that clever."

Charley was so drunk that she could barely stop laughing long enough to speak. She felt one of the little pearl buttons pop.

Edmund poured another round and raised his glass to hers.

"Ah death, here's to you dark lady. You know, perhaps the best cure for the fear of death as my old friend Will Hazlitt once said, '…is to reflect that life has a beginning as well as an end. There was a time when we were not: this gives us no concern—why then should it trouble us that a time will come when we shall cease to be?'"

Charley was surprised at how serious he had just become. She put a comforting hand on top of his.

He pulled his hand away. As quick as his mood had turned serious, it turned back again.

"Well enough about death and dying my dear…here's to fucking."

He downed his drink in one clean shot. "Now come with me. Let's stroll."

He held out his elbow and she took it. He drew his arm in closer, drawing her to his side, so that her arm was pressed against his body.

They strolled side by side through the dusky, narrow streets. He pulled her into a darkened alleyway, backed her up against the wall of a building, leaned in close, his lips almost touching hers. He pressed his body against her so that she could feel him through the dress, through the crinolines, through her skin. He bent toward the curve of her neck, kissing her where just inside the skin and fragile pipe of cartilage the moan lay, curled inside, waiting.

She was silent for a moment, and then…the moan escaped at long last from the bottom of her throat. When he began to undo the tiny buttons of her dress, she stopped him, took his hand and led him down the street towards her hotel.

 NINETEEN

A t the door of her room, Charley realized with some amusement that her whip clothes were left scattered all over the bed.

She stepped in and closed the door, leaving Edmund alone and laughing in surprise outside in the hall. He knocked.

She called through the closed door. "Wait…wait a moment."

"I've waited for you forever. I'll wait as long as you like, my girl."

She stumbled around in the dark, kicking and pushing the clothing under the bed. Not that it mattered, but for some reason she just didn't want to break the illusion of this game they were playing.

Moments later, with a semblance of nonchalance, she opened the door to admit Edmund, closing it behind him.

In the darkness, he struck a match, illuminating his beguiled and intoxicated face. He looked over the flame at her and then turned to light the candle by the bed. She reached out and stopped him. She took his hand in hers and blew out the match.

"You are an amazing puzzle, my girl. The last thing I would have expected from you is modesty."

He then seized her and roamed her body until he found the line of buttons. He bit off the top one and spat it onto the ground. He then began to undo the rest of the tiny pearl buttons. He was used to undressing a lady.

Charley laughed out loud in her drunkenness. It seemed he was better at those damn buttons than she was.

He skillfully continued to lift, unhook and untie. They lost their balance and fell onto the bed. He was again laughing and he was kissing her breasts and he was sucking on her nipple so hard, stretching it toward him using his teeth, that it hurt.

They went on like that, their two bodies colliding with a pleasure that was part pain. Together, they achieved a kind of passion that Charley had not felt before. She cared less than she had with Byron but…she followed wherever Edmund led, and she gasped as she broke open to new, unfamiliar sensations.

Soon afterward Edmund was sound asleep. Lulled by the stillness of the room and the sound of his deep breathing, she drifted into a brief shallow sleep herself.

In the moonlight she dressed once again in her riding clothes, white strips of cotton bound around her breasts—her hat, gloves and boots in their familiar place. She collected from the floor all of the night's costumes, and stuffed them into her saddle bags. She watched Edmund for a moment as he lay there. He looked somehow like a young boy, his arms wrapped around his body protectively.

As she opened the door to leave, a soft voice from the bed murmured, "See you in Hangtown, Charley."

TWENTY

It had been over a month and Charley hadn't seen hide nor hair of Edmund. Strange what a little mystery can do for a man…puts him in your head like a tune that won't go away…drives you mad. She had been looking for him in every coach she drove, in every swing station she stopped at and in every saloon she downed a whiskey. She had not realized how remarkable it would feel to have someone else know her secret.

One rainy night, Charley walked into the Hangtown Saloon, and by God there he was. Finally. She sauntered over to his table, whiskey in hand.

Edmund looked up from his cards, not missing a beat. "Well, well, look who's here. If it isn't my favorite whip…Stagecoach Charley. How're the horses treating you, m'boy?"

"Got a mind of their own, them horses sometimes," she said. She looked down into her glass, trying to hide the annoying blush on her face. "If it weren't for me keepin 'em in rein, they'd take off to—"

"Frisco, perchance?"

She let out a chuckle.

"You know, I've an inkling to head to Frisco again this week," Edmund said. "Place I go sometimes. Dora's? You'd like it there, m'boy. Stop in sometime. Friday night, payday night is quite… spectacular."

"I think I heard of that place, 'Gaming, whiskey and women,' right?"

"Correct. Emphasis on the women."

He winked and went back to his cards.

When the rain stopped, Charley started the long ride home. The dawn was bursting through the sky in purples and reds, and the smell of the earth was pungent. Her horse felt comforting beneath her. There was the familiar sound of hooves on damp soil, and her body felt light and strong...pulled back into Edmund's entrancement.

For the last hour Tonia had been listening hard while going through the motions of her hateful homework. When at last she heard the sound of Charley's horse plodding on the packed dirt outside the cabin, she jumped up from the table, knocking her schoolbooks and papers askew and almost knocking over the candle as well.

Anna, in the corner by the stove, looked up in surprise. Tonia was already halfway to the door.

"Tonia," called Anna. "Leave Charley alone."

Tonia stopped in her tracks just short of the door. "But mother."

"He's a grown man. He needs his privacy just as you or I do."

"I don't need any privacy. And Charley likes to talk with me. He's told me so. And we never see him anymore. I miss him." She took the last step towards the door, though she knew she'd go no farther.

"Tonia."

"All right, mother," she said in an exaggerated beleaguered tone. She removed her hand from the latch and turned back. "You know I think that Charley gives you more privacy than you want."

At the sudden stricken look on her mother's face, she knew that she'd gone too far. Defused now, she collected her books and papers into a neat pile on the table and got herself ready for bed. She put on her pretty flannel gown, white with little blue flowers, sewn together earlier that summer by her mother. Tonia's heart was breaking with sadness and contrition. She splashed water over her hands and face. She climbed into the hard bed and lay down on her side. The sheets scratched her cheek and she was glad of it.

A few minutes later her mother climbed into bed and lay stiffly beside her.

"I'm so sorry, mother. I love you," she whispered.

Anna slipped her arm under Tonia's neck and held her close.

As Charley unbridled her horse, she had heard the loud voices coming from Anna and Tonia's cabin. That cinched it. She wouldn't be heading in there for some late night grub tonight. In truth, she hadn't seen very much of them at all this last month. Charley and Anna had not discussed that thing that had happened between them that night. Easier to avoid the whole conversation… as though nothing had happened. Just slip back into their daily rhythms.

The following day Charley went into work to request a San Francisco run for the weekend.

When she arrived in San Francisco that Friday, she checked back into the Oriental Hotel. And once again, button by button by button, her clumsy fingers transformed herself from man to woman.

TWENTY-ONE

T he paint was peeling on the cracked sign hanging high above the door.

DORA'S
12 Dupont Street.
GAMING ∗ WHISKEY ∗ WOMEN

The sign was shaped like a giant golden coin. Charley smiled... it looked just like the coin that had dropped out of Edmund's pocket that first night she had tucked him in.

Edmund was at the gaming table, no visible sign that he'd noticed her come in. She went up to the bar to order a whiskey.

A man with crooked teeth leered at her. "Lemme buy you a drink, girlie."

"No thanks, I can—"

"The man pays in these parts." He sidled close, sniffing at Charley's cool neck. He emanated sour sweat, bad breath and beer. "So, what'll it be?"

When Charley did not respond but drew back, the man shouted to the barkeep, "Bring the gal a draft."

Charley turned back to the gaming table. Edmund was gone. Had he not seen her?

Her drink arrived, frothy, and in a tall glass. She did not relish playing whore to a man with crooked teeth and a nasty smell. Then she felt a warm hand on the middle of her back, heard a familiar voice. Coins slapped on the bar.

"That'll be on me Andy," said Edmund.

Charley was relieved to feel his firm hand on her back, steering her away from the bar, away from the crooked teeth.

Edmund handed her the cold beer and she brought it to her lips. "Why don't you take a long sip, my dear."

She drained her beer in a most unladylike fashion. He allowed his hand to drift along her body in a most ungentlemanly fashion. He tugged at her hand, planted a kiss on the curve of her neck. She moaned her little moan, tugged back at him, and together they moved as one figure out the door, down the street, and up to her room.

Edmund taught her that weekend, among other things, his favorite card game, Ace-Deuce-Jack. But not before she was given a lecture on the ethics of card playing. Edmund believed all was fair in love and war, with one exception…he said in the game of chance, he never cheated—and despised anyone who did. Cheating at cards was something a gentleman should never do.

After one of their hands that Charley happened to win, Edmund tilted back the last of his brandy, turned Charley around, pushed her down on the bed and sat on her. She didn't know what the hell he was doing. Her face was smashed into the mattress. Then, instead of the usual unbuttoning and tearing and lifting, she heard him singing. Full throated above her. An Irish ballad. A love song to Molly O'Flannery…whoever the hell that was. She started to laugh. Her laughter caused the bed to sway in such a way that she felt almost seasick. But she couldn't stop…her head arched backward. Edmund's tenor notes grew sweeter and higher. Her sides hurt. She felt breathless. Waves of elation grew inside her. Her body rocked as Edmund's voice wound itself around her.

Early Sunday morning, Edmund lazily watched from their bed as Charley once again dressed back into her skivvies, trousers, shirt and boots. Nodding at her crotch, he threw Charley one of his socks.

"Aren't you missing something this morning, my dear?"

Grinning, Charley stuffed the sock down the front of her pants. "There. Big enough for you now?"

"The bigger the better, my dear. Actually…on second thought, why don't you drive your coach back today in your low-cut dress? I'm sure the miners would be as delighted as I have been."

"Are you speaking of your delight with my dress or the sex?"

"My delight with fucking you, my darling. Always the delicious fucking."

Blushing hard, she grabbed her saddle bags, leaned over the bed and kissed him.

He whispered in her ear, "See you on the road sometime, Charley girl."

TWENTY-TWO

At the edge of San Francisco Bay on Montgomery Street, sat the new, red brick, green shuttered Wells Fargo stagecoach office. After checking in, Charley breakfasted next door at the Union Saloon on excellent bread, potatoes, hung beef, eggs, and strong tea. Upon arriving back at the station, she was surprised to see Edmund standing there with that insinuating smile he gave to everyone. Standing there as if he were just passing the time of day.

"Fancy seeing you again, Mr. Bennett."

"Hey there Charley, my good fellow. Spur of the moment... figured I'd join you on the ride back to Sacramento. From there I'll be heading up to Knights Landing for a good game."

"Suit yourself," Charley said with some sniffing and pretense of indifference. She cut herself a chunk of plug tobacco with her jack-knife, put the fresh chew under her lip, and climbed up onto the driver's seat.

Edmund went to climb up to the seat of honor next to Charley but it was already taken. With his usual charm and silver dollars however, he persuaded the gentleman who had been occupying the seat to move inside the coach. Edmund said the rocking made him ill within, and that the other passengers would bless the gentleman for his good deed, saving them all from his breakfast.

As soon as Edmund was seated, Charley grabbed the reins and shouted, "Git acoup. Git alang, my beauties." Her hoarse cry cut through the damp morning air. And they were off.

Fifty miles, seven hours, and four swing-stations later, the coach pulled up to the home station in Suisun City, the half-way point between San Francisco and Sacramento. Dusty and fatigued, the passengers crawled out of the coach—all trying to outrun each other on their way to the outhouse.

Charley yelled out, "Coach leaves at 1:30 sharp. You got thirty minutes."

After leaving the stagecoach in the hands of the two young stock tenders, Charley went inside with Edmund and sat down at the communal table with some of the other passengers for a quick meal.

They were about finished when Edmund looked down into his grease-laden plate. "Hog and hominy is not quite what our appetites deserved after our weekend of drunkenness and debauchery, eh Charley?"

Before she could even react, one of Charley's regular passengers, Ennis Christman, piped up. "Well, this is a whole lot fucking better than what we get at the mining camps…a cup of coffee strong enough to float a millstone—worse than this shit if you can imagine. Beaver liver and tail stew plus a piece of fat pork, fried, or should I say burned, and to top this god-awful mess off, a pancake apiece fried in the pork fat, and about as heavy as its size in lead. And it ain't cheap either. The coffee alone is two bucks."

"Thank-you my good man," laughed Edmund. "You have now ruined all of our appetites for at least the rest of the day."

He stood up and headed back out to the waiting coach, with Charley and the rest of the amused passengers in tow.

Following the group, Christman continued his chatterings, "…but still cheaper than fucking raisins. I know one miner who bought a box of raisins and paid weight for weight about four thousand dollars in gold dust for 'em. It's true. Shit. Can you believe that? Does cure scurvy though. Hell, maybe I should be picking grapes instead of diggin' for gold…"

In time, Edmund and Charley would develop a tacit understanding. They never spoke of her secret. The great game just added to their pleasure. That something unspoken always slipping in and out of their arms.

Charley could sense Edmund not only made love to Charlotte, but to Charley as well. The vision of Charley on the driver's box, sweaty, dirty, whipping the six-team, powerful and brave as any man. She imagined it excited him to feel Charley beneath him or on top. As it excited her…the freedom to be a man and a woman in the same body…at the same time.

TWENTY-THREE

O ne afternoon Charley knocked on Anna's cabin door.
"It's open. Come in," she called out.
Charley walked in to find her chopping vegetables.
"I heard you come home this morning," Anna said. "We haven't seen you in a while. Tonia misses you. Can you have dinner with us tonight?"

"Sure. I just came over though to tell you that I'm leaving again for San Francisco first thing in the morning."

Anna's chopping got faster and harder.

"You know something Charley...I've been thinking...It's time for Tonia and me to leave. I'm going to talk to her when she gets home from school. We'll be gone by the time you get back from your trip."

"What? Why? What the hell are you talking about?"

"You don't want us in your life anymore. Since that night you ran away from me, you are always gone. All those long runs to San Francisco. You don't even have your days off anymore. I don't know if you have someone there. It's okay if you do. You don't have to tell me. But Tonia misses you. We never see you. It's lonely here."

"What do you mean? I thought you were happy. Of course I want you and Tonia in my life...Christ, where are you going?"

"I don't know. Maybe we'll go to San Francisco too. I can find work. I've always taken care of Tonia. I'm grateful for our time here and all you've done but I...I just think it's time."

"This is fucking crazy. You have a good life. Why would you give that up? What will you do? I won't let you go back to Luigi... to that kind of life you used to live."

"At least then I was never bored. And that is not your decision, Charley. You're not my husband."

"You're being selfish, Anna. Tonia is happy here. She likes her school. She has a home. Don't go."

"I don't want to talk about it anymore. We're leaving." Anna went back to her chopping.

Charley didn't know what to do. She poured herself a whiskey. She downed it. She poured another and sat down.

What could she do? Tell her about her "friend" and she'd still leave. Maybe this was the moment that she had to tell Anna the truth…everything. All of it. She took a breath. Please God, don't let Anna and Tonia leave. She willed herself to speak. But nothing came out.

Anna was just busying about making dinner, acting as though Charley wasn't even in the room. It seemed like an hour had passed. Why couldn't she just say the fucking words to Anna? Because she was a coward. That's why.

"Quit staring into space, Charley. Go to the garden and get me some parsley. Make yourself useful."

Charley stood up and started towards the door. But then she stopped. She turned around.

"Anna." Tears had started. "I'm…so sorry. I don't want you to go. I know I haven't been around for you and Tonia. I just…" She shook her head trying to stop the tears. "That night I left you…I didn't know what to do. I didn't know what to say. So I just avoided you. I kept avoiding you. I'm sorry. I didn't realize…I didn't think that you might be lonely. If you want to leave, that's one thing, but please don't leave because of me. I didn't mean to hurt you. Would never hurt you. Please don't go. I promise I'll be here more."

Anna put the knife down. She stared at Charley for a long moment. She had never seen him cry. What did this mean? She walked over to him. She put her hand on his arm.

"Thank-you. I needed to hear that. Let me think...maybe. We'll see. Let me finish dinner. How about we talk more when you get back from San Francisco? Yes?"

Charley looked into Anna's eyes. "Yes," she said. She couldn't stop the damn tears.

TWENTY-FOUR

Jim Birch looked through the shutters of the Sacramento Wells Fargo office, toward the waiting stagecoach outside.

"This is an important job, Charley. Gold run. No passengers. San Francisco office is expecting you as soon as you can get there."

They both watched as two bank guards loaded the shipment into the secured strongbox on the coach.

"There'll be a couple hired guns riding with you," Jim continued. "One'll ride shotgun and one'll be in the coach. Both are professionals. As usual, just let them do their job. You got your gun as well, right?"

"As always Jim."

Across the street, two men exited a neighboring saloon shouldering their shotguns, and ambled toward the stagecoach.

"There's your coach guns now," said Birch.

The two men had the same look: they both seemed to have lost the need to connect with the human race. But one of them, the one on the right with a beard—Charley stopped breathing—that walk, that lanky, insolent stride.

An alarm rang through every part of Charley's body. Had she been an animal she might have put her head down at that moment and bolted, only the warm ripple of the air left as a sign of the creature who'd been there. Or she'd have charged forward at the man, screaming and baring her teeth; she'd have torn with her nails great handfuls of skin from him; and she'd have killed him with her bare hands.

Her palms were sweating, her heart was pounding, pushing a storm-surge of blood through her, expanding her body almost

visibly; her muscles were charged. She was running to the end
of each of the possible paths ahead of her. Death after death was
happening in her mind.

Jim Birch looked at her. "Something the matter, Charley?"

She took a deep breath, trying to shake her head clear of it.
"Nope. I'm fine."

He wasn't quite convinced. "Hell, you sure you're okay?"

"Never better," she said, forcing a smile.

"Well, okay, if you say so," said Birch. "Good luck then. Have
a safe trip. I'll see you in two days."

Charley walked through the door to the red coach glimmer-
ing in the morning sunlight. She pulled her hat down low on her
brow, hunched her shoulders up…her body a tight fist.

The hired guns were standing by the coach waiting. They nodded to Charley and Jim. Charley turned away, but then her body
twisted without her will, to look…just her eyes showing, shoulder
and hat hiding the rest of her face. The man she'd thought was
Lee glanced over at her. His eyes squinted as though he were
looking into the sun. It was Lee Colton. It was Lee. He was barely
recognizable under his hat and full beard, but she knew those
fucked up eyes. She was petrified. Part of her wanted to run. She
needed to gather herself.

If he recognized her, he gave no sign of it.

Charley willed herself to climb up onto the driver's box. Swift
and silent, the two gunslingers took their place; Lee inside the
coach, and the other man on the spare end of the driver's seat.
He nodded to Charley and settled down next to her with his gun
resting comfortably in his lap, staring straight ahead. He reeked
of strong liquor. Charley scanned the horses, the position of the
reins. She could feel movement below her as Lee settled into his
seat. She thought of something.

"Jim," called Charley.

Birch stuck his head out the office door.

"If anything should happen today, you'll see to it Anna gets whatever's coming to me?"

Birch hesitated at the implication, but then gestured assent with a nod and disappeared back into the building.

An eerie unsettled feeling hung in the air. She felt a rising rush of dread and energy building up inside of her. She picked up the reins and started the horses moving.

He had returned again. To drag her down into her nightmare.

How could this be happening? Life had, these last years, become pleasurable. She had her job. Her horses. She had Edmund, Anna, Tonia. Life was good.

Fucking Lee. What should she do now? Pull out her gun, kill him? Finally get her revenge. Did she even want revenge anymore? She had tried to let go. She had almost forgotten about him.

All these thoughts were jumbled in her head. For the first time in a long time, she felt fear…her fate sitting in the coach below.

Their last encounter she had lost everything.

And that was it. Her head cleared. Her body grew still, cool, alert. She could not let that happen again.

The right moment would come. She just had to recognize that moment and not flinch when it came.

TWENTY-FIVE

About an hour out of town they reached a narrow pass. A sheer rock face on the north side and rolling rocky hills to the south, an arroyo long since dried up.

Lee was staring out the coach window. Killing was his profession and he was good at it. Already he'd emptied his gaze in readiness, in trance…in such a way a hawk dreams over the landscape—detached, yet attentive. The smallest movement and he plunges.

The six-team kicked up dust as Charley's stagecoach rounded a bend. The rocks glittered on their left and right. The light was brilliant and Charley shielded her eyes with one hand.

High above them, the bandit shielded his eyes for a moment as well, looking down through the blinding sunlight at the coach navigating the dusty trail. He wore a pair of burlap sugar sacks tied at the ankles and another one over his face.

Down below, Charley guided the team through the rough terrain. She scanned the rocky hills that hemmed the coach. She was radiating tension, and the horses were picking up the unfamiliar scent of it, the strange jaggedness in the feeling of the reins. They snorted.

Charley and the horses would all have liked to make a run for it, to leave this ominous, glittering corridor. But the road was too narrow to move faster than a walk.

All of a sudden, the lead horses began to whinny and toss their necks. They strained against their bits. The swing and wheel horses joined in the confusion. Charley reacted, reining them back under control.

Lee's eyes scanned the hillside, his gun trained through the open window. The gun up top next to Charley sat chewing tobacco, eyes scanning as well.

Not a second had passed when they heard the characteristic rattle of a diamond-backed rattlesnake. Charley saw it coiled on a rock near the road. That is what spooked the horses. She cracked the whip at the snake and it slithered off, away from the road. She relaxed. Just a rattler. The guns relaxed. At Charley's urging the team moved on slowly.

She heard a gunshot. She ducked. The horses frightened and unable to bolt in the narrow pass, came to a confused, disorganized halt.

Up on the hillside, four masked outlaws were silhouetted against the bright sky, their rifles trained on the stagecoach.

Charley looked up from the driver's box. "Oh, shit," she said.

Charley and the hired gun leapt off the coach and hunched down behind the front wheel, guns drawn.

Atop the hill, three of the bandits were raining down bullets. Sugarfoot was moving down the slope, covered by their gunfire. Inside the coach, Lee was kneeling on the floor, the barrel of his rifle resting on the window ledge, returning fire.

The second gun started to move down the length of the coach to the cover of the larger rear wheel.

Sugarfoot was now crouched behind a boulder, taking aim just as the second gun's legs appeared through the undercarriage. His eyes followed the movement of the legs, and his finger squeezed the trigger. A shot rang out and the man fell to the ground. As he tried to defend himself under the coach, Sugarfoot fired a second shot, this time to the man's head. He collapsed.

"Put your hands up," commanded Sugarfoot. "I know what you're carrying."

Lee took careful aim out the window. There was a quick flash as he got a bead on the bandit and fired. The bullet nicked

Sugarfoot's shoulder. He recoiled, falling behind the rock. The three men up on the ridge were still firing down at them. The bullets ripping into the fine wood body of the Concord stage-coach.

Charley, still crouched behind the front wheel, saw Lee jump out of the carriage.

"Get in the coach and cover me," Lee yelled.

Without hesitation, she climbed inside and began firing back at the bandits on the hill.

Lee, dodging from rock cover to rock cover, headed up the steep hillside.

Sugarfoot jumped out from behind the boulder, gun trained on Lee as he fired—missed. Lee flung his body against the ground. In that same moment, Charley's finger squeezed off a shot and her bullet hit Sugarfoot in the chest.

On the ridge, the bandits saw him fall. Sensing the jig was up, they fled to their horses tied nearby. Lee picked off two of them as they were mounting up. The remaining rider galloped away, disappearing down the other side of the hill.

Everything got very quiet.

Charley climbed out of the coach. She walked up the hillside toward the man she had just shot. She stood for a moment staring down at the body and then knelt down next to him. She rolled him over and pulled off the sack from his face. Sugarfoot was staring up at the clear blue sky, the life draining out of him.

"Oh, my God," uttered Charley. "Edmund?"

He attempted a feeble smile. "Guess you broke even with me…"

Charley shook her head, astonished beyond belief, "I didn't know."

Edmund emitted a short, painful laugh, blood spurting from his mouth.

"I'm sorry. I'm sorry. I'm sorry." She kept repeating it over and over. She was too stunned to even weep.

"No hard feelings, my girl. We had—" He struggled to catch his breath. There was a long moment of stillness and then Charley heard that sound, that sound she had heard before, that rattle of the soul escaping.

And he was gone. Her gloved hand closed Edmund's eyes.

A shadow fell across the body. Charley glanced up to see Lee looming over her.

"What the hell are you doing?" he said as he bent down and picked up Sugarfoot's rifle. "Help me load up these bastards so as we can collect the reward."

A sharp cold pain filled her craw. Now. Now was the moment.

Charley stood up. Where the fuck was her gun? She felt as though she might vomit with rage and impotence. It was gone. The gun was gone. "I got to go to the horses."

Lee's eyebrows went up at that. "Well hurry the hell up. I ain't carrying three dead bodies myself."

At the coach she searched for her gun. Where the fuck did she drop it? Wait. The hired gun under the coach. She would grab his rifle. She couldn't see it though. It must be underneath his body. She began to pull him out from under the coach. She was struggling at it when Lee came up behind her dragging Edmund's limp body. He let Edmund's feet drop to the ground. He bent down and helped Charley drag the guard's body out. Lee rolled him over with his foot and picked up the rifle before Charley could get it.

She stood there for a moment, dumbfounded. All she wanted was a fucking gun and Lee was standing there with three of them slung over his shoulder.

He demanded that Charley help with the other two bodies that remained up on the hill. She had no choice but to comply.

She'd had her moment and now it was gone. All these guns and all these bodies and still she fucked it up. She didn't even know if she had the will left to pull the trigger, even if she had a gun. She was numb.

She helped Lee drag the remaining bodies down the hill. And together they hoisted all of them into the coach—he made Charley help with that as well.

They started back to Sacramento; Edmund, piled together with the others, taking his last earthly ride.

Lee rode shotgun next to Charley, swigging from a flask of whiskey. He offered the flask to her. She gave no response.

"Suit yourself," he said. "Don't know why, but killin' a man always gives me a powerful thirst. Always has." He took another long swig.

The sound of Lee's voice was buzzing through her head. She was unable to speak…unable to make sense of anything. How was it possible that she had not known? Had not recognized? Edmund had seen through her disguise. And yet she had not even considered the possibility that he was also living an invented existence. A life of masks and sacks and games and fantasies. Her mind flew backwards to the gal in the saloon so many moons ago sitting on Edmund's lap. Charley remembered that brief second that she had seen revealed, the gal's tiny fragile truth within. Why had she not seen the truth in Edmund? Why had he not trusted her with his truth? If he had, he would still be alive. Enough. Enough. She could not, would not think of what she had just done…killed a man. A man whose moving flesh had found its way deep inside her.

Enough. Her pain was looming beyond the breath. And now crawling somewhere deep inside the dark side of her brain she heard her mind speak. It was seductive. It told her to be glad that it was not Lee that she had killed. Not sad.

Lee, whose smell and voice and eyes were here close…so close. They were so intertwined. The truth…she was never going to be able to kill him.

If she could have gone somewhere, anywhere, to be beaten into stupid insensibility, she'd have galloped there directly. If a tree trunk had fallen to halt the coach and break them, she'd have lain on the road and muttered blessings to that tree trunk with each red drop of the river of blood that poured from her mouth.

Her mind was slipping from her...floating like the wind that blew the dust from the graves of men.

TWENTY-SIX

The stagecoach was pulling up to the Sacramento Wells Fargo office. Lee was booze blind by now. "We got a hundred for each man comin' to us in reward money, plus five for Sugarfoot," he slurred. "What did you say your name was?"

"I didn't."

"I figure, seein' as how you're an amateur and all, we ought to split it five hundred for me and two hundred for you. True, you pulled the trigger on Sugarfoot, but I flushed him out for you and put away them other two critters as well."

Charley stopped the coach and got down, moving away from Lee.

Lee pursued it. "Hey, now, don't git your rattle up. Fifty-fifty, hell, I don't mind."

Charley turned, and for the first time, looked him in the eye. "I don't want it. Take it all."

Lee stopped in his tracks, staring at Charley through whiskey-glazed eyes.

"What the hell did you say your name was?"

At that moment, Jim Birch came running out of the office. "Charley? What happened?"

"Jim, you better get your guards to put the gold back in the safe. We got held up an hour out of town. Got four bodies to remove to the undertaker."

A few nosy townsfolk, seeing the bullet-riddled coach, were starting to gather around. Lee was looking at Charley, befuddled. His eyes sliding over her. The realization of her identity was dawning on him, through the liquor and the strangeness of the thought. But by the time he'd gathered his whiskey soaked wits enough to do anything about it, Charley was gone.

TWENTY-SEVEN

Tonia woke up to the familiar clip-clop of Charley's horse. Anna lay sleeping, undisturbed at her side. Tonia lifted herself onto her elbow and stared at her mother's face. In the starlight that filtered through the window, she could see that her mother's eyes were twitching under her eyelids...her habitual frown was gone and there was a faint smile on her face. She still has her dreams, thought Tonia.

With mischievous anticipation she slid out from her side of the bed, stepping down with her bare feet. She began to tiptoe towards the front door, taking care to avoid the squeaky spots in the wooden floor.

Outside, the summer night sky was brilliant with enormous stars. A sliver of a moon hung low overhead. What Tonia's eyes focused on, however, was not that enchanted sky, but Charley's little cabin.

His door was open tonight, an unusual occurrence she thought; perhaps it was because of the muggy evening. The lantern light streamed out, cutting a sharp wedge of illumination between their two cabins. It was like a pathway directing her. She stepped out onto the dirt and headed towards Charley's cabin. At his doorway she paused for just a moment before stepping into the rectangle of light outlined by the rough frame. She could see through into the bedroom.

Charley was on his knees on the floor with his back to her, unaware of her presence. What was he doing? She took in the tousled hair and the broad back straining the coarse blue broadcloth shirt. She could hear a sound that might be weeping. Charley's shoulders rose and fell. He was weeping.

Tonia wanted to leave now, but she couldn't seem to move. She stood there awkward...anxious, longing to be back in bed safe alongside her mother.

Charley stood up and teetered for a moment. Tonia thought he was going to fall over. He must be drunk she thought.

In a single gesture Charley pulled his shirt over his head. Puzzlement upon puzzlement: Tonia saw that his back and chest were wrapped round with wide cotton bands. An injury? Poor dear Charley—he must be in pain. That was why he was weeping.

Charley began to unwind the cloths. They fell to the floor. In a moment he was finished. His back, naked and pale.

Perhaps Tonia made a sound then, perhaps Charley felt a presence. She spun around and saw Tonia outlined in the doorway.

Tonia's breath stopped. What she saw at that moment...the shock of the revelation tore through her...disbelief, fear, disgust.

"Charley," she whispered. She turned and ran.

Charley threw on her shirt and hurried after Tonia. In a few long steps she'd caught up with her and wrapped her arms around the girl. Tonia struggled and kicked.

"Let me go. Let me go. You're disgusting."

"Shhh," said Charley, tightening her clutch around her.

"Don't touch me. Let me go."

"Be quiet, Tonia. It's all right. It's all right."

Tonia stopped struggling. She twisted around and looked up at Charley's tear-sodden face. She had thought him such a handsome man with his etched and sun-darkened skin. When he sat at dusty high speed on the driver's box, and the sweat-streaked horses responded to the crack of his whip, she caught her breath at the romance of it. She'd admired him so. Fatherless as she was, she was proud of the gift of his special, enviable friendship. The way he'd listen to her sagas of school and support her determined opinions and imaginings. His quiet, common-sense philosophies were so different from those of her drama-ridden mother's. A woman. A woman? Tonia started to cry.

Charley held the girl close until she quieted. She glanced over at the other cabin. Thank God. No sign they had woken Anna.

"But Charley, why? I don't understand why. How can you be a woman?" Tonia couldn't look her in the eyes.

There was nothing else for Charley to do. "Come inside and I'll tell you why Tonia." She turned back to the cabin.

Tonia hesitated, then followed. She flashed on a memory of that first time years earlier when, holding onto her mother's hand, she had followed Charley out of an old life and into a new one.

TWENTY-EIGHT

At dawn, the door opened and the two of them stepped out. Charley's face was sagging with fatigue and sadness, but also relief. Tonia's was glowing with exhilaration and new understanding. Tonia now knew as much as Charley could find the words to tell.

"There's a freedom, my girl, that comes from speaking one's truth," Charley said, as they stood in the doorway of the cabin. "I've been in and out of men's britches so much that half the time I don't know myself what I am anymore. And if truth be told, I don't much care. But too much has passed between your mama and me as I am, for her to know. If she ever found out the truth about me, she would feel betrayed. It's my secret that I trust in your hands now, Tonia."

"But she loves you."

"I know," Charley nodded. "But think for a moment about what this would do to her. Finding out. No matter how your mother's life has been turned upside down by this man or that, she's always landed on her feet. But this is different. This would shame her."

Tonia thought about this for a moment. "Okay. I won't say anything. I promise. It'll be our secret. I love you Charley."

"Me too."

There was a long silence as they walked towards Anna's cabin.

"You know, if I had the chance I'd kill that bastard Lee Colton for you," Tonia whispered. "After what he did to you, and Byron, and your baby. I hate him."

"I don't even know if I could kill Lee if I had another chance. For years I've had dreams of killing him. It's why I came out west. But I don't know anymore."

The front door of Anna's cabin creaked open, and she appeared, looking stern and rumpled with sleep.

"Antonia. What are you doing?"

Charley spoke up. "It's all right, Anna. I was up early feeding the horses and Tonia just came out to help."

"Why are you home so soon? We weren't expecting you until tomorrow."

"There was a hold-up."

"Oh my God. Are you alright?"

"I'm fine. Just tired. We'll talk later?"

"Alright. Tonia, come inside and start getting ready for school."

Tonia hugged Charley and gave her a kiss on the cheek. Following her mother inside, she turned and looked at Charley with a gaze full of affection as she closed the door behind her.

TWENTY-NINE

The following morning, while Charley was grooming the horses, Tonia, carrying her school bag, sneaked unseen through the front door of Charley's cabin. She rifled through the dresser drawer until she found the gun, the one she and Charley practiced with when her mother wasn't around. Charley had said every girl should know how to protect herself.

She found it tucked away under a pile of much-darned socks. She checked it; it was loaded. Her heart knocking in her chest, she hid the gun in her bag and then with feigned innocence, walked out of the cabin towards the barn.

As she mounted her horse, Charley called out, "You riding to school with Dwayne today?"

"Yes. You know I always do."

"Well, tell him to come over after to pick up an old saddle I want to give him."

"Okay."

"And have a good day at school."

"I hate school."

"That's a bad attitude. Never hurt a girl to be able to read and write." Charley winked at her. "Now git, girl. You'll be late."

"Bye. See you tonight."

Charley slapped the horse on the rear, sending it and Tonia out of the barn.

Tonia rode not to her friend Dwayne's or school that morning, but instead, to the Wells Fargo stagecoach office. She tied her horse to the hitching post out front. Inside was Jim Birch, sitting behind his desk drinking his morning tea.

"Tonia, why aren't you at school?"

"I'm on my way there sir. But Charley asked me to stop by your office first and find out if Lee Colton is still in town and how to find him."

"He sure is. For a few more days. We put him up at the old Clinton place."

"Oh. I know where that is."

"How 'bout that Uncle Charley of yours? Took down Sugarfoot in one shot!"

"Yes, he told me all about it. He wants to talk to Mr. Colton. I don't know about what. He just said it was important that he caught up with him before he left town."

"Glad to be of help. Now I have to get back to work, and you have to get to school young lady. Remind Charley I got a run for him in two days."

"Thank-you Mr. Birch. See you soon."

THIRTY

Tonia rode up to the old Clinton place. It was just a small one-room shack on a clear and level bit of ground. She was nervous, but determined to see this adventure through. She slid down off her horse and tied it to a small cottonwood tree. She rummaged in the bag for the gun. This she held before her, making her way to the shack.

So much was going on inside of her. She was thrilled with herself. She was terrified. She wanted to pee. Just shoot the gun like Charley had taught her. That's all she had to do. She would pretend she was on the stage with her mama. She would make Charley proud. She could imagine Charley's expression later tonight; how very pleased she would be with her. After this they'd be together for life.

Her cheeks were flushed with excitement. Her whole body was quivering. On rubbery legs she walked to the door, took a breath, and tried to push it open. Stuck. It took great pushing and shoving, but she got the creaky door unstuck. No one was home.

The interior of the shack was dark and sparsely furnished and smelled of stale tobacco. Tonia felt a surge of disappointment, mixed with the faintest taste of relief. Her heart pounding, she went inside and looked around. This was the place where the man lived who'd hurt Charley so. And she, Tonia, who believed she possessed a courage beyond her years, was about to show her bravery and loyalty to Charley.

She took a chair and maneuvered it to face the half-closed door, then sat down on it, the heavy gun in her lap. She'd wait.

It must have been half the day before Lee rode up, pausing to observe the unfamiliar horse tied to the tree. Tonia hadn't quite thought of that. Lee wheeled his horse, moving in toward the shack. The half-open front door creaked in the light breeze. He dismounted a short distance away, then pulled his pistol from its holster and cocked it.

Tonia had fallen asleep in the chair. A low melodious whistle sounded from outside. She stirred, awakening, her eyes opening, her hands closing around the gun.

Lee, back pressed against the outside wall of the shack to the side of the door, swung out his arm. The door banged open.

Tonia sprang up from the chair, bracing herself behind the gun. She spoke, her voice and body trembling. "Lee Colton?"

Lee stepped into the doorway.

Tonia took a breath and squeezed the trigger with all her might.

Lee heard the bullet hit the wall beside him. He fired several rounds into the dim interior. He heard the word "Mama." Then the sound of a body falling to the floor.

He strode over to the body and turned it face up to get a look at her. "What the hell?" he muttered.

She was thoroughly dead. Who was this girl? Why had she been here? He played it out in his mind. She was in his cabin, waiting for him with a gun. She tried to shoot him. He'd done the right thing. Still: a young girl. He was bewildered and angry. He wondered what to do now. He stomped around the room for a few moments, avoiding looking at the girl's face, her empty staring eyes.

He left the cabin, leaving her there on the floor where she'd fallen, and went back out to his horse. He'd go into town and tell the sheriff that young girls were now attacking people in their own homes.

A few hours later, Sheriff Halstead arrived at the old Clinton cabin with Lee in tow.

"Fuck," he said. "It's Charley's little girl, Tonia. What the hell? You sure you don't know her?"

Lee shook his head, "Never met her in my life."

"You know Charley Parkhurst right? You just did that job together."

Lee's breath stopped. Parkhurst? He was right. Shit. That driver was Charlotte. He had been so liquored up. Charley's girl? What the hell did that mean? Charlotte sent a girl to kill him? Was he going crazy? Was the booze getting to him?

"Hey." The sheriff raised his voice trying to get Lee's attention. "When are you planning on leaving town?"

"Uh...I got one more job for Jim Birch in two days. Then headin' out to Frisco."

"Well, you're coming with me first. I've got some more questions for you. And plan on sticking around till we get this matter sorted out. Get your damn blanket off the bed. I'm gonna wrap her up and take her body back to her mama."

THIRTY-ONE

T he next morning the birds were singing as usual. The sun was shining as usual. The sunlight streamed in through the cabin window onto Tonia's body, dressed in white, laid out on the bed. Anna was kneeling next to her; her face expressionless as she plaited white ribbons into her dead daughter's hair.

A short time later a small group gathered around the grave: Jim Birch, Ben, Hank and a few other whips and neighbors, Charley and Anna. The rough homemade wooden box containing Tonia's body lay at the bottom of the freshly dug hole. The soft spring earth was heaped to one side, awaiting the moment to cover her.

Birch was speaking, "...there is no death. Only a change of worlds..."

Anna was on her knees sobbing. Over and over she sobbed, *"Perché? Perché?"*

The whips were awed by her grief. There weren't many mothers in their midst. They thought of their own mothers: would they grieve like this at their death?

Charley's eyes were frozen into an expression of rage... remorse...loss. She knew the "why"—if only she hadn't told Tonia...if only she had closed the cabin door that night. If only, if only....

It was time.

She broke away from the group, striding off toward her cabin. She grabbed Byron's pistol from off the hooks on the wall, loaded it and headed to the corral. A time to every purpose, a time to be born, she was thinking. A time. A time. She saddled up the horse. A time to die. Hell, even the Good Book was telling her it was time.

Charley mounted her horse. As she passed the little group around the grave, Anna looked up for an instant, her eyes like great black stones. It won't change anything she was probably thinking. You stupid man, it won't change anything. Anna dropped her face back into her hands. Her body shook with anguish.

Charley glared at the grave, at the sky, at the road, at God. She gave the horse a hard slap of the reins.

This was that moment she had lived in her dream. But the horror in the dream had been that the trigger would not move, no matter how hard she pulled, no matter how she willed it, no matter how she begged God. The trigger was always frozen in place, and she would wake up in bed sweating, shaking. And now this moment felt like her dream. It was hard to know the difference. Just breathe. Breathe. She would move her finger against the curved metal of the trigger. She would pull with all her strength. This time the gun would fire. She would kill Lee. She would finish this nightmare forever.

THIRTY-TWO

C harley rode up to the Clinton place and saw a horse in a small corral. She saw a bit of wood smoke curling up from the stovepipe sticking out of the roof. He was home.

She paused for a moment at the tree where Tonia must have tied her horse. She rode in closer. Her hand gripped the butt of the pistol in her holster. He would probably kill her, she thought in passing. But it didn't matter.

Just outside the shack she dismounted. The front door creaked open and Lee appeared. He was leaning against the door frame, gun dangling from his fingers, his veiled eyes glittering.

"Well, hello there. Shit. I wasn't sure back then at the coach it was you Charlotte. Or should I say Char...lee? Looks like you took my name advice after all."

Charley just stared at him.

"Guess I been sorta expecting you," Lee said. "You're lookin' mighty tough and serious these days. Oh, and sorry about the girl...it was a mistake. Don't know what the fuck she was doing. You send her out as your hired gun?"

He ambled out onto the porch, taking a few steps along the length of it, laughing. The laugh at this moment was forced, but he'd had plenty of time on his own to think how funny it was, the way things turned out—the girl and all. And Charlotte, like this. And the way his life became, and hers. You'd never have expected it. Not in a million years. He turned to look at her as she raised her gun and trained it on him.

Eyes cold, Charley cocked it.

Lee quietly cocked his gun as well, except his he left dangling at his side.

"Come on now, Charlotte," he continued. "You can't kill me. I'm the one took care of you. I raised you. I'm the one that loves you. I'm all you've got in the world. I'm your brother."

And then he pursed his lips and whistled their private whistle and smiled the way he smiled—the fetching, lopsided way he used to reserve for her alone.

"You're not my fucking brother," Charley whispered. Lee winced at the words. He wheeled, raising his gun toward her—but Charley was already aimed and ready.

She squeezed the trigger hitting Lee square in the chest. As Lee fell he got off a single wild shot, missing Charley entirely. She followed with her eyes and with her gun the trajectory of his falling body.

She fired again.

On Lee's face was a look of utter surprise. He was already just about dead.

She stepped in close to Lee's body. Her thoughts were wrapping themselves tight around her feelings. There was no joy or relief, no satisfaction, no sense of revenge now fulfilled. The time had come. She had done what she had to do for Tonia, for Anna, for Byron, for the baby. Done what she had to do for herself. And now it looked as if she had not been killed.

Lee was right, but not the way he'd meant it. The world was different for her now, without him. Better, maybe. Alone, but emptied of some curse that had followed her since a child.

It was so strange, she thought, these moments we pray for; they happen so quick and then they're gone. "Just like that," Charley said out loud.

She left Lee staring at the sun. Someone else would have to close his eyes.

THIRTY-THREE

Charley sat alone, hunched over a glass of 40 Rod Whiskey, a half empty bottle on the table next to her. The barkeep came over. He wiped the whiskey bottle and put a cork in it.

"Closing time again, my friend. Time to go home. Maybe you should take a night off."

By now everyone in town had a different theory about what had happened. Someone had revenged Tonia and killed Lee Colton, a good for nothing gunslinger. Charley was the likely candidate. But maybe it had been Anna…maybe some other enemy of Lee's out for revenge, or maybe even that drunk Ben. Folks still could not fathom though, what in the world Tonia had been doing at the Clinton place. With a gun no less. Some thought perhaps there was more to the coach robbery than they had been told. Colton and Charley kill a famous outlaw, and two days later Tonia is killed by Colton? It was all very confusing. But if it was Charley, nobody could blame him. After all, Tonia had been like Charley's daughter, for Christ sake. Even the sheriff, with no proof, had eventually dropped the matter. Anybody would have done the same thing. No doubt about it.

Charley looked up at the barkeep. She nodded, staggered out and headed home.

She rode her horse up to her cabin. Dismounting, she slide down the side of the horse and crumpled into a heap on the ground. After a few minutes of lying there staring at the moonless sky, she managed to get herself up. She stumbled into the cabin heading straight for the bedroom—ignoring Anna, who was waiting at the table.

"Life is so simple for you, Charley. Isn't it? So easy for a man. You go out and you kill somebody. You get away with it. And then you get drunk every night. I wish it was so simple for me."

"Nothing simple about killing a man," Charley said. She pulled a cigar out and tried to light it. "Can't rightly say as to how I feel about it." She got the cigar to light.

"That is all you ever say to me, 'Can't rightly say as to how I feel about it.' Even with Tonia gone, you can't say how you feel about anything. You can't say how you feel about her? She's dead, Charley. Rotting. Maybe someday God will tell me why my daughter did what she did and why he took her. Maybe in exchange for the pain, God will give me that gift. But now I need you to speak to me. I need you to help me. I feel like you're not telling me something. Are you protecting me? Why...why did she do what she did?"

Charley's inebriated body had to sit down. She sat in her old rocker and turned toward the fireplace, staring into the flames.

Anna stood up from the table. Her voice got softer. "Why won't you look at me? Why won't you speak? Tell me how we can live together, side by side for all this time, through everything that has happened and you won't say anything to me. Tell me something. Anything."

There was a long pause as Charley drew on her cigar.

Anna erupted, screaming, "Good. I'm leaving. Why would I stay? You don't care about me enough to speak. You never loved me and you never loved Tonia. I don't think you know how to love anybody."

Charley threw her cigar into the fireplace and turned towards Anna. "You're right. I don't—I can't love you Anna, not the way that you want. I care for you, and I need you, and that's a kind of love, isn't it? It's the best I can do. Please don't ask any more of me."

"More? I get nothing from you Charley. I feel only empty holes. Forget about me. I have never even heard you speak once of love for Tonia. Or love for God...what kind of man are you that you cannot even love God?"

Charley looked at Anna with her glazed, drunken eyes. "Please understand, it's always been hard for me to put into words what I feel."

Anna sat down in front of the fire next to Charley. "Well, try. I need your help," she said.

"I can't explain. I...fuck." Charley pushed herself up out of the chair and grabbed a bottle of whiskey. She took a slug and sat back down. "I...I think a lot Anna...when I drive..."

She was struggling to get the words out.

"Have you...have you ever seen a slab of towering mountain rock...so powerful, so perfect. You have to lean back on something when you release the tears that snap into your eyes because you know that God has a face. The poppy growing out of the side of the rock. The waterfall that claws its way through the stone. That force...that face. I've come to believe everything that causes me awe, must be what you call God...So yes, Anna, I love God. And I do love Tonia."

Anna stood up and walked to the window. There was a long moment before she spoke. "I need to leave in the morning."

"Where will you be going?"

"I don't know. I don't know anything anymore. I don't know why Tonia's dead. I don't know why you could never love me. All I know is there's nothing for me here anymore."

It was so quiet. Charley could hear the scratching of the branches against the cabin. A possum or some other creature ran across the roof. She could see Anna's chest moving in and out, holding back her tears. She walked over to where Anna was standing. She reached out and touched her.

Anna started to sob. "Oh Charley...where is there to go in this world?"

"Nowhere," Charley said. "Nowhere." She had thought about these things. "Here is all we got."

For a long while they both stood there, Charley's arm protectively around Anna.

It was time to tell her the truth, Charley thought. It was the least she could do, she told herself, for the part she'd played in Tonia's death. And how could she go on living with herself, if she allowed Anna to believe that she was unloved for the wrong reasons. Let her vent her fury. She has a right to know. Hell, whatever Anna might say or do to her, she deserved worse. For thinking of no one but herself all these years...putting all her thoughts into protecting her damn, worthless self.

She took a deep breath. "Anna. There's something you need to know...about why Tonia went to Lee Colton's...she went because of me."

Anna pulled back from Charley. "What?"

"I'm not who you think I am. I'm so sorry. I don't want you to feel I've betrayed you. But I've kept a secret from you, from everyone, all these years. I don't know how to tell you this. I guess there's no other way than to just tell you that I'm a woman."

There was a stunned silence.

Anna threw back her head and laughed in disbelief. "What? Are you so drunk...what kind of trick are you playing? Why are you being so cruel? Why are you doing this to me?"

"I'm sorry, Anna. I'm not being cruel. I'm not playing a trick."

Charley took off her shirt and began unwinding the long strips of cloth wrapped round her chest.

At the sight of Charley's breasts Anna's mouth dropped in horror.

Charley put her shirt back on and took another long slug of whiskey.

She began to tell Anna everything. All of it. The whole story. It was like unwrapping her breasts from their tight bindings. In the beginning it hurt, but then, as the wrappings came off, she felt free, light, released. At last...Anna now knew.

But her release lasted just a few breaths.

"You bastard...I don't even know what to call you."

Anna was beside herself. She grabbed the poker from the fire and held it up to Charley's face. She was roaring: "Assassino. That's who you are. It was you murdered my little girl. Not that Lee Colton."

"Anna. Forgive me." Charley grabbed the iron tool from her hand. "This won't put anything right. I'm so sorry. I'm sorry."

"No. No you're not. You were just thinking to protect yourself with your awful secret. Never thinking about how you'd influence a girl who worshipped and loved you with all her beautiful heart."

"I had no notion of what she'd do, Anna. Believe me. I wish it was me instead of Tonia got that bullet. Seems like my whole life people I love most have gotten killed because of me."

"People you love?" Anna screamed. "All this time you let me fall in love. Let me care for you. You should have told me. You made me such a fool."

"I'm the one's a fool. You're right. I should have told you. I shouldn't have told Tonia. But I was afraid I would lose you both. You'd become my family. I needed you. Please forgive me. I've been a damn coward. Forgive me." She sat down and she wept.

Charley's tears were all it took…to turn Anna's rage to pity. Anna looked down at her. She watched Charley for a moment and then walked out the door.

The morning after Charley's truth-telling, Anna packed up her few belongings in her old cloth valise. By the time Charley woke up, she was gone.

THIRTY-FOUR

With Anna gone, Charley's life-long coat of loss acquired yet another layer. It was what she deserved she told herself. For all the bad choices she'd made. All the secrets she'd kept. Anna. Tonia. Edmund. Byron. The baby. Hadn't she somehow brought it on them all? Lee as well.

With a heavy heart, Charley turned to her horses. Animals could do you no wrong. Horses did not give a damn if you were man, woman, or anything in between. Animals valued a person, judged a person, loved a person by simple things. Her horses judged her by how hard or gentle she tugged at the bit in their mouths, how often she held out her palm so they could nibble a crisp carrot or an apple and how she spoke to them, groomed them and respected them. She took comfort in the beasts' warmth and silence, the soft sound of their breathing as they slept...comfort she had discovered so long ago when she'd been taken in by Jonas. She'd been a girl then. My God. A girl with ribbons in her hair. She remembered the time she'd held the reins with such confidence, and then the wagon overturned, hurling her and Jonas to the ground. What was it he had said as they dusted themselves off? "Life's going to upset your wagon. Maybe someone's riding next to you can help you set it right. Maybe not." Maybe not... Wasn't that the truth.

Tonia was dead and Anna had left and now Charley wasn't sure how she'd set it right. Maybe she wasn't supposed to set it right. We find a being who we somehow think can fill us, mend us, make us whole. And then they abandon us, or we them. Maybe loneliness was the answer. Maybe the key was accepting that.

So Charley accepted it. And she did so by embracing her old pal, 40 Rod Whiskey. If she wasn't on her coach, she was with her bottle. She slowly stopped spending time with her friends in the saloon, preferring instead the seclusion of her cabin and horses. She mustered up the energy to take care of the animals but that was about it.

THIRTY-FIVE

Jim Birch found Charley passed out on her porch one afternoon. He had stopped by the cabin to see if she was okay as she had missed her last run. She had obviously tripped, in a drunken stupor no doubt, and was splayed out on the front steps. She began to wake up as he lifted and dragged her into the rocker on the porch.

"Hey Jim," she muttered. "What the hell you doing here?"

"You realize you've missed your last run, right? And the one before that I got three complaints that you were drunk and weaving the coach all over creation. You alright?"

"Oh shit…I forgot. Sorry Jim."

"You got to ease up on the drinking, Charley. I know it's hard with Tonia and Anna gone."

"I'm fine Jim. I just forgot is all. I'll be there tomorrow."

"No you won't. You're taking a few weeks off. Get sobered up and pull yourself together. Then you can come back to work."

"No, no. I don't want to take any time off. 'Sides, Ben drinks all the time on the job…you don't make him take time off."

"Ben might miss a run or two because he was drinking, but I've never had a complaint from a passenger about him. Look, Charley, we've known each other a long time. We're good friends. But I'm the boss here. You're taking the time until you get your drinking under control. I don't want to have to fire you."

"C'mon Jim. You're making a big thing out of this. I'm not drinking too much."

"I'm not here to argue with you, Charley. You used to be responsible. Nowadays, I can't even trust you. Get your damn self together…you want some help getting inside?"

"No. I don't need your help."

"Suit yourself. Hope to see you in couple weeks."

He then got on his horse and left Charley sitting there.

Thirty-Six

Somewhere in the back of her mind Charley knew that Jim was right. But try as she may, she couldn't let go of the whiskey.

It was during her involuntary time off that a new horse came under her care, a mature, chestnut-colored gelding. He was an unpredictable and temperamental horse and therefore was about to be put down. So she took him in. The horse had been passed around so much that no one could pinpoint his exact history, but wherever he came from, Charley thought, people must've treated him rough. Tabbris was his name.

Tabbris was a jittery gent who tossed his head and stomped his feet as if to show that he was always ready to bolt or rear. He had wild eyes...even when he seemed to be resting.

One morning Charley entered Tabbris' stall. She called out to the horse, as she always did with him before she entered, and held out an apple for him. He gobbled it from her hand. "Come on now, boy, we're going give you some new shoes."

Tabbris snorted and stomped.

"You're going to like them," she said. "Won't be any trouble at all and afterward you're going feel like a fine young colt again. Now don't be nervous, boy...it don't hurt at all."

Charley led the stubborn horse from his narrow confines and into a larger space cleared out for doctoring the horses. Tabbris seemed more restless and anxious than usual. But Charley overlooked it and her good instincts. She had always tried to follow her instincts with her animals but age was beginning to creep up on her. Her patience was not at all like it used to be...and neither was her once agile body. It was stiffening and hurting as she leaned in toward the horse. She felt a damn ache in her knees and another down her back into her leg. An ache like wire twisting around bone. And as usual these days, her head was pounding from her days and nights drinking. She pulled a bottle of Paines Celery Compound out of her pocket and took a healthy swig. It seemed like she was also living on every snake oil remedy she could find.

She sidestepped the large snorting animal, turned to the open window, looked up at the approaching rain clouds overhead and took a deep breath of crisp air. Out of nowhere a rough cough erupted from her chest. And another…and again. It left her breathless and surprised and dizzy. Shit…was it the beginning of old age or the influenza? Neither a good sign.

Still coughing, she turned back to Tabbris and knelt down to begin shoeing him. All of a sudden she was overcome by the faintest memory of her first rain. What a strange sensation…her mind floating backwards so far…so fast. She smelled straw, dampness. Her jarring memory took only a tenth of a second but that was a tenth of a second too long. She shook her head, trying to get rid of the image. And then she glimpsed the horse turning but was not quick enough to dodge the explosive hoof coming toward her face. She did not hear her own scream. She felt an unbearable, searing, infinite pain. And then, darkness.

THIRTY-SEVEN

C harley became aware of a familiar voice.
"You think he'll come out of it?" said Ben.
"Sure was a nasty kick," said Jim.
Charley moaned. Her head was throbbing.

The moon-faced Doc Jarvis came into focus. "Looks like our patient is coming around. Charley...you've had a bad accident. Your horse must have kicked you in the head. Somehow you managed to stumble across the road to your neighbors, and they found you and brought you here. I've cleaned you up and stitched you up and you're going to be okay. Jim and Ben are here."

Charley's hand went up to her left eye. She felt rough cloth.

"That's a bandage," Doc Jarvis went on.

Charley remembered another time in this room when she had removed bandages from her chest and Jarvis had repaired her rib. The woman had been revealed that day under the dirty flannel shirt. Today, nothing in his voice seemed to betray that secret.

"You're going to keep the bandage on until you've had a chance to heal." His tone was even, yet somehow foreboding.

Charley felt Jim's hand on her shoulder.

"You've lost the eye, Charley," said Jarvis. "You'll be able to see just fine from the one that's left. When the healing is done you'd best wear a patch. You know you're very lucky. You could have been killed."

"A patch," Ben chimed in. "One-eyed Charley. That sounds pretty fine to me."

"As soon as you heal up," Jim said, "you got your job waiting for you...on the terms that we spoke of a couple of weeks ago, of course. Looking forward to having you back. Now, we'll help you get home. And we'll all stop in to check on you and see if you need anything."

Charley closed her one good eye and felt herself bathed in darkness. She opened the eye and saw the hairs in Doc Jarvis's nose. Closed it and saw nothing. Opened it and saw Ben's tobacco-stained teeth. Her head was throbbing.

"Got me a headache something awful," she groaned. "Got any whiskey?"

"Glad to oblige," said Ben. He sidled over and lifted her back so she could rest against his arm. With his free hand he poured spirits from his flask into Charley's mouth. How tender a man can be was what Charley thought as she grimaced and swallowed and then lay back on Jarvis's doctoring table to rest.

A good kick to the head, if you survive it, is bound to make you examine your life, one way or the other. You might think the loss of an eye would have sent Charley further down into her dark spiral. But oddly, it seemed to do the opposite.

You get a choice when you hit the bottom. And half-blind Charley felt like she was now spread-eagled, face-down in manure. For a moment it was such a relief to be lying there...to not struggle anymore.

But as she lay on her bed recovering, she kept hearing Jonas' voice over and over. That under all the shit was something good... if you were willing to dig through it. What the hell good could come out of losing an eye? Losing a baby? What about all the other bad things that had happened? What was the fucking good in them? She thought about it—for a long time.

She realized that her work as a whip had been good. Her freedom. Her friends. Even the ones that were gone...the time she had with them. All that still didn't change the lonesomeness though.

But then it came to her...just change your mind about it. About everything. Shit. That was it. What an idiot she was. It was that simple. Just decide to stop struggling and embrace it all as a gift. And in a single second, everything is different.

She was feeling somehow restored, revived. All her senses were on fire. And now from atop the stagecoach there was plenty for Charley, even with one eye, to see. From her perch she could see California growing, changing as more and more people took root. Her attire now included a black patch. People, even the newspapers, called her One-eyed Charley. Cock-Eyed Charley. That Wicked Hoss Done You Charley. She had become famous in her own little world. She had made peace with her loneliness. What she saw and felt now, even more than before, was wind and speed and mastery.

Thirty-Eight

Three years later Charley made the decision to move to a steadier climate. The changes from season to season in Sacramento were aggravating her constant cough and rheumatism. She discussed her situation with Jim, and he suggested that she move down south to the Watsonville area and start taking fewer and shorter runs out of that office. So she sold her property at a fair price, packed her belongings and headed down to the Pajaro Valley. She purchased a twenty-six acre ranch with a two-room cabin, stable and apple orchard for six hundred dollars just outside of Watsonville, California, near the Seven Mile House stage stop.

With much more time on her hands now, she became an avid reader of newspapers—*The Watsonville Pajaronian*—in particular.

The world around her seemed to speed and twist and tumble in ways she could not fathom. In 1860, the year the United States was brawling and wrestling with itself over slavery issues, the Pony Express advertised for young riders but stated that only orphans need apply. The Pony Express made its first run to the west carrying 49 letters and 3 newspapers, delivered to Sacramento in tip top shape, all the way from St. Joseph, Missouri in the record speed of eleven days. The new hero of the day was young Tom Hamilton, who had weathered everything from hostile Indians on the prairies to storms on the mountains to make that first delivery.

Hell, Charley thought, as she turned the page to more interesting news...if she was seventeen again, she could've done it in nine days.

Charley was becoming political. Her usual routine, when she wasn't working, was sitting in the saloon with her newspaper spread across the table, debating the issues. She loved to read aloud and have great violent arguments with anyone and everyone willing to disagree with her, particularly about the issue of equal rights for both Negroes and women.

She even voted in the election of 1868 for General Grant. As she made her mark on the ballot, she wondered in passing, if she might be the first women to vote in these United States. Of course, as a man.

THIRTY-NINE

Charley was finishing her lunch when she heard someone coming up the porch steps of her cabin. She opened the front door to find an older woman standing there... she had sun baked skin and silver hair. Her eyes...something familiar about them. In that second, Charley looked down and saw at the woman's feet, a valise. Oh my God...the perpetual bestowing valise.

"Anna?"

"Of course it's me, Charley. What the hell happened to your eye?" Anna peered into the cabin. "My God...your place looks like shit. And so do you. How long since you've eaten a decent meal? Are you going to let me in?"

"I'm sorry, Anna. It's just that you look...I mean it's been how many years? What a shock to see you. It's been a long time...I'm sorry...come in." Charley grabbed the valise. "Are you hungry?"

"Yes, thank-you. I haven't eaten since last night at the stage-coach stop."

Anna followed Charley inside. She took off her coat and hat.

Charley poured a bowl of soup and placed it on the table with a tin of crackers. "Sit. Please. It's not much."

Anna sat down and began to devour her soup. Charley watched her eat in silence. It was so hard to believe that after all this time it was Anna sitting in front of her. It felt like another one of her dreams.

"You want something to drink?" Charley said. "All I got in the place is whiskey."

"Sure. Why not."

Charley poured both of them a glass.

"Thank-you, Charley. Funny. Yes? You cooking for me."

Charley smiled.

There was a long pause as they both sipped their whiskey.

"I swore I'd never cook another meal after Silvio died," Anna said.

"Silvio?"

"My late husband. Old Italian gentleman. We lived in the Salinas Valley. He owned a small lettuce ranch. Oh God, Charley. I learned to hate lettuce. He made me work with him in the fields. He left me the ranch though. I sold it and made a little money. I lived in a boarding house for a while but despised it. All those gossipy old biddies."

"How the hell did you find me?"

"I went to Sacramento. The man who bought your place said you had moved down to Watsonville. So I went to the Wells Fargo office here in town, and they gave me directions to your place. What about you? What happened to your eye?"

"Horse kicked me in the head. Was drinking too much after you left. Didn't have my wits about me. No matter though...can see just fine."

"Why'd you move down here? I thought you loved Sacramento."

"Wanted some easier weather. My sciatica was getting to me in the cold. So Jim, you remember Jim Birch? He's gone now. Went down with a ship in a gale south of Cape Hatteras. Anyway... he suggested for me to move down here and do fewer runs. You know I'm not a young colt anymore."

"I'm so sorry about Jim. I liked him. Aren't you lonely without all your friends though?"

"Ben and Hank drop in whenever they're down this way. I'm friends with the neighbors, the Harmon's and their son, George. And I'm an Odd Fellow...a great group of men...we do a lot of good things for people. I like Watsonville. It's simple here...and peaceful. Life has been good. Except for the fucking sciatica...I've thought of you often, Anna. Hoped life was good for you, too."

"I have a favor to ask you Charley. For old time's sake. I was wondering...what you thought about me coming back. To live here. With you."

"Live with me? I didn't ever think that you'd forgive me, Anna. I never thought I'd see you again."

"I'm not angry with you anymore. I understand now why you chose to live your life the way you did. In my travels, I've heard of other woman just like you. And I know you didn't mean to hurt Tonia...that you loved her." Anna took a little sip of her whiskey. "Life is empty, still. Sad. Thought maybe...thought it might be less so if I came back."

Charley stared into her glass. Strange how once in a while God gives you what you didn't even know you needed. She hadn't realized how she missed Anna until she saw her again.

"I'd like that," Charley said. "I'd like you to stay here with me. If that would make you happy. Whatever I can do. Thank-you for saying that you aren't angry with me anymore. That means a lot to me...unpack your things Anna. Make yourself at home. Welcome back."

Anna continued to call her Charley. Charley continued to pass as a man. And at this point, it's not like she could have gone back even if she had wanted to. What with lips and teeth stained brown by chewing tobacco, her raspy voice, leathery skin shaded under a battered hat, a particular swagger to her walk, and an ease with cigars, whiskey and cards—her act had long ago become truer to who she was than the truth of her anatomy. The other whips, her passengers, and the world at large, all treated one-eyed Charley as a man. No use in changing who she'd become. She'd tried that once.

The balance between Charley and Anna had tipped, however. No longer was Anna a doe-eyed female pining for Charley's affection. She had wandered, and all she had found was that she missed the comfort and security of her old friend Charley. She also knew that she didn't want to die alone in a damn boarding house.

So Charley and Anna slept together in the same big bed in the Watsonville cabin. They had talked about how if only Charley were a man, this relationship could have been one of Watsonville's happiest marriages. The community already saw them as the perfect couple.

One summer night, in that big bed after more than a few glasses of wine, they had tried to find some comfort in each other's body. But it had come to no avail.

They ended up roaring with laughter. They both agreed what an incredible joke life sometimes brings you in the end...not exactly what you planned. So even without the blessings of connubial bliss, the two friends made a vow that they would be there for each other.

Friendship, true friendship is a curious dance. Why does one recognize and embrace one soul and yet not another. What is that? That something unspoken. Perhaps it is a long ago remembrance of another time, another place, those same familiar eyes shining out. Always we are searching for those recognizable eyes...so that we might at last be recognized ourselves.

FORTY

Watsonville, California
December 28, 1879

T he table had been covered with a red cloth and set
for two. The interior of the small cabin glowed in the
candlelight. Homemade curtains rippled from the dark
recesses of the windows inward towards the illumination. Deliciousness hung in the air; something savory was cooking. Anna
bent over the wood stove for a moment, adding fuel, the glow of
the fire playing over her face.

At sixty, one could still see in the secret places of that face,
now covered over by shadows and hard lines, what a beauty she
had been...a pressed rose now lost in the dusty pages of some
nameless book.

Anna heard the sound of slow hoof beats approaching the
cabin. Out of habit, she reached up to smooth her hair, her dark
eyes tightening, apprehensive. A few minutes later the door of the
cabin opened and Charley entered. Anna put her hands, protected
by two checkered cloths, around the rim of a steaming tureen of
soup, and carried it from the stove to the table.

Charley reached with difficulty to hang her coat and hat
on their customary hooks beside the door. She paused, trying to catch her breath. Then she rinsed her hands and face
in the basin of water, turned and limped toward the table and
sat down.

Anna watched her with concern. Not a word had been spoken.

Charley brought the spoon to her mouth, blew on it to cool
it, and then tried to sip the broth. She could not swallow...the

liquid spewed from her mouth. The exertion brought on a racking cough. Pain clouded her eyes.

"Please let me help you Charley. Let me go get the doctor."

Charley's face was ashen, sweat beading down. When the cough subsided, she grunted no. She heaved herself up out of her chair. Anna watched as Charley moved in a slow painful shuffle toward their bedroom. She vanished into the room, closing the door behind her.

Charley sat on the bed patting her pockets till she found matches and a cigar. She bit off the end, lit the cigar and took a deep draw…her exhalation became another wrenching cough.

In the other room Anna sniffed the air, her eyes flickering with unease. She stood up and made her way to the closed door.

"Charley? Are you alright? Let me help you." She tried the knob. The door was bolted. "Damn it, answer me. You know what the doctor said. You've got to at least try to drink something. To keep up your strength."

"We all got to go sometime, Anna." Her voice was raspy and winded.

"This is not a joke. Why do you lock the door?"

There was no reply.

"Alright. I don't care. Even if you don't like it, I'm going across to the Harmon's, so George can go and get Doctor Irelan. Just lie down on the bed and rest. I'll be back soon, I promise."

A few minutes later when Charley opened the door, she saw that Anna was gone.

She turned back, shutting the bedroom door again. She started to take another pull on the cigar but her lips had no strength. Her arm felt heavy holding it. The cigar fell from her fingers to the floor. She stared down at it, then put it out with her boot. A stabbing pain ran down her arm and her neck.

She sat back down on the bed…her breathing still labored. She took from her pocket a small tin. Sliding open the top she removed several opium tablets from inside. It pained her but she managed to swallow them.

Willing herself, she bent and pulled off her boots. She felt winded...like she had been kicked in the gut. With great expense to her body, she slid down to the floor on her knees in front of the bed.

Reaching under it, she pulled towards her the little trunk hidden there. She brushed a thick layer of dust off the top and stared at it for a moment, as though it were a stranger. She took a little key from her pocket, turned it in its lock and then raised the lid. Reaching in, she pulled out something small and fragile and red. She held it up in her hands. It was a tiny embroidered homespun dress...the dress of her child.

She lifted the dress to her face, breathing from it as though it might give her life. She put it down on the floor alongside her, and reached back into the trunk: a tiny pair of crocheted shoes. With care, she placed them below the little red dress. Her shoulders rose and fell. Next: Byron's tattered copy of Emerson's *Essays*. And then lastly, Jonas' coiled, dusty old whip.

It meant something, she thought, that she'd held onto these souvenirs from a life that had long since ceased to be hers.

She pulled herself up from the floor. She was feeling ensnared beneath her garments...as though she might smother within their bindings. She had to remove them and free herself from their grasp.

She stripped off her shirt. She began to unwind the coarse cloths that bound her and they fell in loops onto the floor. In a moment she was finished.

Fighting against the waves of nausea, she bent down to remove her pants and undergarments. Her breath was short and strained and made a hollow yellow sound in her chest.

She was naked now. She felt liberated, weightless, euphoric.

In the dark glow of the candlelight, she stood in front of a small silver framed mirror perched on her bureau. There she watched herself remove the last little bit of cover on her body...the black patch from her left eye, revealing an opaque, sightless orb.

Next she took the mirror, her hands trembling, and moved it all around her body, every inch that she could see. She put the mirror back in its place.

She took her hands and moved them to her waist and onto the hair of her groin. She touched the roughness of her face. Then her hands held her breasts. They were round and full and heavy.

Unexpected tears came to her eyes.

She lay down naked and spent on top of the blanket and looked up into the shadows of the air above. In the distance, she could hear her breath rattling. How strange it was. All that seemed to be left of this world now was breath.

Then a sound came to her. A whistle. And fluttering...tiny flapping; orange against the blue.

The candle next to the bed sputtered, trying to keep its flame. Warm blood escaped from her mouth.

She sensed now that she was a stranger to that flesh beneath. Without fear, without surprise...the realization that in that moment she was about to die.

She struggled fiercely—holding tight to that last breath. Why had it felt she'd been holding it in, holding everything in, her whole life...waiting for its release. And in this moment now, a path was opening, and she was still struggling to let it all go.

There was a flash of blue sky. The whistle. She was reaching for a butterfly as it fluttered away. Her hand was pudgy. The light was brilliant and warm. Lee was there, and she turned and smiled at him.

"Don't move, Charlotte," he whispered. "Hold still..." The butterfly hovered for an instant above her before spiraling down in a single smooth arc to her hand.

"See it didn't die," whispered back Charlotte, after the butterfly floated off her finger towards the sky.

Charley let go. She let it all go. She released that breath with a long rattling sigh, the light ebbing out of her eyes.

In the end it was so quick. In the end, it was so easy.

EPILOGUE

"Fuck me—Parkie was a damn female? Don't that fucking beat all," Ben said. He was shit-face drunk.

Ben and Hank were sitting at the bar with Joe, one of the other whips who had helped build Anna's cabin. They were staring at the newspaper.

"Go ahead. Keep reading Hank."

"Stop yelling in my ear Ben. Say's here…'rumors that in early years she loved not wisely, but too well, have been numerous and from the reports of those who saw her body, these rumors receive some color of truth. It is generally believed that she had been a mother'—"

"A mother? What the fuck?" Ben screamed.

"Goddamnit. Will you let me finish? '—and that from that event, dated her strange career.' That's the end of the article."

There was a moment of silence as they all took this information in.

"Hell, I knew," said Ben.

"You're so full of shit," said Hank.

"The hell I am. Hey, back me up on this, Joe."

Joe looked up from his drink. "You never said nothing to me."

"C'mon. Remember those gloves he always wore? I saw his hands once. Soft n' smooth, they was. And now that I think of it…he never had no beard, neither."

"Says in the paper he died of cancer of the tongue," said Hank. "Anna told me she thought his heart went."

"Tongue cancer huh? Probably from going against nature to hold it still," said Ben.

"She was shaped kinda funny," said Joe.

"That's right," said Ben. "I thought he was a morphodite."

"A what?"

"A morphodite. Half man, half woman, kinda."

"Shit Ben," said Hank. "I think you didn't know nothing. If you did, it would have been all around town with your big mouth. Didn't act like no female when he got kicked in the eye, did he?"

"No. Guess not. Just took his medicine like a good ole boy."

There was a long pause as the three men mulled over the newspaper, drinking, shaking their heads.

"Well, here's to Six-Horse Charley Parkhurst, one of God's great mysteries!" said Joe.

"A damn fine reinsman," said Hank.

"A helluva guy," said Ben. "Never did see him take a piss, though."

"May he rest in peace," said Hank.

"She. She," said Joe.

"I can't fucking believe it. I can't," said Hank. "I know it's true, but I never suspected a thing. Jehoshaphat! I camped out with Parkie once for over a week, and we slept on the same buffalo robe right along; wonder if Curly Bill's been playin' me the same way."

"Probably," said Ben.

They all laughed. Tears rolling down their drunken faces.

"Hell. Here's to you Parkie," said Ben. "You one crazy son-of-a-bitch."

THE END

Charley's grave stands in
the Pioneer Odd Fellows Cemetery
in Watsonville, California.

It reads...

CHARLEY DARKEY PARKHURST

1812 – 1879

NOTED WHIP OF THE GOLD RUSH DAYS
DROVE STAGE OVER Mt. MADONNA IN
EARLY DAYS OF VALLEY. LAST RUN
San Juan TO Santa Cruz. DEATH IN
CABIN NEAR THE 7 MILE HOUSE,
REVEALED "ONE EYED CHARLIE,"
A WOMAN. THE FIRST WOMAN TO VOTE
IN THE U.S. NOV. 3, 1868

Obituary for Charley Darkey Parkhurst
The New York Times January 9, 1880.

 OBITUARY

*"Truth is stranger than fiction,
but it is because Fiction is obliged to stick
to possibilities; Truth is not."*
—Mark Twain

THIRTY YEARS IN DISGUISE.
A NOTED OLD CALIFORNIAN STAGE-DRIVER
DISCOVERED, AFTER DEATH, TO BE A WOMAN.
Correspondence of the San Francisco Call

WATSONVILLE, Cal., Dec. 31.—There is hardly a city or town
or hamlet of the Pacific coast that includes among its citizens a
few of the gold-hunters of the early days where at least one person
cannot be found who will remember Charley Parkhurst. For in
the early days the gold-hunters were, by rapidly-succeeding gold
discoveries, drawn back to San Francisco as a head-quarters, and
again distributed from it to the most recently found diggings, and
in those same early days Charley Parkhurst was a stage-driver on
the more important routes leading out from the city. He was in
his day one of the most dexterous and celebrated of the famous
California drivers, ranking with Foss, Hank Monk, and George
Gordon, and it was an honor to be striven for to occupy the spare
end of the driver's seat when the fearless Charley Parkhurst held
the reins of a four or six in hand. California coaching had, and
has even yet, one exciting adjunct that was wanting in all preced-
ing coaching. It was when the organized bands of highwaymen
waylaid the coaches, leaped to the leaders' heads, and over leveled shot-guns, issued the grim command made so often that it

has crystallized into the felonious formula of "Throw down the box." Drivers of a phlegmatic temperament become accustomed to these interruptions, expertly reckon up the killing capacity of the gun-barrels leveled at them, accept the inevitable, throw down the treasure-box and drive on. Charley Parkhurst was high-strung, and this was one requirement of the driver of the early days he could never master. He drove for a while between Stockton and Mariposa, and once was stopped and had to cut away the treasure-box to get his coach and passengers clear. But he did it, even under the "drop" of the robbers' fire-arms, with all ill-grace, and he defiantly told the highwaymen that he would "break even with them." He was as good as his word, for, being subsequently stopped on a return trip from Mariposa to Stockton, he watched his opportunity, and contemporaneously, turned his wild mustangs and his wicked revolver loose, and brought everything through safe. That his shooting was to the mark was subsequently ascertained by the confession of "Sugarfoot," a notorious highwayman, who, mortally wounded, found his way to a miner's cabin in the hills, and *in articulo mortis* told how he had been shot by Charley Parkhurst, the famous driver, in a desperate attempt, with others, to stop his stage.

Charley Parkhurst also afterward drove on the great stage route from Oakland to San Jose, and later, and for a long time, he was "the boss of the road" between San Juan and Santa Cruz, when San Francisco was reached by way of San Juan. But Parkhurst was of both an energetic and a thrifty nature, and when rapid improvements in the means of locomotion relegated coaches further out toward the frontiers, and made the driving of them less profitable, it was not sufficient for him that he was acknowledged as one of the three or four crack whips of the coast. He resolutely abandoned driving and went to farming. For 15 years he prosecuted this calling, varying it in the Winter times by working in the woods, where he was known as one of the most skillful and powerful of choppers and lumbermen, and where his services were eagerly sought for, and always commanded the highest wages. Although, in his stage-coaching days, he was hail fellow well met with the migratory miners, and during the succeeding years of his life as farmer and lumberman he was social and generous with his fellows, he was never intemperate, immoral, or reckless, and the sure result was that his years of labor had been rewarded with a competency of several thousands of dollars. For several years past he had been so severely afflicted with rheumatism as not only to be unable to do physical labor, but the malady had even resulted in partial shriveling and distortion of some of his limbs. He was also attacked by a cancer on his tongue. As the combined diseases became more aggressive, the genial Charley Parkhurst became, not morose, but less and less communicative, till of late he has conversed with no one except on the ordinary topics of the day.

Last Sunday [December 28, 1879], in a little cabin on the Moss Ranch, about six miles from Watsonville, Charley Parkhurst, the famous coachman, the fearless fighter, the industrious farmer and expert woodman died of the cancer on his tongue. He knew that death was approaching, but he did not relax the reticence of his later years other than to express a few wishes as to certain things to be done at his death. Then, when the hands of the kind friends who had ministered to his dying wants came to lay out the dead body of the adventurous Argonaut, a discovery was made that was literally astounding. Charley Parkhurst was a woman. The discoveries of the successful concealment for protracted periods of the female sex under the disguise of the masculine are not infrequent, but the case of Charley Parkhurst may fairly claim to rank as by all odds the most astonishing of all of them. That a young woman should assume man's attire and, friendless and alone, defy the dangers of the voyage of 1849, to the then almost mythical California—dangers over which hardy pioneers still grow boastful—has in it sufficient of the wonderful. That she should achieve distinction in an occupation above all professions calling for the best physical qualities of nerve, courage, coolness, and endurance and that she should add to them the almost romantic personal bravery that enables one to fight one's way through the ambush of an enemy, seems almost fabulous, and that for 30 years she should be in constant and intimate association with men and women, and that her true sex should never have been even suspected, and that she should finally go knowingly down to her death, without disclosing by word or deed who she was, or why she had assumed man's dress and responsibilities, are things that a reader might be justified in doubting, if the proof of their exact truth was not so abundant and conclusive. On the great [voting] register of Santa Cruz County for the year 1867 appears this entry: "Parkhurst, Charles Durkee [Darkey], 55, New-Hampshire, farmer, Soquel," where he then lived. It is said by several who knew her intimately, that she came from Providence, R. I.

LETTER TO THE EDITOR

March 15, 1930
Watsonville Register—Pajaronian

Dear Editor,

My father met Charley Parkhurst in the fall of 1873. At that time she lived on her place, which is located on the Santa Cruz road, about six miles from Watsonville, and was opposite what is now known as the "Risdon Place."

My people lived on the opposite side of the road. This place at that time was known as the "Moss Ranch."

In my boyhood days I knew Charley Parkhurst as a man; in fact, she dressed and acted the part perfectly. She often spoke of her early life, which she claimed was spent in Providence, R.I.

I often heard her tell of working as a stable boy in that city when gold was discovered in this state. She joined the rush and if I remember right, she landed in San Francisco in 1851, coming via the Isthmus of Panama. She was a great lover of horses, and had no trouble getting employment as a stage driver.

She drove from San Francisco to San Jose, from San Jose to San Juan and Watsonville. While driving the stage from San Francisco to San Jose, she was kicked by a horse and thus lost one of her eyes....

During the early part of 1879, she complained of a sore throat and a swelling on the side of her tongue. This trouble proved to be cancer, which was the cause of her death, December 28, 1879.... She did not die alone, as an old acquaintance of hers was present when she passed away....

What caused Parkhurst to adopt male attire and follow a man's work will never be known, as the secret died with her....

A short time before her death, she said that she had something to tell (my father), but there was no hurry about it. She kept postponing telling him, and he was not present when the end came. I have no doubt that she intended to tell him the secret of her life, what caused her to dress and live in the way she did.

After her death, all kinds of stories were told about her early life. So far as the writer knows, these stories were all fictitious. No letters or papers were ever found, (and articles in the newspapers brought forth no inquires or relatives.) Nothing that would give the least inkling about anything else than (my) above statement.

During a period of six years, I saw a great deal of her, and what I have written is her own story of her life. Charley Parkhurst was a kind and good natured person, but could, if occasion justified, be rather profane. She was very charitable, and helped those in need.

She was buried in the Odd Fellows cemetery at Watsonville. The grave was donated by the late Mr. Stoesser.

In the summer of 1880, my father placed a small head stone at the grave. I do not know if the stone is still there or not, as I have not been in the cemetery for many years.

George F. Harmon
San Francisco, California

NEWSPAPER REPORTS

"Charley Parkhurst used to be with Hank Monk (another famous whip) a good deal in early days and when Hank heard the report that Charley had turned out to be a woman, he was so overcome for several minutes that he gasped for breath, and drawled out: 'Jehoshaphat! I camped out with Parkie once for over a week, and we slept on the same buffalo robe right along; wonder if Curly Bill's been playin' me the same way.'"
—Santa Cruz Sentinel, Oct. 1, 1880

"Rumors that in early years she loved not wisely, but too well, have been numerous and from the reports of those who saw her body, these rumors receive some color of truth. It is generally believed that she had been a mother and that from that event, dated her strange career."
—Watsonville Pajaronian, Jan. 8, 1880

"Being thrifty, industrious and economical, temperate and a full hand at any employment in which she engaged, often cutting the heart of a tree from genuine masculines of double her avoirdupois, her accumulations were regular and her wealth considerable at the time of her death, which took place in a lonely cabin, with no one near and her secret her own. Why this woman should live a life of disguise, always afraid her sex would be discovered, doing the work of a man, may never be known. A mother she is represented to have been, and it may date back to that proud eminence from which virtuous women alone can fall, fall by the deception of some man monster, but there must have been a cause, a mighty cause."
—Santa Cruz Sentinel, 1880

"Charley Parkhurst was one of this city's finest stage drivers. The only people who have any occasion to be disturbed by the career of Charley are the gentlemen who have so much to say about 'women's sphere' and the 'weaker vessel.'"

—*Providence Journal, 1880*

SELECTED BIBLIOGRAPHY

The following books have been sources of information, quotes background and inspiration for both setting and characters in this book:

Abbott, E. C. & Smith, Helena Huntington, *We Pointed Them North*, New York: Farrar & Rinehart, 1939.

Adams, Ramon F., *Western Words*, New York: Hippocrene Books, 1998.

Boyer, Paul S., *The Oxford Companion to United States History*, New York: Oxford University Press, 2001.

Brighton, Marylee, *Windhorse Relations Inc. Meet the Mustangs*.

Brown, John Ross, *Adventures in the Apache Country*, New York: Harper & Brothers, 1869.

Chronicle of America, Mount Kisco, N.Y.: Chronicle Publications, 1989.

Curtis, Mabel Rowe, *The Coachman was a Lady*, The Pajaro Valley Historical Association, 1959.

"Father's a Drunkard and Mother is Dead." 1866. Words by Stella Washington. Music by Mrs. E. A. Parkhurst.

Johnson, Theodore, *Sights in the Gold Region, and Scenes by the Way*, New York: Baker and Scribner, 1849.

Judd, A. N., *Watsonville Pajaronian*, October 3, 1917.

McCutcheon, Marc, *The Writer's Guide to Everyday Life in the 1800s*, Cincinnati, Ohio: Writer's Digest Books, 1993.

Moulton, Candy, *The Writer's Guide to Everyday Life in the Wild West*, Cincinnati, Ohio: Writer's Digest Books, 1993.

Reader's Digest, January 1957.

Stegner, Page, *Winning the Wild West*, New York: The Free Press, 2002.

ACKNOWLEDGEMENTS

In his collection of poetry *The Leaning Tree*, my friend Patrick Overton wrote:

When you walk to the edge of all the light you have
and take that first step into the darkness of the unknown,
you must believe that one of two things will happen:

There will be something solid for you to stand upon,
or, you will be taught how to fly.

(This is from The Leaning Tree, a collection of poems by Patrick Overton. Copyright © 1975 by Patrick Overton. Reprinted by permission of the author.)

****

In writing *The Whip*, the people in these acknowledgements have either given me something solid to stand upon or have endeavored to teach me to fly. All of them, some even serendipitously, shared in the creation and or publication of this book…

Jon and Jody Hansen: you took a chance publishing a "new voice." You had the courage, the true grit, to take Charley and me on. For that I will always be grateful, more than you will ever know. And hopefully those readers who are entertained, perhaps even inspired by *The Whip*, have ultimately you to thank.

Jason Baerg: without your keen editing eye, your patience and wicked sense of humor, Charley might still be resting in a large stack of typewritten pages.

Simon Levy: my maestro and friend. Twenty-seven drafts ago, you were the first I trusted to read the book. Thank you for your constant inspiration, honesty and humor. Everyone should have a Simon in their life who points to the sky and says "fly baby, fly"...and then trusts they can do it!

Jeffry DeCola: I will always be grateful to your talent. You created an extraordinary book cover for *The Whip* that gave a face to my imaginings.

Elise Ballard: many years ago, after reading my film script of *The Whip* you said, "Hey, why don't you write a novel of this amazing story." It was you who put the seed in the ground. Thank you for your inspiration and your beautiful heart.

Barbara Lyons: you helped me understand the truth that anything is possible if you believe it to be. Your constant friendship, encouragement and kindness has been apart of my life since I was your shy little 'flower-girl,' a thousand years ago.

My grateful thanks to Regan Huerta and Geri Anne Solano-Simmons and the staff of the Pajaro Valley Historical Association, Watsonville, California...for your patience and assistance in locating historical information regarding Charley Parkhurst—and most especially, your kindness and warmth in the face of deadline emergencies.

Edward Achorn, Loreen Arbus, Jim Beaver, Deborah Behrens, Steve Bennett, Greg Berkin, Tara Boles Williams, Reiner Boller, Yvonne P. Borroto, Mary Lee Brighton@WindhorseRelations, Colby Chester, Nicole David, Judy Davidson@Davidson&Choy, Robert and Debra Deyan@Deyen Audio Services, Jan Deen, Lisa England, Tom Fleming, Peter Flood, Julie Garfield, Victor Gulotta@booktours.com, Jack Heller, Allan Hitchcock, Ara Keshishian, Sonia Keshishian, Eduardo Machado, Valerie McCaffrey, Lee Melville, Richardson Morse, Ryan Oksenberg, Mary Oliver, Patrick Overton, Michael Peretzian, Mike Rice, Peter Robinson, Barbara Witkin Sanders, Brad Schreiber, Sue Terry, Barbara Teszler, Robin Weigert, Eric Weissmann, Esq.

About the Author

K aren Kondazian's career as an actor, author and journalist is as diverse as it is long. She was born in Boston, Massachusetts. At the age of eight Karen was chosen to be one of the infamous children on Art Linkletter's *Kids Say the Darndest Things*. The opportunity to miss school during tapings was all it took for Karen to abandon her life's goal of becoming a CIA spy and focus on acting.

She completed her schooling at The London Academy of Music and Dramatic Arts (LAMDA), The University of Vienna and San Francisco State University, where she received her B.A., after which she began her acting career in New York. Her first professional work was in the award winning production of Michael Cacoyannis' *The Trojan Women* at the Circle in the Square Theatre.

In 1979, she won the Los Angeles Drama Critics Circle Award for Best Actress in *The Rose Tattoo*, (in which her work as actor and producer so impressed Tennessee Williams that they became friends, and he gave her carte blanche to produce any of his work in his lifetime).

Her theater career has included starring opposite Ed Harris in *Sweet Bird of Youth*, Richard Chamberlain in *Richard II* (dir. Jonathan Miller), Stacey Keach in *Hamlet*, (dir. Gordon Davidson). She also starred in the world premiere of *Mixed Blessings* with Raul Esparza, and in Eduardo Machado's off-Broadway play, *Broken Eggs* (world premiere). Her latest awards have been through her work at the Fountain Theatre in Los Angeles where she played Maria Callas in the Ovation Award winning, *Master Class, Orpheus Descending, Night of the Iguana*, and *The Milk Train Doesn't Stop Here Anymore*, all directed by Simon Levy.

She has appeared as series regular lead in CBS's *Shannon* and guest starred in over 50 television shows and films including, TNT's *James Dean* with James Franco (dir. Mark Rydell), *NYPD Blue, Fraiser, Yes Giorgio* with Luciano Pavarotti, and played Kate Holiday in *The Shootout at OK Corral.*

She is a lifetime member of the Actors Studio and a member of the Academy of Television Arts and Sciences. She is also a member of Women in Film. She occasionally teaches at the Lee Strasberg School of Theater and Film in Hollywood.

Kondazian is a published writer. She is the author of the best-selling book *The Actor's Encyclopedia of Casting Director,* (the second edition of the book will be released in 2012–13). Her long running weekly column, *Sculpting Your Own Career* appeared in Back Stage West.

The Whip, published November 2011, is her debut novel.

She currently resides in Los Angeles, California.

For more information on Karen Kondazian, please visit her web site:

http://kondazian.com